Not Easily Broken

Ruth Smith Meyer

By Ruth Smith Meyer

NOT EASILY BROKEN

By
Ruth Smith Meyer

ISBN: 1-897373-10-4

This book is a work of fiction. Names, characters, places, and incidents are the product of the author's imagination or are used fictitiously. Any resemblance to actual events, locales, or persons, living or dead, is coincidental.

All scripture quotations, unless otherwise indicated, are taken from the King James Version.

Hymns: "How Happy Are They" by Isaac Watts and "Oh, For a Heart to Praise My God" by Charles Wesley.

Published by Word Alive Press
131 Cordite Road, Winnipeg, MB R3W 1S1
www.wordalivepress.ca

Dedication

This book is dedicated to:

... the seniors who shared their wisdom, their lives and their stories, enriching my life immeasurably.

... especially to Freda Litt, a delightfully young late-90's woman who was an inspiration extraordinaire. She not only stayed vitally interested in her ten children, but also in their offspring—grands, greats and great-grands. As long as there were such things, they each got a card with a two-dollar bill tucked inside when their birthday rolled around. It was the story of Freda's mother, though, whose true-life triumph over difficulty and despair provided the basis for this book. Because Freda (the Rina in *Not Easily Broken*) was gone before this book had its debut, the basic facts are true, but the details are mine.

... the men in my life: Norman, my love of thirty-nine years whose departure from this life conferred reality to Ellie's story; and to Paul, who proved that love can bloom again.

By Ruth Smith Meyer
NotEasilyBroken.book@gmail.com
www.inscribe.org/ruthsmithmeyer

Table of Contents

Preface

Rina 1998

The sun shining through the remaining leaves on the big maple created moving patterns on the wallpaper and crowded shelves at which Rina stared from her sick bed. All morning her thoughts had drifted between her mother's life and her own.

Those shifting patterns are like the influences of our parents and other important people on our lives, Rina thought. *There's a pattern to our lives like the wallpaper, but the lives of others move like sunshine and shadows on what we are and what we do*. "Like father, like son" often applied to mothers and daughters as well. Contrary to her reaction when younger, at ninety-eight she deemed herself old enough to not mind being likened to her mother. In fact, it pleased her to think that she may have inherited her mother's strength. If her mother, Ellie Kurtz, was anything, she was strong—in both faith and determination!

What was that verse Mama used to quote from Proverbs?—or was it Ecclesiastes? Something about a cord of three strands being not easily broken…

Not easily broken—that described her mother. She supposed it might apply to her own life as well. *If I can hang on and live until the year 2000 like I always hoped I will get to see most of one century. I guess even lasting this long took some strength,* she mused.

The perspiration from her fever dampened the sheet. She was too old to fight the pneumonia that kept plaguing her. Maybe it would be better to give up the dream of living so long. At the present moment it hardly seemed worth the distinction. Her forced inactivity and so much time spent in seclusion allowed her thoughts to become filled with memories. Sometimes she remembered her children when they were small, sometimes she thought about her beloved husband, and sometimes it was her own childhood memories that warmed her heart or brought a smile. Her mind could wander the space of twenty or thirty years in a matter of minutes! She smiled to think how the early memories were so much clearer than events that had happened a week or a month ago.

Rina's back and hips creaked in protest as she turned to ease the pain in her lower back. Her shoulder didn't cooperate in moving the covers, and it took almost more strength than she had to make the last lap of the turn. She groaned with the effort. She couldn't believe how her body had aged even though she didn't feel that old inside. What a long way from what she once was! She, who could run across meadows, traverse small streams with a flying leap and dance up a storm long after others were nursing tired feet and sore limbs—who had merrily worked long days and still had energy left for reading long into the nights by candlelight or bed lamp— now required a major effort to gather the strength to turn from one side to the other! A wry grin spread over her face as she saw the humor and irony of it all.

Hey! Let's really have an adventure and do something really daring! Let's turn to the other side so I can look out the window instead of staring at the purple-flowered wall paper, overflowing shelves and packed bookcases holding the remnants of my life's accumulations! Perhaps, if I try hard enough, I could write a whole chapter about this, my most recent daring escapade—turning over in bed! She gave a little snort of laughter at her attempt at comedy.

Escapades! How often her beleaguered mother had used that word to describe her daughter's frequent efforts to circumvent the carefully explained rules set for her offspring. *The same determination and fortitude have been the compelling force in both mother and daughter*, Rina thought, *they have just been expressed in different ways*. Her mother's story deserved to be told. How often had she rehearsed it in her mind, meaning to put it on paper—some day? Oh, she did jot down many of the stories her mother had told her, but she never finished the job. She often wished she'd have asked her mother more questions.

"Be honest! Mom didn't readily talk about the difficult times. She was so determined to make the best of whatever situation came along—Ha! Just listen to this old woman talking out loud with no one in the room to hear me!"

She, herself, had been younger than her mother when life took an unexpected twist. But the twist in Rina's life was of her own making, whereas her mother's had been forced upon her. Probably no young woman in this day and age would even consider doing what her mother did out of honour and loyalty to her parents.

Fiddlesticks! Why am I putting down the present generation? Even I wouldn't have done it! Goodness knows I was headstrong in doing things my own way. I was only sixteen when Bart begged me to make a commitment to him before he left for the Great War—and I did, even though my parents thought it unwise.

Being three years older, Bart had volunteered to join the troops in Europe. She had succumbed to his pleadings, even though she knew to be engaged would curtail some of the fun to which she had become accustomed. A sly grin spread over Rina's face.

I don't know if Bart ever found out that I did go out the occasional night with other young men while he was gone, but goodness, I was young and had to have some fun!

Bart came back a greatly altered man. No longer the fun-loving, carefree joker, instead Rena found him morose, demanding and moody. Her parents, distressed that she would even consider going through with her commitment, urged her to reconsider, but she felt she shouldn't go back on her promise.

Bart, in the years of trenches, artillery and death, had also found another mistress in liquor. Repeated promises to change floated away like the morning mists at the very next opportunity to drown his memories and nightmares in the gulps of sweet release as cheap gin flowed down his throat. She loved him, and at first, felt that she could be his salvation. Even after doubts began to push their way into her mind, her sense of loyalty kept her from stopping their plans for a wedding.

If I hadn't met David Litz on the train trip back home from Strafford, I probably would have married Bart. Poor man! He ended up drinking himself to an early grave, leaving behind a poor widow and three small children. My life would have been much harder if I had married him.

She and David hadn't entirely been strangers—over the years they had met at several neighbourhood parties so their conversation on that first train trip began quite naturally. During the ride they delighted each other with tales of one another's breaks with convention and the thrills they experienced in shocking those who lived by established customs. She slipped back in time and let herself relive the beginning of their courtship.

"You know, Rina," David laughed as they neared his destination that first day, "I think we could make a good team. Maybe we should get married."

Rina laughed, "Don't you think that's a little sudden and drastic? After all, I'm an already-engaged woman!"

"But you know I would be a much better husband. Just tell him you've changed your mind since a better offer came your way." David's lips smiled in fun, but his eyes belied the depth of his desire and seriousness.

They shared the train ride the following two weeks. On the homeward trip only three weeks later, David begged in earnest for her to marry him. When his station was called, he took her hand between the two of his and told her, "I'm not leaving until you say 'Yes.'"

As Rina stared at him with an incredulous gaze, the train began to move from the stop.

"David!" she protested, "What are you going to do? Where will you spend the night?"

"If you don't say 'Yes,' I'll sleep on your doorstep until you do. If you do, I, in my elation, will walk all the way home singing, and I won't mind a bit!"

I didn't say "Yes" to marrying him, but I did say "Yes", on a whim—or perhaps it was because I knew I had to get to bed if I was to work the next day. I did agree to go with him and eight other young people, two of them girls, on an excursion to the western provinces to work in the harvest for the summer. True to his word, David did walk the six miles back to his home. What a round of arguments that plan raised with Mama and Papa and Bart! I guess it was a combination of fear and desire that made me stand firm—fear of what marrying Bart would mean, and desire for a real adventure. I guess the fun I had with David and the insistence of his love helped a bit too!

From her present vantage point Rina had much more sympathy for her parents now than had entered her young heart and mind at that time. Deep down, she had probably surmised it would be an easy way out of her commitment that, more and more, was beginning to feel like a trap. Going away was easier than face-to-face confrontation. She really was a self-absorbed and willful young woman! She grinned and gave a little chuckle.

A little late to admit that now!

She stared out the window at the falling leaves as they released their grip on the tiny branches that had supported them and given life for a season.

I guess I'm a little like those stubborn leaves that are hanging onto the branch for dear life, not knowing enough to let go and let nature take its course. Rina closed her eyes and let out a big sigh.

Chapter One

Ellie 1877

Ellie's face flushed and her eyes sparkled as she glanced in the mirror. In just moments her sister Regina and her beau would drive in the lane to stay for the weekend. At Christmas, when she was home for the holiday, Regina told the family that John Kurtz had come calling on her at the Schwartz home in Monkville. Regina had been working there since the Schwartz's fifth child was born in October. She described John's striking features—his wavy dark hair and blue eyes. The balance of his sense of humour and his quiet wisdom delighted her.

Even the idea of her sister having a beau thrilled thirteen-year-old Ellie's heart. Now Regina was bringing John home to meet her parents and family in reality. It wasn't just a dream—Willy and Martin were bringing them from the train station right now.

Yesterday a big ham cooking on the stove filled the house with its smoky aroma, mingling with the smell of freshly-baked bread, cakes and cookies. Today coleslaw, too, cooled in the cellar and Mama's soup simmered on the stove. All morning they worked, cleaning the house and getting everything in place. Ellie personally aired the spare bed and dusted every piece of furniture to make sure they would make a good impression. Martin and Willy should be back before long.

She peeked in the door again on her way back downstairs after changing her dress in readiness for the company. The tall carved headboard stood against the blue-gray wall. Above it hung a picture of a guardian angel grasping the coattail of a young boy reaching from the bridge to pick a cattail from the reeds growing in the stream. Ellie loved that picture. The ivory crocheted bedspread her mother had made before her marriage gave the room a distinguished look. As Ellie smoothed out a small wrinkle she felt the pattern under her hand and admired the beautiful coverlet. The blue tatted lace that edged the pillowcases highlighted the blue embroidered flowers on the hems and on the runners that protected the high bureau. The freshly filled lamp waited to light the room at night. She straightened the towel on the rod at the back of the washstand as she reached for the pitcher from the water set. She would take that downstairs and fill it in the morning with warm water for John. Through the white dimity curtain she saw a movement. In the twinkling of an eye she was rushing down the stairs.

"Mama, Papa, they're coming in the lane. John and Regina and the boys are coming in the lane!"

"All right, all right, Ellie. Just calm down!" Daniel Kessler rose from the chair where he had been reading. Daniel smiled at his wife, Elizabeth, as she untied her apron and hung it on the hook beside the kitchen door.

Much as Mom is trying to hide her excitement, her face betrays her with flushed cheeks and bright eyes, Ellie thought. "Come on, Mom! They're getting out of the buggy. Come quick!"

Smoothing a few strands of hair and fixing them to the bun at the back of her head, Elizabeth joined Daniel and Ellie at the front door, ready to meet the new man in her daughter's life. Through the window they saw the young couple approaching.

"Regina was right, John is a very handsome man!" Elizabeth hastily whispered to her husband before she opened the door.

"Regina, come on in!"

"Hello, Mama and Papa and Ellie! I would like you to meet John Kurtz." She smiled as she looked into John's eyes, "John, these are my parents and my sister, Ellie."

Warmth filled his eyes as John reached out to shake hands. "So glad to meet you, Mr. and Mrs. Kessler and Ellie. Regina has told me so many wonderful stories about you and her life here on the farm. I am pleased to become better acquainted."

"Come into the parlor," Elizabeth invited. "We've got a little while to visit and get to know each other before supper time."

"Do you want Ellie and me to get the supper on?" Regina asked.

"Oh, no, Regina. Thanks for the offer, but everything is pretty well ready. Ellie and I will go in a few minutes and get things on the table. The boys aren't in from the barn yet."

"So, John," said Daniel when they were all seated, "Regina says you are from a farm family too?"

"Yes, I am, Mr. Kessler. Abe and Sarah are my parents, and I have two brothers and two sisters. My brother Albert's farm is right across the road and my Uncle Henry's have the one right beside my parents' farm, so we all work together. My brother Isaac and his wife Emma live in town, but I like farming. I've bought one for myself, but it isn't as close to home. It is about ten miles west of my parents'."

"Have you had it for awhile, or did you just buy it recently?"

"I bought it last fall, so this spring will be the first for me to work the land."

"Are there buildings on the farm?"

"Yes, it has a good barn and a nice brick house. Not as large as the ones in our immediate area, but it's big enough."

The men continued their conversation about farming while Ellie and her mother went to make final preparations. Martin and Willie soon came from the barn and joined the others in the parlor.

After supper they got out the crokinole board and the young people played a few rousing games at the kitchen table. John and Regina made a good team and Willy and Ellie had to work hard to keep the score anywhere near even. John's and Regina's encouraging remarks when the other made an especially good shot were always accompanied by a look of love and pride in each other. Ellie, so enamored with the romance of it all, almost missed her turn.

"Come on Ellie! Where have you been? There are a whole lot of black buttons on the board just waiting for you to shoot them off!"

Thoroughly embarrassed, Ellie tried to keep her mind on the game for the remainder of the time.

As the weekend progressed, Ellie found herself entranced with this handsome young man. Willy and Martin, coming into their manhood, also felt captivated with the maturity of their sister's beau. Ellie smiled to see Martin's attempts at imitating the way John crossed his legs and hooked his arm over the back of his chair.

By the time Regina and John took their leave on Sunday afternoon the last visages of discomfort had disappeared. John had begun to fit into the family with ease.

A year after they began seeing each other—on a bright spring morning—John and Regina's wedding day dawned. The orchard trees, arrayed in pink and white blossoms, filled the air with sweetness. The neatly mowed grass made a nice setting for rows of chairs and an altar where the minister would stand to marry the happy couple. At fourteen, Ellie's sense of romance bloomed as vivid and intense as the apple trees in the orchard. She thought her sister a lucky woman to be married to such a stalwart man. How could she ever hope to find a man as handsome as John, with such an impeccable list of attributes to satisfy her own longings?

"Regina, does my hair look all right?"

"Yes, Ellie, you look radiant in that light green dress with your hair done up. That colour is perfect with your chestnut hair and fair skin. You could almost be the bride!"

Ellie blushed with pleasure. "You're the bride, Regina, but I want to look my best for you too!"

"For me, or for some of the young gentlemen who will be here?" her sister teased.

"Come on, Regina! John and Jake are out there waiting, the minister looks impatient and John's dad is beginning to play the violin, so we'd better get going, or else John will think you got cold feet!

Regina smoothed out her dress of soft rose silk and patted her dark hair once more. She took a deep breath.

"Are you nervous, Regina? I think I would be."

"I guess a little. But it's what I've been looking forward to for months now. Let's go."

Moments later, the sisters emerged from the house. Their father stood waiting on the porch. Ellie led the way and Regina and her father followed several steps behind. They crossed the lane and entered a chapel decorated by nature's abundance. John had eyes only for Regina as she slowly walked between the rows of chairs and reached his side.

Ellie's eyes shone as John and Regina repeated their vows and the ring was placed on her sister's finger. When the minister said, "You may kiss the bride," Ellie's cheeks reddened as she imagined what it would be like, were she to be the bride!

John and Regina set up housekeeping on a farm only five miles from home so it was relatively easy to visit them often. What fun Ellie had helping unpack Regina's things! The two girls examined the coverlets Regina had knitted over the years, the embroidered runners and doilies, the needlepoint samplers for the walls. They tried them out in various spots until everything felt right. By the time they placed all the wedding gifts and items from her dowry in the farmhouse it was transformed into a lovely home. Ellie became the main help for her mother, but she often went to assist her older sister, and the two cemented their friendship during those days.

The following year, just as the apples ripened on the trees and the mornings dawned with a nip in the air, John came to get Ellie to help them for a few weeks. Little Maria had made her appearance through the night. What a welcome the wee one received! Being the first grandchild for Regina and Ellie's parents, the blue-eyed child with curly dark hair was the recipient of much loving attention.

Those days were good for the sisters. Ellie did the cooking and cleaning and laundry, but she still had time to spend with her sister and new niece. Ellie felt so privileged to be entrusted to assist with her care. As she held her little niece she gently ran her finger across the silky softness of the tiny cheek. Maria's mouth made a sucking motion but her eyes remained closed. A wave of protectiveness washed over Ellie. "*Someday, dear little Maria, I hope I will have a baby of my own to love and cherish. She will be your cousin and perhaps by then you will be old enough to help me care for her."* The thoughts were too private and too precious to say aloud, but her heart swelled with the thought.

Regina was such a good mother. John, too, thrilled with this new little member of the family, openly demonstrated his pride and sense of responsibility. Many men, in Ellie's experience, waited until their children grew a little older before they had much to do with them, but after the departure of the midwife, John hopped out of bed at night to attend to the baby's cries. He seemed to derive a great deal of pleasure in giving this care. Again, Ellie thought her sister an extremely fortunate woman.

Three years later, Marta joined the family. Once more, Ellie helped with the housework while Regina recuperated. Ellie and Gerhard Hirsch, a well-respected young man in the community, had already been dating for a year by then, so he took Ellie to John and Regina's on Sunday nights and picked her up on Saturdays. Ellie's dreams of having wee ones of her own seemed within reach.

Marta, a happy little girl whose constant chatter delighted the whole family, was only two and a half when the next baby was on the way. This time, however, Regina went several weeks over her due date. Then one morning John brought Maria and Marta to stay with their grandparents. Regina was in active labour, so Ellie went back with John. Dr. Mitchell stood beside Regina's bed while the nurse readied the equipment. Through the day and into the night, Regina laboured in vain. In the early morning hours Dr Mitchell came to the kitchen asking for a cup of tea. John stopped his pacing.

"Dr. Mitchell, how much longer can Regina stand this? She is going to be all right, isn't she?"

Dr Mitchell wiped his brow with his handkerchief. In undertones, he replied, "John, I wish I could truthfully tell you that she will be, but I just don't know. The baby is turned the wrong way, and I haven't been successful in righting it. I really don't know." He gulped the last of the tea. "I will do my best."

It was almost morning when Regina breathed her last. Dr. Mitchell made a grand effort to spare the baby, but the little son, awaiting a welcome with love and pride, never took a breath of air.

Dr. Mitchell wearily emerged from the bedroom and put an arm on John's shoulder as he sat at the table, head resting on his folded arms. "John, my man, I am so sorry, but both Regina and the boy are gone. I tried my best! "

John stared at him with blank, disbelieving eyes. It took a full minute or more for the reality of the Doctor's pronouncement to sink in. His mouth dropped open before he cried out in horror.

"NO! Not Regina!" He bolted into the bedroom, lifted Regina's shoulders and cradled her in his arms. "No, Regina! I need you! Regina, please come back to me!" Again and again he called out her name, kissed her face and called again.

Dr. Mitchell stood by for a while then went to John.

"John, John, its no use. She is gone. I am so sorry!"

A few days later, the combined Kurtz and Kessler families, enveloped in a cloud of shock and sadness, buried Regina and her little son in the same casket. Maria and Marta spent the days with their grandparents while John did the farm work, but he usually took them home for the nights. Ellie did some cleaning for him once a week, and took the laundry back home with her.

Only a month after Regina's death her parents requested to meet with Ellie in the parlor. Daniel shut the door firmly behind them. What's going on? Ellie wondered, with a sense of foreboding.

Her Dad cleared his throat; her mother twisted the hem of her apron.

"Ellie, at times like this, families have to stick together. Your mother and I have talked it over, and we have decided what would be best for everyone involved. We do not want to lose Maria and Marta from our family. If John marries someone else, we cannot be sure that the new wife would want to keep us involved. That has happened too often. We don't want to see it repeated in our family. So we are asking you to break your engagement to Gerhard and to marry John so that the girls will be assured of a continuing relationship with us."

Ellie's mouth dropped open and she looked askance. "Dad, you can't possibly mean that!"

"Yes, Ellie, we do mean just that."

"But Dad, how do we know that John would want me for a wife? I love Gerhard, and I've promised to be his wife. Surely you don't want me to break that promise? Dad, of course you wouldn't ask me to do that. I like John but I don't love him that way. I love Gerhard." Ellie sat down, stood up, paced back and forth and sat down again as she spoke. Now she sat twisting the handkerchief in her hands, her knee jiggling up and down in agitation.

"Ellie, calm down. We don't know for sure, but John does need a wife with two small girls. It may as well be you. And as for love, that can grow if you set your mind to it and commit yourself to it."

"But Dad, Gerhard loves me; he will be terribly hurt if I break our engagement now. We have so many plans. Oh, Dad, I can't do that!" Ellie pounded her right fist into her open left hand.

"Yes, Ellie, you can. We've been good parents to you, and you have an obligation to this family. Maria and Marta share your blood in their veins, and you have an obligation to them, too. We are not just suggesting, we are asking you to do this. The sooner the better."

Ellie felt the tears come to her eyes. When she saw the determination in her father's face, she began to cry. Her shoulders shook with sobs. "Dad, I can't!"

"Yes, you can, Ellie, and you will. I will talk to John just as soon as you tell Gerhard. I suggest the time to do that is Sunday night when he comes."

What a tortuous two days followed! Ellie tossed and turned in her bed and hardly slept at night. Through her mind raced all kinds of arguments she could present to her dad to get him to understand just how unreasonable he was being. Her pale face and lack of appetite did not seem to break his resolve. Every time she looked at him with pleading eyes and said, "Papa…" he would interrupt before she could go further.

"Ellie—no arguments! Just do what you need to do. You can and you will!"

They were standing on the verandah when she told Gerhard about her parents' request. His eyes widened in disbelief. He shook his head as if to clear the confusion and looked into her eyes as if he expected it to be a joke. Ellie's eyes held large unshed tears and her eyes reflected deep pain and uncertainty. She nodded her head at his unasked question.

"You mean you would actually think of going through with this fool plan? You committed yourself to me! You promised to be my wife!"

He clenched his hands on her shoulders and gave her a little shake as if to bring her to her senses.

"Gerhard! You're hurting me!"

"Oh, I'm sorry, Ellie, but don't you see? John is just a farmer, and he is more than ten years older than you. Does he even want you? You'd always be just a substitute for your sister. I can give you so much more than John could! Ellie, I love you and want you to be my wife."

He changed his tone, put his arms around her and spoke as if explaining logic to a child. "I know we were starting off with a small house, but I have my eye on that estate just outside Bolton, with plans for a big lovely home with you the matron of it. Ellie, we love each other! You can't just throw your life away like that!"

Ellie hung her head in grief and indecision.

"Gerhard, it's not about things you or John can or cannot provide! It's because I love you that I wanted to marry you—I shared your dreams. However, John does need someone to look after the girls, and Mama and Papa want so much to keep them in the family. If I marry John, that will be assured. Papa says I have no choice; it is my responsibility. "

Gerhard dropped his arms. His eyes narrowed in anger. His voice was barely controlled and his cheeks flushed red.

"Your parents are being absolutely selfish in this. They are not thinking of your good. They are thinking only of themselves." He stamped his foot and slammed his fist against the side of the house. His red face and angry eyes matched his voice, which sounded somewhere between an angry shout and a desperate cry that emanated from deep inside him.

"Ellie, I forbid you to do this! You can't do this to us!"

Tears of anger and confusion sprang from Ellie's eyes.

"Stop that, Gerhard! Who are you thinking of? Are you really thinking of me more than my parents? This isn't easy for me, either!" Ellie stopped to wipe the tears from her eyes with the back of her hand.

"Gerhard, my parents love me too. At first I didn't want to listen because it seemed preposterous, but they insisted that it was the wise and right thing to do. I still don't want to—it tears my insides—but I feel an obligation to do it." She looked up, hoping Gerhard could understand the turmoil she had experienced in making her decision.

"Yes, John is just a farmer, but he is a kind, considerate man. I cannot take lightly the request and desire of my parents. They have been good parents to me, and I do owe them something—probably I owe it to Maria and Marta as well. They are almost like daughters to me. Since Regina's death, I have taken care of them more than anyone except their father." She paused to catch her breath. The anger still simmered in Gerhard's eyes. His fingers dug into her upper arms where he once more held her firmly in his grip.

Tears spilled from her eyes, and her shoulders drooped in defeat. "Gerhard, I had looked forward to life with you. It breaks my heart, too, but please understand I have to do this. Oh Gerhard, please understand. Believe me, I want you with my whole heart, but I have to do what my parents ask."

She leaned against Gerhard and sobbed with abandon. Gerhard held her close and kissed her forehead. "Oh Ellie, please don't do this!"

Ellie released herself slightly from his embrace. Slowly, but with determination, she took the ring from her finger, took Gerhard's hand from her arm and placed the ring in it, closing his fingers over it. She placed her hands on each side of his face and stood on her tiptoes to kiss him. She saw the desperation and humiliation in his eyes and the pallor of his face, and her heart tightened in a dreadful pang. He drew his breath to speak, but she placed her finger over his lips.

"Shh-hh! Please just go now before I weaken. I know you will find someone to love who loves you and will make your dreams come true. I will always remember the good times we shared. But I must do what I must do. I hope you can wish me well, for I will have some big hurdles in the days ahead. Oh dear, dear Gerhard, may God be with you!"

Gerhard reached out for her hands and gave a heart-wrenching cry.

"Ellie!"

But then he did as she had bid him. He turned and ran toward the gate. She watched him go before turning to enter the house. Her stomach lurched and her heart twisted in grief and uncertainty. Even though she felt she had done what was her responsibility to her parents, sobs of grief surged up as she ran to her room and wracked her body as she fell on her bed.

In the days following the break with Gerhard, Ellie resumed her schedule and immersed herself in the care of the two motherless little girls. When she would first wake in the morning things seemed as usual. Then reality would roll over her like a heavy load that almost crushed her. Her heart would cry out in loneliness to Gerhard and then to God for help to face the day.

Most days, the girls came to her parents' house. Occasionally, she would go to John's house to do cleaning. John went about the work of the farm as if in a daze. It was only at the end of the day, with his girls in his arms, that he seemed to feel any life or meaning. He insisted on caring for them at night, answering their calls, explaining over and over again that Mama couldn't come back but that he loved them and would take care of them, and to remember how much Mama had loved them. When they were at home, Mrs. Miller, a neighbour, would come early in the morning to stay in the house until after morning chores, and then the girls would go once more to their grandparents' house.

When the days ended Ellie escaped to her room. Even though her body was tired from the busy days, her mind played over and over the events that had led to that final scene with Gerhard. There were times when anger at her parents almost overwhelmed her, but just as often her anger was aimed at herself for consenting to their plan. She missed Gerhard so—what had she been thinking, to cut off their engagement, to trash their dreams?

When Ellie broke off her engagement to Gerhard her parents approached John with their plan. At first John seemed horrified at the thought, but as Mama and Papa gently kept suggesting this as a solution to his loneliness and need, he began to think of it as a possibility.

Ellie felt suspended in a difficult grief journey. She longed to just talk with Gerhard. She had always felt so special as they discussed so many things, dreaming about their future and deciding together what steps they should take and when. Now she felt afloat on a large sea without an anchor. She longed for the safety of the love that had been theirs.

At times she wondered if she had made a big sacrifice for nothing. She felt so alone. What if John decided that marrying her was not something he could do? She couldn't very well go back to Gerhard and ask him to take her back. Sunday and Wednesday nights were the worst, for it had been those evenings she and Gerhard would spend together. In the dark of night her fears loomed large and she often cried herself to sleep. When John made no moves toward her, a large part of

Ellie's heart hoped that Gerhard would come again and plead with her to reconsider, but she saw nothing of him.

Her heart ached for John's obvious sorrow and became all mixed up in her own grief for her sister, the pain of letting Gerhard go and the fear for her future. As she watched Maria and Marta at play, her heart bled with anguish to realize all her sister would miss; yet she enjoyed the interaction with them and their growing trust in her care.

She had always been a loving and well-loved aunt, but now her heart warmed when they turned to her to solve their problems or soothe their hurts. What if John didn't go along with the plan and they would have to make another adjustment? She felt suspended in uncertainty—tossed from resolution to desperation and back again. Privately, in those weeks Ellie's prayers became earnest pleas that God would move both her and John's hearts to know the right path—and if marrying John was the right path, that he would remove from her own heart the ardor and longing for Gerhard and replace it with a love for John.

Sundays, after church, John came to her parents' house for dinner. Afterward they went for walks in the woods, sat in the orchard while the girls played in the long grass, or went for a drive through the countryside. A few times, they took the girls and a picnic lunch along.

Gradually, the strangeness disappeared; the girls seemed to enjoy the sense of family, and she and John became more comfortable with each other. One afternoon in late summer, John reached out to take her hands.

"Ellie," he said, looking into her eyes, "If you are still willing, I would like to ask you to marry me. I am ready to make a commitment to you, and I hope we can be a real family."

Ellie looked deep into John's eyes. It was a declaration of commitment, not love.

"Are you really sure this is what you want, John?"

Taking a deep breath, John replied, "Yes, Ellie, this is what I want."

Again, she searched his eyes for any doubt. Seeing only a quiet assurance, she spoke, "Then my answer to your question is yes."

He pulled her into his arms and lifted her chin to kiss her on her lips. That kiss seemed to seal their agreement and

Trying to calm herself, she hung her coat in the front closet and placed her hat on the shelf. She smoothed her gray velvet skirt and glanced at the lacy blouse that had topped her wedding outfit. Fixing the loose chestnut curls that had escaped her pompadour, she walked slowly into the kitchen where she had shared so many heart-to-heart talks with her sister. She laid her hand on the back of the chair where she had often sat. She could almost feel Regina's presence. The thought left her feeling uneasy. *Oh God! What have I done?* If Regina could see her, what would she think of her sister, seven years her junior, stepping into her shoes? Her stomach tightened into a hard knot as grief, fear and uncertainty washed over her. Tears welled in her eyes, but she quickly wiped them away when she heard John coming in the woodshed door. He mustn't see her crying on their wedding night. The kitchen door opened and John looked at her. Perhaps she hadn't hidden her feelings well enough, for his first question was, "Ellie? Are you sure you are all right?"

Quietly she nodded in the affirmative. He reached to put an arm around her shoulder.

"This is going to be difficult for you and me, Ellie," he went on, "Regina was important to both of us. We both loved her dearly. Neither of us has had enough time to get over missing her."

His kindness and understanding melted something in her heart, and she felt the tears once more. This time, she couldn't hold them back.

"Oh John!" she turned toward him. He held her closely. After her outburst subsided, she lifted her tear-stained face to look into his eyes. There she saw tears as well.

"Are you still sure this is really what you want, John?" she asked.

John, visibly moved, swallowed and paused before replying.

"Ellie, it's not easy to know what I really want. Regina was my first love. We had only a few years together, but our love was a deep, abiding and comfortable love. I wanted to live on with her. We weren't finished with our life together! I miss her so much! However, the girls do need a mother, they are comfortable with you and I know you love them." John paused, and seemed lost in memories and thoughts of his own.

Even surrounded by John's arms, Ellie's heart sank. Sure, she loved the children, and she had always admired John, but this was not all she wanted for her life. Again, dread clutched her heart as she thought of all she had surrendered for this plan. Should she have listened to her parents? Should she have let Gerhard go? She and Gerhard had courted for two and a half years—had been engaged for six months. She knew he loved her and she loved him.

It's a little late to be asking that now! She mentally chided herself even while her heart remained weighted as a heavy stone within her breast.

With a gentle squeeze, John continued, "But Ellie, I am committed to loving you too. You may need to be patient with me, but I do care for you, and I'm sure love will grow."

Again he paused as he led her to the settee in front of the kitchen window and sat down beside her.

"I know what you gave up, too, Ellie. We both have some adjustments. It'll take some time."

He lifted her chin and looked into her eyes. His lips met hers in a tender kiss. "Are you still sure that this is what you want?"

Ellie forced a smile, "Let me answer as you did, John. We both have some adjustments to make and learning to do." She reached over to place a kiss on his cheek, "Some time has passed, and much has happened since, but I admired you when Regina first brought you home. I imagined then what it would be like to love a man like you. Now I will find out!"

John pulled Ellie close.

"Thank you, Ellie, for your courage and willingness to take 'us' on. I promise to do my best to be all I can be for you!"

They sat in silence for some time. The scene felt unreal, as though they were actors on a stage. A surge of despair washed over her. *Stop it, Ellie!* she remonstrated. She would not allow herself to look back; it would be of no help in her present situation. She must put those things out of her mind and move forward. Now was the time for her to let one of her personality traits get to work—the one she called "determination" while the rest of her family was wont to say "stubbornness." She lifted her chin in resolve. There would be some times of learning ahead, but she'd never been one to turn away from a challenge. She would do her part to be what John needed and give Maria and Marta the kind of mothering Regina would have wished to give them. They would be a family, and they would learn to love each other even if it took everything she had within her.

Chapter Two

The kettle sang a merry tune on the kitchen range as Ellie set the table for breakfast. She had roused when John left the bed to go to the barn.

"Just stay there for awhile," he said, "I'll start the fire before I do the chores, so wait until the chill is off before you get up. There will be lots of mornings ahead when you have to get up!"

He bent to kiss her before he got dressed and left the room. By that time Ellie was almost asleep again, but as she heard John light the fire and adjust the dampers, her thoughts turned again to last night. John's gentleness, kindness and consideration of her, in spite of his own grief, touched her deeply. Even though she had promised herself not to let her mind go there, she couldn't help remembering that, only a short while ago, she had imagined sharing those special first moments of marriage with Gerhard. It felt odd to change those expectations and let John into her private dreams. Much as he had loved her, however, she could not imagine Gerhard being so solicitous and patient with her. She had loved him so much, and she had to admit that she still did to a great extent. Gerhard was much more flamboyant than John. He was a man with a plan for his life. No farming for him! He was going to establish himself in the textile business and had great plans for the growth of the industry. Already, he worked long hours and spent much of his time with plans for progress.

Coming back to the present, Ellie stretched and yawned. She had better get out of bed. The air was definitely warmer; she could almost smell the warmth! Perhaps it was the bit of wood smoke, but it was a comforting odor. John would be finished with chores soon. It wouldn't do for him to come in to find her still in reverie with no breakfast on the table.

She chose a light-green cotton dress with tiny gold flowers—one of her better everyday dresses, and pulled it over her head. After brushing her long hair, she pinned it in a figure eight on the back of her head and went to the kitchen. She added a bit of wood to the fire and filled the teakettle. Tomorrow afternoon Mama and Papa would bring Maria and Marta, so she and John would have until tomorrow evening to themselves. Since they could spend a leisurely day today, John had suggested taking a picnic lunch to the woods at the back of the farm.

The nights were getting to be chilly, but this morning the sun was shining. It looked as though it would be a nice day, warm enough to carry through with their plans. She put eggs on to boil. Egg salad sandwiches were one of John's favorites, she knew. She went down to the damp, dark cellar for a jar of pickles. The shelves were lined with jars of produce from her parents' garden. When they were preserving these things, Ellie thought, she still hadn't known if she and John would be using them or if they would stay in the Kessler cellar. Some of the ambivalence she experienced in the summer washed over her. *But this food and I are in this house now, and John and I have these two days for getting used to each other*, she thought. *I will do my best to let him know that I am ready to do my part.*

Upon her return to the kitchen, she took the eggs from the stove, drained the hot water and poured cold water over them to help them cool. *Fresh water from the well would be colder!* She reached for her sweater, then the granite water pail, and went out to the well. She filled the pail, breathing the fresh air as she pumped the wooden handle. The air was rather nippy, so she hurried back to the warmth of the kitchen.

As she added more cold water to the eggs, she mentally finished the menu for their picnic lunch. A few pieces of the pie she had brought to the house at the beginning of the week and a couple cookies from the well-filled tin would complete the meal. If she put coffee in a jar and wrapped it in paper and towels, it would still be warm enough by the time they were ready for it.

She put the pan on the stove and added some lard. Fried potatoes and slices of ham ought to satisfy John after choring. The coffee was percolating, so she set the table. On a whim, she went outside and clipped a few flowers that were still blooming close to the house. She found a bit of greenery to add to the nosegay to put in a vase on the table. Not all men would fully appreciate that touch, but she knew John liked helping to care for the flowerbeds even after working all day in the fields. Regina had often said that the beauty in nature was a delight to John. The mingling smells of hot food as she reentered the kitchen made her smile. Probably that aroma was more pleasing to a man than expensive bottled perfumes dabbed behind the ear.

Ellie reached for a vase and arranged and rearranged the flowers to give them gracefully flowing lines. She set them on the table and stood there in reverie. The first time John had asked Ellie to go for a drive on a Sunday afternoon, he had brought her a small bouquet of flowers from Regina's garden.

That afternoon had started with a level of discomfort, but John had been quite honest in stating his need and discussing the plan her parents suggested. She was still impressed at his kindness and concern for her in asking how she felt about such a possibility.

"John, believe me, I have given this a lot of thought. I must admit I have struggled, but I wouldn't have broken my engagement to Gerhard if I hadn't been willing to do what Papa and Mama wish. However, in order for the plan to work, it must also be what you want," she told him.

John had been quiet for a moment. "Ellie, let's spend some time together and test it out before we make any final decisions. We can see how we feel about it when we have had a chance to talk more seriously about ourselves and each other."

Glancing out the window, Ellie saw John emerging from the barn. Quickly, she added the potatoes to the frying pan, took a momentary look in the mirror, and then turned the slices of ham.

If the saying is true that the way to a man's heart is through his stomach, I can at least try to use it as one method to help love grow. Her face broke into a grin at her own conniving to make love develop.

"Mmm-mm! Smells good!" John remarked as he came through the door from the back entry. "It's nice to have breakfast ready and waiting after chores!"

Ellie smiled again. His remark seemed to confirm what she had just been thinking. John went to the basin in the corner to wash up. After toweling dry and combing his hair, he took his customary place at the table as Ellie served up the breakfast.

"Nice touch!" he said when he noticed the flowers. "It makes our first morning together extra special."

"Thanks, John." She felt rather self-conscious and a bit uncomfortable—still like a visitor. "I like having flowers in the house."

She sat at the place around the corner from John's seat at the table. John reached for her hand and cupped it in his on top of the table.

"Let's pray."

They bowed their heads.

"Gracious Father, you have led us through dark and difficult days. Our hearts have been broken and our lives torn apart. We thank you that you are the healer of broken hearts.

"This day, as Ellie and I begin our life together, we pray for your presence and guidance and blessing on our lives. Teach us to love each other, to be honest and open with each other and to be patient with each other, just as you are with us. Our trust is in you.

"Bless, now, this food that you have provided and that Ellie has prepared, that we may be strengthened to do your will this day.

"In Jesus' name we pray, Amen."

Tears shone in Ellie's eyes as she lifted her head. "Oh John!" she murmured, "Thank you for that prayer. If we keep that our intent, God will surely bless us and help us build our marriage into all that it can be."

John lifted her hand to his lips. He placed a kiss on the top of her hand.

"That, by his grace, is what we will do. Now let us eat this delicious breakfast before it gets cold!"

"Looks like a nice day for a picnic!" John commented after a few bites. "Will you pack a lunch for us?"

"I already have eggs boiled to make sandwiches, and I have pickles and pie and cookies ready to go. The coffee is perking too, and there is enough to take along after we have our morning cups."

"Great! I'll just turn the cows out after breakfast, then I will be ready to go."

After eating his fill, John pushed back his chair and patted his stomach.

"Good breakfast, Mrs. Kurtz!" His eyes twinkled with merriment, "If this is evidence of what I'm in for, I will have to work extra hard to keep from getting a middle-age spread!"

"Mr. Kurtz, you may be a lot older than your beautiful young wife, but I don't think of you as middle-aged! With as hard as you've been working, not to mention losing weight while eating your own cooking, it will take you awhile just to catch up! I will not have it said that my handsome husband is looking poorly!"

John chuckled as he rose from his chair.

"You get that lunch ready, and as soon as I can finish in the barn, we will be off to the woods."

"Don't worry, I'll be ready and waiting with bells on!"

John reached for his hat and light jacket and went out the door. Ellie turned to the table to clear the dishes. Getting out the dishpan, she got warm water from the stove and a block of homemade soap to add suds. Quickly, she washed the dishes and wiped the oilcloth that covered the table, the routine acts bringing her some comfort in her new situation. She looked through Regina's cupboard drawers until she found a doily to put underneath the vase of flowers, thankful that John had enjoyed her efforts. Her eyes lingered on the flowers as she remembered John's prayer. Thankfulness arose in her heart, and she prayed, "Thank you that you will walk with us, Father!"

She took the cooked eggs from their shells and mashed them with a fork to make the sandwich filling. Going to the pantry, she got the large wicker basket and some clean tea towels. Carefully, she wrapped the dish that held two good-sized pieces of pie. She put some pickles in a small jar and tucked it into the side of the basket. Slicing a fresh loaf of bread, she liberally buttered the slabs and made the sandwiches. Cutting them diagonally, she wrapped them in a clean tea towel and put them in the basket. She was just stirring sugar and cream into the coffee when John came in from the barn.

"Ready to go?" he asked as he washed up again.

"Just as soon as I wrap this coffee to keep it warm."

"Take your time! I want get out of these barn clothes," said John as he headed for the bedroom.

John emerged from the bedroom minutes later in clean overalls and a blue plaid shirt, carrying a blanket. Picking up the basket with that hand, he laid the other on her shoulder.

"Let's go, Ellie. It's quite a ways to the back of the farm and I have a lot to show you along the way. We could make it in half an hour or so if we had to do it quick, but I'm glad we can take our time today."

Hand in hand, they walked past the weathered barn and through the gate to the grassy lane that led to the wood lot at the back of the farm. Ellie sniffed the barn smells and smiled.

"I guess city folk would think it stinks around a barn, but to me, there is something homey about the aroma."

"Perhaps that's because you are used to it and you know that those smells are the evidence that good living and plenty of food come from within."

Ellie smiled. John's observations sometimes sounded so formal and almost poetic. Perhaps he, too, was feeling as though they were actors on a stage just play-acting the parts that had been assigned to them. She wondered how long it would take before they felt comfortable and at home with each other.

They walked in silence down the back lane. In the brush that lined the fencerows on either side birds flitted silently from branch to branch.

"If this were springtime, you would hear much more singing. The birds are on their way south now. No time for singing along the way. They are foraging for food to make the long journey. In the spring we will come this way again. When the warblers are coming through, you'll be surprised at how many kinds there are. They are such colorful birds, but hard to spot if you aren't patient. The best way to see them is to just sit and watch them as they go by."

They walked through long grass at the edge of the field. John made a right turn and held back the branches of the thick shrubs and trees so Ellie could get through the thick brush. When they emerged on the other side, they were at the top of the riverbank. Huge maples and oaks spread their limbs out over the bank. There was a clearing right at the top, covered by a thick carpet of leaves. John brushed off a fallen log and sat down, drawing Ellie with him.

"This is where I like to sit in the spring and watch for my feathered friends."

Ellie looked up to see his face lit with pleasure.

"How do you know what they are? I know there are different kinds of birds, but other than the more common ones, I have just looked at them as—" she hesitated, "well, as—birds! I don't think I could even name fifteen different varieties."

"I couldn't have, either, at one time, but I saw John James Audubon's book *Birds of America* advertised in a paper once and sent for it. I really enjoy being able to identify them and to know what an endless variety God created. I'll show you the book when we get back to the house. Look up at that big maple. There's a white-breasted nuthatch. You can always identify them because they are usually upside-down on a tree trunk. They're handsome little fellows!"

Ellie strained to see where John was pointing.

"Oh, yes, I see it now. He has a little black cap! Oh, there he goes!"

"We may see him again."

They sat in silence for awhile, watching the activity of the birds as they passed by.

Occasionally John would whisper the name of another species. After some time, he arose.

"Are you rested and ready to go on?"

When Ellie moved to get up, John reached for her hand to help her, then kept holding it as he led her on to descend a ravine to the left. At the bottom John stepped out on a stone in the middle of the small rivulet that led to the river and extended his hand to her.

"Here, let me help you over this little stream. You can step on this other stone, Ellie, then hop over to the other side."

When Ellie had successfully negotiated the jump, John joined her, taking her hand again as they ascended the steep hill on the other side. Pausing part way up, John patted the trunk of a tall pine.

"This is my favorite pine tree. I've been measuring its circumference each year to log its growth. Just see how straight and tall it is. I always think it's reaching up to God to say thanks and perhaps even to kiss the clouds as they go by!" John smiled. "There is something about pines that inspires a man to be straight and true."

"What a beautiful comparison," responded Ellie. "I guess we can learn a lot by observing nature. I've always enjoyed the trees too, but I hadn't thought of them in that way. Now that you have pointed it out, I'll keep my eyes open for other lessons I can learn."

"It's one advantage of being a farmer," John said. "Being out in the open through the year gives lots of chances to listen to God's creation."

"True," observed Ellie, "but not all farmers listen, even when surrounded by the evidence! I think, perhaps, you're rather exceptional in your understanding; I admire that quality in you."

"I hope I'm not that exceptional," remarked John. "It would be too bad to miss all that we can appreciate in the plants and wildlife around us. Come to my 'Dining Glade.' We'll leave our lunch basket there until I show you something else."

Through the trees they wended their way, stopping now and then while John identified other kinds of trees, until once again they were in sight of the river. There, high on the bank stood a grove of hemlocks forming a circle around a sheltered spot, the ground covered by a thick mat of hemlock needles. John set the basket down and covered it with the blanket.

"We've taken a long time getting here, but I wanted to show you why this acreage at the back of the farm is so special to me. Now we still have enough time for me to show you the grand matriarch of the woods before lunch time." John, again taking her by the hand, led her along a narrow path at the top of the riverbank, down a gully, and up to the other side. In another five minutes or so they came to an opening in the thick woods. They found themselves in a clearing where a giant oak, its leaves turning a dark brownish red, spread its branches over a vast grassy area. The trunk itself was immense. Ellie felt a sense of awe.

"What a huge tree! It must be ancient!"

"It is. The only way to know its age for sure would be to cut it down and count the rings, but I would think it must be at least one hundred years old. It helps me put my own life in perspective when I stand here beneath its shelter."

He put his arm around her.

"See how many babies she has? I don't know if that means she is preparing to die or not, but in the last few years there have been a lot of acorns, and now the little oaks are thick at the far edges of her branches. I would like to transplant a few of the bigger ones closer to the house. We would never see them this big, but they have to start somewhere."

"Why don't we plant a few between the house and barn? Some day they may be big enough to attach a rope for a swing for our grandchildren—or great-grandchildren," Ellie laughed.

"Now that's what I call forward thinking!" John chuckled. "Meanwhile, we can bring the children here to show them the possibilities!"

"It is a lovely place!" remarked Ellie. "Almost like a cathedral!"

She picked up a few of the acorns, rubbing her finger over the smooth lower part of the nuts while admiring the little cap on each one. She dropped a few into the pocket of her dress.

"I guess it's as good a place as any to worship," John agreed. "Our hearts should worship whenever we feel awe and wonder at God's beauty and goodness. It's getting close to noon so let's go back to the dining room!"

As they walked, arm in arm, back to the hemlock glade, Ellie marveled at the depth and sensitivity of this man she had married. She felt privileged to share some of the insights and understanding he had revealed. She treasured it as a precious gift. Surely, he was making an effort to share himself with her and help to establish a bond. She fingered the acorns in her pocket. She would put them in her jewelry box to remind her of this day.

When they reached the hemlocks, John laid the blanket on the soft mat and Ellie spread out their lunch. Small hemlocks grew at the outer edge of the glade, sheltering them from any breeze. The sun shone warmly into the little haven, forming a private dining room with décor only nature could provide. Carefully, she poured two cups of coffee and wrapped the remainder to keep it warm. John sat down close to her and reached for her hand as he bowed his head in prayer.

"Father, in this outdoor chapel we again bring you thanks for your love, for each other and for the food we are about to partake. We thank you for your blessings through Jesus Christ our Lord. Amen."

Pressing her hand, he smiled at her. "I've enjoyed sharing my woods with you. It's been a good day already."

Ellie passed him a napkin and a sandwich.

"I've enjoyed it too. I agree that it's been a good day. Would you like a pickle with that?"

John reached for one. Quietly, they enjoyed the food. As they finished their pie, Ellie was conscious of the closeness of John's arm as it brushed hers. She felt a quiver through her body. She bent her head to touch John's shoulder. He looked tenderly down at her and put his arm around her waist.

"More coffee?" Ellie inquired.

"I think I will."

Ellie unwrapped the jar and refilled his cup. As he sipped his coffee, he talked about his joy in sitting quietly observing nature.

"There is such a vast variety of plants and animals. Nature is so carefully balanced. Not much grows beneath these hemlocks, but what does grow here is entirely different from what grows beneath a maple or oak tree. There are many flowers here in the spring, yet later on there isn't that much evidence of the color and beauty that we see earlier in the season. Mushrooms of all kinds grow in the woods too, and then later in the fall I look for puffballs. They're so good fried in a bit of butter. I am always fascinated at their short life span. They go from nothing at all to a huge ball to a small pile of dust in a matter of a few days."

John emptied his cup.

"Let's put these towels and things back in the basket."

When they had everything tucked away, John reached for her and stretched back on the blanket, taking her with him in his arms.

"So, my dear, how are you feeling about your new station in life?"

She raised herself on one elbow and leaned on his chest so she could look him straight in eyes.

"Mr. Kurtz, give me time, but I think I'm going to like being married to you. What I have learned about you this morning has been a precious insight into your heart. I just hope I can give you the same kind of gift."

He drew her close and kissed her.

"I'm glad you like the things I like. It helps if we have common interests. As I said last night, it'll take some time, but I believe that we'll learn to truly love each other."

Ellie laid her head on his chest and he held her close. The warmth of the sunshine in the little glade shone assurance and blessing on them. It was some time later when John roused.

"It's about time to head back to the house. Cousin Jake did the chores for me last night, but tonight, it's up to me! It's getting a little cool anyway." John folded the blanket and put it on top of the basket, picked everything up and took Ellie by the arm, heading back by the way they came.

As they walked, Ellie realized she was beginning to see through John's eyes, for she recognized some of the birds and varieties of trees he had pointed out.

"Oh God," she silently prayed, "How often we miss blessings because we are too busy to notice! Help me to have open eyes and ears to the people and things around me."

She pressed John's arm close to her and wondered what all was in store for them.

Chapter Three

Slowly, Ellie opened her eyes. The moon shone in through the bedroom window. She quietly turned her head to see the outline of her husband's sleeping form. It must be close to morning. She could still hardly believe that she was married to John Kurtz. Yesterday had been such a beautiful day, yet she wondered how it would be when the girls came home this afternoon and she and John would not have so much time for one another. Would she be able to be both wife and mother?

She had been looking after the girls for some time now, but her mother had also been there most of the time and Martin had often played with the girls when she was washing dishes. Would she really be able to handle it all by herself?

Get a hold on it, Ellie! Put your chin up and take a moment at a time! You have come this far and there's no going back, so it's straight ahead!

She lay quiet, her thoughts alternating between hope and self-doubt.

Lord, I know that I do not need to walk this way alone. You have promised to be with me to the end of the world, and John is a good man. Help me to remember that. But God, right now I feel as though the job is too big—that I have started something that I don't know if I can do. We care for one another, but I long to feel the love that a husband and wife should have between them. It all seems so unreal, as though we were playing house. It is hard to wait for love to grow, but please let it come."

Beside her, John heaved a big sigh as he awoke. Becoming aware of her wakefulness, he asked, "Did you sleep?"

"Oh, yes, I just woke up early and got to thinking."

He reached for her hand. "And what were you thinking that kept you from sleeping?"

"Guess I was just wondering if I could measure up to all my responsibilities. I mean, all of a sudden, I have a husband and two daughters."

"The parenting we'll do together, Ellie," John assured her, "and as to being a wife, you've made a good start. Let's take one day at a time and stay open with each other."

Glancing out the window, John moved to get up. "I guess it's time to get up and at the chores," he commented.

"Do you want me to come out to feed the chickens and gather the eggs?"

"Thanks, Ellie, but I can do that. Tomorrow you will have the girls in the house and you won't be able to leave them." As he rose, he chuckled, "If you do it this morning, I might get used to it and get lazy!"

Ellie threw back the blankets and got up. "At least I can start the fire this morning. I'd like to do a few things before breakfast anyway; I still have some unpacking to do."

"All right, if you are sure you want to. There's lots of kindling in the wood box behind the stove. I'll do the chores, and then maybe before noon we can work at getting the flowerbeds ready for winter."

"Are you sure you have time?"

"These few days are for us. Tomorrow I will have to return to the more regular farm work, but today we will work together."

As Ellie buttoned her dress, John came to give her a kiss before he left for the barn. Ellie laid the blankets back to air the bed and went to the kitchen to start the fire. When the wood began to blaze, she filled the teakettle and set it on to heat. She shivered in the cool room and reached for a sweater from the hooks inside the back door. *If only it could be this easy to take the chill off my fears this morning! I feel as though I have cold feet in figurative ways as well as literal,* she thought as she felt the coziness of the wool on her body and held her hands over the fire to warm them.

Back in the bedroom, she lifted the lid of the trunk her father had brought to the house earlier in the week. Whether it was because they felt responsible for Ellie and John's tenuous liaison or not, Mama and Papa had been very helpful in doing everything they could to give them a good start. Mama had made sure there were enough canned goods and root vegetables to see them through the winter. She had even baked extra pies, cookies and biscuits and made soup to send along for their first days.

Now, as Ellie hung her dresses in the wardrobe and put her underclothes in drawers, the permanence of the change in her life became more real. Her jewelry chest, with the few pins and hair ornaments she possessed, she put on top of the chest of drawers. She placed the acorns she had picked up yesterday in the corner beside her combs.

Tenderly, she laid out the dresser set on top of John's dresser. That had been a gift from Gerhard, which he insisted Ellie should keep. The hand mirror, brush handle and top of the comb were polished walnut inlaid with tiny bits of mother-of-pearl in a dainty floral pattern. She felt a pang in her heart as she remembered the precious moment she and Gerhard had shared and his words of love and admiration when she had opened the gift. She lifted the mirror and looked at her reflection. Curly, chestnut hair surrounded a light complexion, although a few freckles still sprinkled across her nose. In spite of all Ellie's efforts, those last freckles just would not completely fade. Soft pink highlighted her cheekbones and green eyes, fringed with long lashes, stared back at her. Perhaps not a startling beauty, but as Mama always said, "You look nice enough to act nice!"

What conflicting emotions those outer attributes kept hidden! Gerhard had loved her and taken such pride in introducing her as his bride-to-be. She had in turn felt pride in Gerhard and looked forward to fulfilling the promises they had made to one another.

"Oh God! What have I done?"

Tears came to her eyes and her throat tightened to restrain a sob. She laid the mirror down.

"Enough of that!" she said out loud. "Life with Gerhard is past. Get on with the doing of what lies before you."

Finally, she reached the last items. Setting the shoes in the lower drawer of the wardrobe, she shut the lid of the trunk. John could carry it upstairs to the spare room. The chest would be a good place to store extra bedding. Or perhaps, she could put some of Regina's things in there.

Someday, she thought with sudden insight, *Maria and Marta will treasure some of the things their mother lovingly made.*

Ellie certainly had enough things in her own hope chest to replace the items that would hold special meaning to the girls.

Carefully, she made the bed, making sure there were no wrinkles on the counterpane. She ran her hand across the smooth finish of the rich cherry wood. It was beautiful furniture. The high posts were decoratively turned and the intricate carving on the headboard was repeated on the top drawers of the dresser, chest of drawers and side panels of the wardrobe. The lovely grain and deep color brought her delight, even though the big pieces almost overpowered the small bedroom. A spacious room with high ceilings would probably have done it more justice, she thought.

She returned to the kitchen to add wood to the fire and make breakfast. To still her anxious thoughts, she began to sing some old familiar hymns.

How happy they whose hopes rely on Israel's God,
Who made the sky and earth and sea with all their train,
Whose word forever stands secure,
Who heals the sick and feeds the poor,
And none shall find His promise vain.

She sang the verse over several times, and then hummed the tune while the words sank into her soul.

And none shall find his promise vain. So, I have to set my heart to accept that promise—my heart!

Into her mind drifted the last verse of another song, "Oh for a heart to praise my God." She sang that softly as her heart responded to God's promises.

A heart in every thought renewed and full of love divine, perfect and right and pure and good, a copy, Lord, of Thine.

She put the coffee on.

"Oh yes, God! I need to let you renew my heart. Make it a copy of yours!"

She put bacon in the pan and set the table. She was contentedly humming when John opened the door and entered the kitchen. She looked up in surprise.

"I didn't hear you coming!"

"Caught you in the act, did I?" his eyes sparkled as they reflected the smile on his lips. "Sounds as though I have a happy wife, though."

Ellie pulled the frying pan to the front of the stove and started to break the eggs into the hot bacon fat. She was not sure she wanted John to know about the struggle that had been quelled by her humming.

"It's nice to get settled in a bit. It still feels as though it is Regina's house, but I guess that will take some time to overcome—not that I want to forget Regina," she hastened to add. She reached for the turner and flipped the eggs.

"John, I was just thinking that perhaps you could take my trunk upstairs to the spare room. Do you think it would be all right if I put some of Regina's table runners, quilts and other things in there to save for Maria and Marta? Someday they may appreciate having some of their mama's things."

As she brought the plate of bacon and eggs to the table, John took them from her hand, set them down and took her into his arms.

"Ellie, that is very thoughtful of you! I'm sure you are right." Tears welled up in his eyes. "Much as we need to be a family, I do want the girls to remember their first mother too. Thank you, so much, for realizing that. I will take the trunk upstairs after breakfast."

They sat down for their breakfast. After John had prayed, Ellie spoke again.

"I remember, as a child, how Aunt Matilda used to take us up to her room when we visited Grandpa's. She was never married, and maybe that is why she was such a special person to us. She had more time to devote to us. She kept our great-grandparents' memories alive as she showed us some of the keepsakes from her bureau and told stories about them. I still cherish those memories and the bits of wisdom from her grandparents that she handed down to us as we went through those things. Do you think that Sunday afternoon we, as a family, could put some of Regina's things in the trunk? Marta is young enough she won't really remember, but I'd like if we could tell them stories about their mother as we put each thing into the trunk. Maria will remember more. Over the years we'll repeat them so that it will keep Regina's memory alive for both of them."

John's eyes mirrored the appreciation he felt. "I think that's a marvelous plan. You gather up the things you think they should keep, and we'll do it after Marta's nap on Sunday afternoon. Perhaps that would be a good place to keep the little knitted outfits Regina made for each of them before they were born. You'll find them in the chest in the upper hallway." He paused and swallowed hard. "The one she made for John Jr. is there too. Let's put that with the rest. Someday the girls may want to remember the brother they never got to know, and understand that he'd been loved already."

Ellie laid her hand on his arm in a comforting gesture.

"John, my heart cries for you too. You have lost so much. Not just a wife and son, but all the dreams you had for them and for life together."

John reached for his handkerchief, wiped his eyes and blew his nose. He paused for a moment to get his emotions in control.

"Thank you for understanding, Ellie. My loss is like a gaping hole. It feels as if a big part of me is gone too. I'm sorry if this makes you feel uncomfortable. I hope, eventually, things will settle into place and life will go on in a more normal fashion. Our life together is important too."

"Oh John!" Ellie exclaimed, "You must never apologize for your grief and sorrow in losing Regina and John Junior! If you need to cry, do! That is another of the things I admire in you. Not all men allow themselves the luxury of shedding tears. To me, it is an indication of the depth of your love and your ability to express it. I see it as another gift in building our lives together."

John pushed his chair back from the table, and pulled Ellie off hers and onto his lap and drew her close.

"Bless you, Ellie! You are a great comfort!"

She put her arms around his neck.

"I hope I can be that and much more!"

After a moment, in which he seemed to be drawing strength and comfort from her, John moved to get up.

"Well, I guess we'd better make use of some of this nice autumn sunshine! Before I came in I loaded the wheelbarrow with some well-rotted manure to put on the beds. I'll take the trunk upstairs, and then let me help you with the dishes. When that is done we'll both work at the flowerbeds."

Ellie scooped some warm water from the tank on the stove and quickly washed the dishes while John dried them and put them away. Giving the table a quick wipe, she opened the back door to empty the dishpan. She wiped it with the dishcloth and hung it on its hook in the pantry. Removing her apron, she slipped into her gardening shoes. As she reached for her sweater, John opened the back door and headed toward the shed. Ellie walked toward the flowerbeds in front of the porch on each side of the low steps. She broke off some slips from the geraniums that had escaped the light frost the week before. These she would plant in pots to put in the windows for the winter. By spring they would be attractive plants to return to front beds once more. Regina had a lovely variety of colors. The geraniums had thick, healthy stems. She should see if she could get a slip of Mama's "Age and Youth" begonia as well. It was her favorite begonia, except for the angel wing, which she had already made sure to bring along for the parlor. In spite of all John had to do in the summer, he had kept the flowerbeds well cared for and weed free.

As John rounded the corner of the house, he noticed the slips Ellie had laid on the front steps.

"I see you have taken some slips off. There are some pots inside the woodshed door, and you can use some soil from the pile right behind the woodshed. I will dig out the geraniums first, and if you would like to shake the loose dirt off of them and lay them on the back stoop on your way to the woodshed, we'll let them dry out for a few days and then I will hang them upside down in the cellar for the winter. They don't all grow again in the spring, but it's worth saving them for those that do."

Ellie eyes widened in surprise. "I didn't know one could do that," she said. "We always just took in slips, then planted those outside in the spring."

"I like lots of flowers," said John, "and the windowsills hold only so many."

Ellie picked up the geraniums as John loosened them from their summer homes, then gathered them in her arms to take to the back stoop. John began to dig up the rest of the plants to clear the beds of growth. When Ellie returned from her planting, John was just finishing spading in the rich natural fertilizer. The freshly turned sod was a dark contrast to the grass of the lawn. She sniffed, with delight, the mingled earthy smells of soil and leaves.

"Perhaps we can still dig out the dahlia roots at the side of the house before dinner," John suggested, "then we can have a rest before we get the gladiola bulbs from the end of the garden. If you wouldn't mind getting one of the hampers from the woodshed, we'll put the dahlia roots in it."

Ellie retrieved the hamper and cleaned off the roots as John unearthed them. Working together, a warm companionship imperceptibly drew them closer. "If you want to get a bit of dinner ready, Ellie, I will put fertilizer on this bed and dig it in and straighten up the edges a bit."

"I'll warm up some of the soup Mama sent home with us," Ellie replied.

Ellie looked back to see how carefully John was edging the bed to make it look neat. It felt good to share the work and enjoy the out-of-doors together. She washed her hands, donned her apron and began to prepare a simple meal for them. With the soup warming on the stove, she sliced bread and cheese, put some of the pickles in a dish and pieces of pie on small plates for dessert. As she set the soup bowls on the table, she ran her fingers over the pattern. How well she remembered Regina's careful decision regarding which pattern of dishes to choose. They were lovely, though. The circle of dark blue with the tiny sprigs of roses was set off by the gold edges that rimmed the plates and bowls.

"Oh, Regina, Regina," she sighed, "It doesn't seem fair that you should not be here to enjoy them." Guiltily, she realized it wasn't only Regina's dishes that she was learning to enjoy.

As if in answer to her thoughts, John came through the back door. He waved a postcard in her direction.

"The Millers just went past and brought our mail from town. There's a postcard from Uncle Henry and Aunt Bertha. Here, have a look!"

On the front an embossed stem of white lily-of-the-valley lay on a light blue background. A ribbon across the bouquet read "Wedding Wishes." The first thing Ellie noticed on the back was that it was addressed to Mr. and Mrs. John Kurtz. It was strange to think that she was included in that address. There was a small personal message and it was signed Uncle Henry and Aunt Bertha.

"How nice of them!" remarked Ellie.

Ellie laid the card on the table. By the time John was sitting at the table, Ellie had the soup in a serving bowl and was also ready to be seated. When they had prayed, he pointed to the card.

"We have always been very close to Uncle Henry and Aunt Bertha," John told her. "We were double cousins, for our fathers were brothers and our mothers, sisters. Because they lived right beside us we cousins played together almost daily when we were small. Uncle Henry and Aunt Bertha were almost a second set of parents. Jake was eight years younger than I was, so it was mostly the older ones I played with. Those my age have moved away, so I don't get to see them often, but as we got older, Jake turned out to be a good friend too. I enjoy working with him. Never thought, as we were growing up, that we older ones would be separated by so many miles!"

"You were lucky to have cousins so close." Ellie observed. "I guess we were the ones to move away. All my mother's brothers and sisters live a hundred miles away, so I didn't get to see them more than a few times in my whole life. We had Grandma and Grandpa Kessler, but Aunt Matilda never married, so there were no cousins on that side of the family."

"That is hard for me to imagine," remarked John. "Although Uncle Henry's lived closest, my cousins—five children on my father's side and six on my mother's—all lived within about ten miles of us as we were growing up."

"It's going to take me a while to get everyone straight with that big a family!" Ellie commented.

"Oh, we're quite a friendly bunch," John said. "We usually have a picnic every summer. Everyone brings some food and we eat very well as we catch up on each other's lives. Of course, some of Uncle Henry's family don't always make it because of the distance, but you'll eventually meet them all."

When they had finished eating, John said, "There are such few dishes, and your parents will be coming with the girls later this afternoon, so let's just rinse them a bit and then I want to show you something before we do the gladiolas. For now, it's a dream, but I'd like to tell you about it."

"Sure!" replied Ellie as she removed her apron. What, she wondered, was this new husband of hers going to surprise her with now?

Unlike many farm lanes that came straight in from the road, this tree-lined lane curved gently toward the end over a bridge spanning a rather deep ditch before it met the road. The large maples met overhead, forming a leafy arch. Many of the leaves had fallen, but some color remained. The leaves lay thick on the lane and Ellie delighted in shuffling through them, hearing them whisper of the winter to come.

John bent over, scooping a handful of leaves and playfully letting them flutter down on Ellie's head. Ellie laughed and bent to scoop her own handful, but John ran ahead to escape from her reprisal. She threw them anyway, missing John entirely. He waited for her to catch up, caught her and planted a kiss on her lips.

"Watch out!" Ellie warned, "the neighbors might see!"

"Think I might make them jealous?"

As they neared the turn of the lane, John reached for her hand and drew her toward the ditch. "There is a very large stone at the back of the farm. Someday, I would like to put it on the stone boat and bring it up here. I think, with a small cedar behind it, and perhaps forsythia on each side, it would be a nice entrance to our property—the whole arrangement would be a focal point of colour and beauty. Even during the rest of the summer, there would be a contrast of greens. With a few irises and daffodils in front of it, we could have a real welcoming sight for our visitors. Perhaps we could even paint a small sign "Maple Lane Farm." Eventually, we could make a rock garden on the slope and a small walking bridge over the ditch to the trees on the other side."

"That would be very pretty!" Ellie exclaimed. "If we have enough geraniums, we could plant a few out here and they could provide colour all summer."

"It's a huge stone, but perhaps I can get cousin Jake and a few others to come and help me get it in place," John surmised.

"It seems to me that part of the dream wouldn't have to wait long to come to pass."

"You're right," John replied, "I'll see if I can get Jake to come yet this fall. We could level off a spot, then, once we have the rock in place, we could find a small cedar from down along the river and transplant it while it's dormant. Next spring we can add the flowers."

"We can get some forsythia shoots from home," Ellie mused.

"Guess we'd better get back to work if we are to finish up before the girls get home."

The gladiola bulbs were harvested and safe in the root cellar when John suggested resting on the bench on the front veranda. From there they could watch for the arrival of the girls. From their vantage point, they chatted amiably as they surveyed the beautiful view of their front lawn and lane. John's arm was on Ellie's shoulder, and her hand rested on his knee.

By and by, John pressed her close to him and kissed her on top of her head. "Here they come!"

Sure enough, her father's horses and buggy were in sight just past their neighbor's trees. John reached for her hand and squeezed it.

"Are you ready? We've had two days alone and I've enjoyed them, but I do miss the girls. I hope we aren't too much for you!"

"We'll take it one day at a time. Actually, I miss the girls too."

They stood at the porch railing to watch as their family came around the bend in the lane.

"Papa!" the girls cried as John and Ellie waved. The buggy hadn't quite come to a standstill when Maria stood up. Her grandfather reached out and grabbed her arm to keep her from falling.

"Just a minute, little lady," John admonished, as he reached to lift her out. Maria wrapped her arms around his neck and buried her face in his shoulder.

"Me too, Papa!" Marta cried.

"I've got room for both of my girls!" John assured her as he lifted her from the buggy into his other arm.

"We had a good time at Grandpa's," Marta excitedly shared. "Uncle Martin lifted me way up in a tree to see a bird's nest, but it didn't have any eggs in it, and he made the leaves in a big pile and let me jump in them and then he covered me all up with the leaves and he couldn't find me so I had to jump up so he could see me, and..."

"Whoa! Girlie," John told her, "You have the whole rest of the evening to tell me all about it. Let's ask Grandma and Grandpa if they would like to come into the house for awhile."

"Would you like to stay for supper?" Ellie asked. Marta ran to Ellie, and was lifted in her arms.

"Oh no, not tonight!" Mama replied, "We brought along some things for you, though. I baked some fresh bread today, and a few more pies. I brought along a part of a ham that I cooked, and Dad dug our potatoes, so we have a few of those for you. If you want to make us a cup of tea while we unload, we'll stay for that, then we'll go again so you can get used to being a family."

Ellie noticed that three-year-old Marta was again gaily running about, glad to be at home, but six-year-old Maria stayed close to her father, leaning closely to him. *She is more aware of her loss and the changes,* thought Ellie. *She is also much quieter than Marta. I will have to find ways to reach her and help her express her feelings.*

Even though Ellie had cared for her much of the time since Regina's death, she wondered if Maria might feel a little resentment toward Ellie's new role in the family.

They all carried something from the buggy inside, and Ellie put the kettle on for tea. Marta was still running about, finding her toys and chatting to anyone who would listen. Maria sat quietly on her father's lap. Ellie put out some cookies, and poured tea for each of them.

"Would you like apple juice," she asked the girls, "or would you rather have some milk?"

"I want milk!" Marta chirped.

What about you, Maria?" Ellie asked.

"Apple juice, please," Maria's requested politely.

Ellie went to the cupboard and got a few of the small glasses from the good dishes they didn't normally use. Those would be a treat for the girls to use for their drink. Into one she poured milk, and in the other, apple juice. "Now, Marta," she admonished, "you must sit down and be careful! Don't break the glass and try not to spill it."

"I be careful!" promised Marta.

"You're a big girl, Maria. I know you will do all right"

Everyone enjoyed the tea, along with good conversation, but it ended when Papa said, "We'd better get going. It's beginning to get dark. Martin said he'd start the chores, but I don't think he meant to do them all."

They all arose to see them out to the buggy. The new family joined in waving good-bye to the grandparents as they went on their way.

Chapter Four

Making use of her parents' gift of potatoes, Ellie added bits of parsley and fresh cream to begin the meal. Along with fried squash, cold ham and slices of fresh apple pie, it made a delicious supper. Marta's chatter about her days with her grandparents and beloved uncle accompanied the entire meal. With the encouragement of John and Ellie, Maria occasionally shared in the storytelling. Before the end of the meal, Marta's narrative was increasingly interrupted by yawns.

John reached over and patted her head. "Looks like it's almost bedtime, little missy! Maria, why don't you get the violin? I will play our lullaby, and then, when you are ready for bed, I will come and read a story after you are tucked in."

Maria brought her father's violin. As she handed it to him, she looked up into his face. "I want you to hear my prayer and tuck me in, Papa."

John laid the violin on the table, set Maria on his lap and put his other arm around Marta. "Girls, I want to tell you something. Your mama will always be your first mama. You know how much she loved you, but now she is in heaven with your little brother, John. Aunt Ellie has taken such good care of you since Mama left. Now she will be your new mama. If you don't feel comfortable calling her that right away, perhaps you want to just call her Ma."

Maria quietly nodded her head, but Marta emphatically proclaimed, "I call Aunt Ellie *Mama*!"

A look of pain crossed Maria's face. John hugged her close. "It will be different, but she loves you too, and don't forget, I love you. I'll always be here for you."

Maria glanced at Ellie, who had kept silent through the conversation. Now she intuitively assured Maria.

"You don't need to call me Ma or Mama until you are ready. I'll answer to Aunt Ellie until then. I do love you, though."

"Now listen to our lullaby," John turned to Ellie to explain. "This is a lullaby that my mother used to sing to us, and her mother before her. It comes from the old country—*Mude ich bin ich geh zur Ruh*"—"I'm Tired and I'm Going to Rest."

John picked up the violin and bow, and soon the strains of the comforting music filled the room. He played it through several times with small variations, then put the violin away.

"I think we'd better get ready for bed and say our prayers, or Marta won't be awake for the story!"

"John," Ellie looked over the girls' heads into his eyes, "Why don't you put the girls to bed tonight as you usually do. Tomorrow night I will join you."

John understood the unspoken message. "What do you say, girls? Shall we let Ellie, er, Ma, finish up in the kitchen while we get tucked in?"

There was relief in Maria's eyes. "That would be nice, Papa. Come on Marta, Papa is going to tuck us into bed!"

Ellie busied herself in the kitchen. Her mind reviewed the day. She remembered, with warmth, the pleasure of working side by side with John. However, as she recalled Maria's quiet reticence, Ellie felt empathy mixed with inadequacy. Maria was old enough to feel her loss more deeply, but young enough that it was hard to fully perceive all the changes and to be able to put them into proper perspective. She could hear the girls voicing their prayers and then John beginning to tell their bedtime story. She hoped this little time together would allay some of Maria's discomfort.

"Oh God, Loving Heavenly Father, help me find ways to meet Maria's needs, calm her fears and dispel her resentment and resistance. I do love her so, but I know you have a love and knowledge that far exceeds mine. Guide me by your Holy Spirit, I pray."

Ellie heard John quietly humming the lullaby, and then all was quiet. Soon, he emerged from the girls' room and joined her on the settee in the kitchen.

"They're asleep," he said. His eyes glistened with tears as he put his arm around her shoulder. "Oh, Ellie!" he whispered, "I wish my little girls didn't have to go through the pain of so much change. They are so young!"

Laying her hand on his cheek, she turned his head toward her. There were no words to adequately express what she felt, so Ellie just looked into his eyes, trying to convey her sympathy and understanding. Tears began to escape from his eyes as he drew her close. Ellie returned the embrace and just quietly held him for several moments.

"You, my little *frau*, are such a comfort!" John murmured as he released her. "I need to go to the barn to check on a cow before we go to bed. I would ask if you'd like to come along, but I wouldn't want the girls to wake and find no one in the house."

Ellie nodded in agreement.

John lit the lantern, "Unless Bessie is closer to giving birth than I thought, I should only be ten or fifteen minutes."

Ellie sat close to the lamplight at the table. She reached for the Bible and turned to Psalms. She often resorted to David's words when she needed strength and assurance. She found the 86th Psalm and read:

Bow down thine ear, O LORD, hear me:
for I am poor and needy.
Preserve my soul; for I am holy:
O thou my God, save thy servant that trusteth in thee.
Be merciful unto me, O Lord:
for I cry unto thee daily.
Rejoice the soul of thy servant:
for unto thee, O Lord, do I lift up my soul.
For thou, Lord, art good, and ready to forgive;
and plenteous in mercy unto all them that call upon thee.
Give ear, O LORD, unto my prayer;
and attend to the voice of my supplications.
In the day of my trouble I will call upon thee:
for thou wilt answer me.
Among the gods there is none like unto thee, O Lord;
neither are there any works like unto thy works.
All nations whom thou hast made shall come and worship before thee,
O Lord; and shall glorify thy name.
For thou art great, and doest wondrous things:
thou art God alone.
Teach me thy way, O LORD; I will walk in thy truth:
unite my heart to fear thy name.

I will praise thee, O Lord my God, with all my heart:
and I will glorify thy name for evermore.

She reread those verses several times, letting them sink down into the need of her soul. Gradually, a deep peace settled into her heart.

A full half hour later she heard John at the back door.

"Bessie did surprise me! She had a nice little heifer calf. She will be a welcome addition to our herd. I've been letting the girls help me name the calves, so they will have something to think about tomorrow."

"So mother and baby are both doing fine?"

"Yes. Bessie had the calf all licked clean and I helped her get started nursing before I came in. They are together in the box stall, bedded down for the night."

As John finished washing up, Ellie motioned to the chair beside her.

"Come here for a minute. Listen to the verses I was reading. They brought peace to me. I hope they will do the same for you. They come from Psalm 86." Softly she read the verses.

"Isn't that a wonderful thought, to know that He WILL answer?"

"Read it over again, Ellie. Those words are a like a soothing ointment to my soul." He encircled her with his arm as she reread the passage.

When she finished they sat in silence. Finally, John took a deep breath and drew her close.

"Let's pray, Ellie." Ellie reached for his free hand and bowed her head.

"Dear God," John began, "we echo the psalmist's words, 'Be merciful unto us, O Lord.' We thank you that you do hear our daily cries. We lift our souls to you tonight. Just as you look on your children with compassion and love, so have we looked on those you have given us to love and care for. We thank you for your plenteous mercy in our days of trouble and for your promise that you will answer. I thank you especially for the comfort and encouragement that you have brought me and are bringing me through Ellie." He firmly squeezed Ellie's hand. "Help us grow together in love toward you. For your glory and honor, we pray. Amen"

"Amen and amen," echoed Ellie as she lifted her face toward John.

Gently he drew her to him and placed a kiss on her lips. "I do really feel blessed by your care and understanding. Thank you for finding those verses that spoke comfort to me tonight."

"Oh, John," Ellie replied softly, "They comforted me too. I longed to bring you some consolation."

They moved toward the bedroom in silence. After they were in bed, Ellie lay quietly in John's arms. "John, are you still awake?"

"Yes?"

"We will find ways to bring comfort to the girls too. Maria especially needs assurance that her mother will keep being remembered. I'm hoping that Sunday afternoon will be a help to her, as we tell stories about Regina and pack some keepsakes in the trunk."

"I believe it will. We'll both think of stories to go along with the things we put away for them, but you may have more than I do. She was your sister, and you shared more years than Regina and I had with one another."

"We'll do it together!" Ellie stated emphatically. She turned to give John a kiss. "We'd better get to sleep or we won't be ready for the morning!"

She turned on her side, as did John. Drawing her close to him, he soon breathed deeply in blessed sleep. Drowsily, the last thought of her day drifted through her mind, "I'm so glad for a God that gives ear to our prayer!"

Saturday was the day for cooking and cleaning. Maria helped Ellie wash some potatoes for boiling. Together they also baked a coffee cake for Sunday. Ellie made sure to comment on how much help Maria was to her. She could see that Maria felt good about being included in the work. There was enough ham left to go with the potatoes for frying and, along with some canned chili sauce and a jar of beans, it would make a quick Sunday meal so they could get on with the planned afternoon activities. She thought of the cabbages in the springhouse, and went to get a small head. Quickly, she grated it and made coleslaw. She put it in a dish, covered it with a board and took it to the cool cellar floor. There was enough that it could last for several days.

With the food preparations done, she turned to cleaning. When all was well swept and dusted, she suggested that perhaps the windows could be washed. The day was warm and sunny for fall.

"Get your sweaters on, girls," she told them. "I'll get things ready, then we'll go outside. I'll wash the windows and you can play in the leaves until I am finished."

"Can't I help you?" asked Maria.

"Well, perhaps I can take the step-stool out so you can reach the bottom ones at least," answered Ellie.

"I want to help too," Marta chimed.

"All right, Marta, we'll let you do one too," Ellie reassured her.

Ellie went to the pantry for the tin pail and some soft rags. She ladled some warm water from the reservoir on the stove and added a splash of vinegar.

"Why do you put vinegar in the water?" asked Maria.

"To help cut the dirt and to make the windows shiny clean," Ellie answered. "Come, let's go!" She opened the door. "Can you hold the door open until I get through with the step stool and bucket?" she asked Maria.

"I can do it!" said Marta.

"Sure enough!" Ellie exclaimed. "That is the perfect job for you. Thank you very much!"

Ellie set the stool beside the first window. "Did you want your turn first, Miss Marta?" she asked.

"I'm Marta, not *Miss* Marta!" the little girl remonstrated.

Ellie laughed. "All right then, Marta, do you want the first turn?"

"Yes, I do!" Marta replied emphatically, her hands firmly on her hips.

Ellie lifted her up and wrung out a rag from the water. "Here, you can start on this one." Ellie retrieved another rag from the water and, with one hand holding onto Marta's skirt, started washing one of the higher panes. The little girl rubbed and rubbed at the center of the pane.

"There! All done!" she exclaimed. "It's Maria's turn now."

Ellie helped her down from the stool and Marta ran off to shuffle through the leaves on the lawn, singing a gay little tune of her own making.

"Did you want to do one now, Maria?" Ellie asked.

"Sure. How do I do it?"

"You can wash it with the wet cloth. Make sure you get the corners clean—the whole window looks cleaner if the corners and edges are nice and clean. When you have washed it well, I will give you a dry cloth to wipe it clean. You'll want to get it nice and dry in the corners too. When Papa comes in for coffee before chores, you can ask him what is different about the windows and see if he can guess."

Diligently, Maria worked at her first pane. "Is this clean enough?" she asked.

"Looks very good! Let me move the stool so you can start the next one."

In spite of Ellie's offers to finish so that Maria could play, she doggedly kept helping until the last window was done.

"Now we'll really surprise Papa!" she commented in anticipation.

Realizing the chatter and singing from the lawn had stopped, Ellie looked about to see where Marta had gone. Under one of the maples, she saw Marta sitting on her heels, her hands on her knees, quietly observing something.

"What do you see, Marta?" Ellie asked.

"It's a big fat stick with a giant thimble on it!" Marta announced. "There's a bug crawling on it."

Ellie emptied the pail across the lawn, hung the rags on the side of it and took Maria's hand.

"Let's go see Marta's thimble!" she suggested.

Together, they walked to Marta's observation post and bent down to see her discovery. "Do you know what that is, Marta?" she asked.

"I know!" Maria exclaimed. "Papa and I saw one when we walked in the woods. It's a mushroom. I forget what kind, though," she added.

"I don't know what kind it is either, Maria. But I do know that some mushrooms can be very poisonous—that means they could make us very sick—so we must never eat them unless someone who knows all about mushrooms tells us they are safe. It's better not to even touch them unless you wash your hands right after. They are pretty to look at, though, aren't they? That is a ladybug that is crawling on it. We used to say a poem when we saw a ladybug. 'Ladybug, ladybug, fly away home, your house is on fire and the children are alone.'"

"Was her house really on fire?" queried Marta. "Was it, Aunt Ellie—oops! Was it, Mama?"

"I don't think so, Marta. It was just a fun rhyme."

Ellie's heart leapt at being called Mama. She glanced at Maria, but her expression didn't reveal anything untoward. Ellie bent down to look again at the mushroom.

"Look, girls! See the ant there in the grass? See what a big load it is carrying? Ants are very busy creatures. They have houses called anthills, rather like a big town full of ants. All summer, they store food for the winter. Did you know the Bible even talks about them? In Proverbs 6:6 it says 'Go to the ant, thou sluggard; consider her ways, and be wise: which having no guide, overseer, or ruler, provideth her meat in the summer, and gathereth her food in the harvest.'"

Marta's brow wrinkled into a frown. "What is a sluggard?"

"A sluggard is someone who is lazy. So the verse is saying that lazy people can learn something by watching the ants, for without anyone telling them what to do, ants work hard to gather food in the summer enough to last all winter."

"We do that, don't we?" observed Maria. "This summer you and Grandma got a lot of food ready for the winter. We have our shelves full of jars and lots of things in the root cellar, too, and some in the spring house."

"You are so right, Maria," Ellie agreed. "Remember, you helped us too. You podded some peas and snapped some beans, and you helped husk the corn. So this winter, when we eat some of those things, you can know that you worked hard like the ants."

"It wasn't all hard work, though," Maria thoughtfully replied. "It was fun when we all sat out under the tree at Grandma's, podding peas. We even played 'I spy' while we were doing it. Remember, I fooled everybody when I spied something red and it was Grandma's cheeks because it was so hot?"

Ellie laughed. "Yes, you sure did fool us! I guess you were just a little smarter than we were! I think we had better go into the house. I see Papa coming in for his coffee."

"Wait!" Marta requested. "I want to show Papa the mush—broom!"

Ellie smiled. "Mushroom."

"Oh, yes! Mush—room! Papa! Papa! Come and see the mush—room!"

"What is it you have found?" he asked as he joined them under the tree.

"It looks like a stick with a big thimble on it, but Maria and Mama said it is a mush—room. There was a ladybug on it, but she had to go home to her children because her house was on fire!"

John looked quizzically at Ellie.

"I just told her the little poem we used to say when we saw a ladybug!"

"Oh, I see!" John replied. "That is a nice mushroom, Marta. But we must never eat those, because they could make us sick."

"I know, Papa! Mama told me."

John and Ellie looked at each other. There was a slight smile on John's face as he reached for Ellie's and Maria's hands. Marta was already running toward the back kitchen door.

When they reached the kitchen, Ellie poured two cups of coffee and two glasses of milk and set the cookie tin on the table. "After all that fresh air, I don't think a cookie will spoil our appetites for supper."

As they sat enjoying their refreshment, Maria asked, "Look outside, Papa! Do you see anything different?"

John looked out the window. "I see the trees in their usual places. I see the leaves on the grass. I see the sun getting low in the sky. What is different?"

"Look again, Papa," she admonished, "but don't look quite so far."

"Oh-hh! The windows! They look so clean I can hardly see there is glass in them! Has someone been washing windows?"

"I have!" she looked uncertainly at Ellie, "and so has—ah," she hesitated, "so has she!" she pointed to Ellie.

Quickly, Ellie came to the rescue. "Maria did such a good job. She stayed at it until the last window was done. She was busier than an ant! No sluggard, our big girl! Are you?"

Ellie laid her hand on Maria's arm. "We had a good time working together, didn't we?"

Marie shyly nodded in the affirmative.

"That's good to hear! Clean windows help us see better and make everything look brighter. If the windows are too dirty, they make everything look messy and dull! Well, I'd better get those cows milked and the rest of the animals fed. I should be in by six o'clock," John said as got up, reached for his hat and headed out the door.

Ellie rose from the table. "I put water on the stove before we went out. I'll bring in the rinse tub and put some water in it. You can have your baths before supper and then you'll be ready for bed. Tomorrow we go to church in the morning and then Papa and I have planned something special for the afternoon."

"What is it? What is it?" Marta begged to know.

"It wouldn't be much of a surprise if I told you now, would it, little one? You go find your nightgowns and robes and I'll get the water ready for your bath. Bring your slippers with you too."

Ellie went to the woodshed to get the rinse tub from the nail where it hung. She set it on the floor in front of the stove and added a good chunk of wood to the fire. From the pantry she brought the clotheshorse, which she put on the side of the tub away from the stove. She hung a blanket on it to keep the heat close to the tub. The girls were still small enough that they could both fit in at once. She got two washcloths and towels ready and put them on the open oven door, and set on a saucer a bar of perfumed soap she had brought along from home. By that time the girls had their nightclothes ready.

"Come, let's get your clothes off so you can get into the tub. I have some special, nice-smelling soap for you. See? It looks like a flower. Here are some washcloths. Make sure you wash behind your ears and between your toes—even if it tickles!" she smiled.

The girls giggled with glee as they got into the water and started washing themselves, and Ellie started getting the supper on. After some time she realized the girls were playing.

"Do you think it's about time to get out?" she asked. "You'll get cold if you stay in too long."

"Just a bit more, ple-ease!" Marta begged.

"I'm ready to get out." Maria said.

Ellie laid a towel on the floor and held another—a warm one—up for Maria. Maria stepped out and Ellie toweled her dry and gave her a clean nightgown.

"Put your feet into your slippers and put your robe on. Now it's your turn!" she looked to Marta as she held out another warm towel. "Come on, you are starting to shiver!"

Ellie toweled the little girl dry and opened the towel to kiss her tummy. Marta wriggled with laughter.

"That tickles!" she objected. "Do it again!"

Ellie complied. "Now let's get your nightgown on!"

She put the nightgown over her head. "Now, where has Marta gone? She was here just a minute ago. Where could she be?"

From the folds of the nightgown, Marta giggled.

"Where is our little girl?"

"Here!" Marta cried, pulling the nightgown down. "I'm here!"

"Well, sure enough!" Ellie exclaimed. "Just in time for supper!"

She picked her up and gave her a big hug. "I'm so glad you're here. You smell so sweet and clean!" She set Marta down.

"So do you, Maria!" she told her, giving her a quick hug. "I think I hear Papa coming into the house. He'll be glad to see his girls all clean and ready for Sunday!"

"I see someone's had a bath!" said John when he came in. "Do you want me to empty the tub?" he asked Ellie.

"Would you, please? I'll take down the clotheshorse and blanket and get supper on the table."

Later, as John sat at the table waiting, he asked the girls, "Do my sweet-smelling girls have a hug for their papa?"

The girls came running. "Mm-mm! Smells good enough to eat! I think I'll just take a bite!"

The girls squealed in delight as he pretended to take bites from under their chins.

"Oh-oh!" said Ellie in alarm. "I'd better get the food on the table so Papa can eat the food instead of his girls!"

The girls laughed. "Papa won't really eat us! He just pretends," Maria assured her.

"But it tickles!" Marta added.

After supper, John asked once more for the violin. This time he played several other songs before the lullaby. "Shall we ask Mama to join us for the bedtime story tonight?"

While Maria shyly nodded her assent, Marta enthusiastically shouted, "Yes!"

Sitting at the foot of the bed, Ellie gave each of the girls a hug and kiss.

"Let's say our prayers," John told the girls. Obediently, the girls knelt at their father's knee on the braided rug beside the bed.

Maria began with a simple child's prayer, adding, "...and thank you, Jesus, that clean windows can help us see better."

When it was Marta's turn, she began, "Father, watch your little child tonight and keep me safe till morning light," then she hastened to add, "Thank you God for breakfast, and thank you for the sun and thank you for the leaves and for mushbrooms and for ladybugs and thank you for my sister Maria and for Papa and for Aunt Ellie—oops! for Mama, and for Grandpa and Grandma Kurtz and Grandpa and Grandma Kessler and Uncle Martin...Aaa-men!"

Breathlessly she hopped into her father's lap. "Is that good, Papa?"

"It's always good to be thankful, little missy!"

Ellie let John do the tucking in. John began, "Tonight I'm going to tell you the story of a little boy who was entrusted to take care of his father's sheep. His name was David..."

After the story, John and Ellie once more kissed the girls and wished them a good night before they left the room, leaving the door slightly ajar.

Chapter Five

Sunday morning dawned with the promise of another sunny day. Ellie rose early again and put a pot of porridge on to cook. She went to the cellar to bring up a jar of strawberries that would accompany the coffee cake at noon. Upstairs, she looked for some of the things they would later put in the trunk. Quietly, so as not to wake the girls, she tiptoed from room to room, gathering some familiar items of Regina's. Placing them in a neat pile on the spare bed beside the trunk, she glanced at the dresser where John had placed Regina's jewelry chest, which, until Tuesday, had still been on the dresser downstairs.

As she slowly opened the lid, the released memories rose to greet her. There lay Regina's wedding ring and the birthstone ring their parents had given her on her sixteenth birthday. She picked up the locket that was John's first Christmas gift. She opened it. Tiny pictures of Regina and John looked back at her. Quickly, before the tears and apprehension could form, she snapped it shut. This, along with the rings, should go into the trunk. There were the lovely combs Regina used to wear in her hair—how Ellie had admired those combs, and wished to wear them in her own tresses. She entertained the idea of bringing them downstairs and adding them to her own jewelry box. Then she thought better of it. It might be hard for John to see her wearing them, and anyway, the girls should have those too.

Perhaps they should just put the whole jewelry box in the trunk. She set it over on the bed. She would ask John as they got ready for church how he felt about it.

Another thought came to her, so she quietly went down the steps straight to the glass cupboard, which held the good dishes. High on the top shelf she found the item that she sought—the silver spoon and cup, engraved with Regina's name and birth date. These had been a gift from Mama's grandmother on the birth of her first daughter. Great-Grandma was no longer living by the time Ellie was born. These, too, would go into the trunk.

She wondered where Regina's little bonnet and shawl were. Her mother had made one for each of her children and they had been given to them when they were grown. Perhaps that, too, was in the chest where John had said the girls' outfits were.

Upstairs she went again, to see if she could find them. Sure enough, she found them tucked away with the children's outfits. She had just added the last items to the pile when she heard Marta calling, "Papa!"

Ellie hurried down the stairs. "I'm here, Marta!"

"Where is Papa?" Marta asked.

"He is still in the barn, but he should be in any minute. Is Maria awake yet?"

"I tried to get out of bed without waking her up, but she woke up anyway!"

"That's all right, Marta. It is time to wake up. We need to get ready for church. We'll put your good dresses on, then you can wear aprons over them to stay clean while you have breakfast," Ellie told her on the way to the girls' bedroom.

"Good morning, Sunshine!" Ellie greeted Maria as she entered the room and raised the blind. "Let's get dressed for church. Papa should be in for breakfast soon."

Ellie laid out the clean clothes and Sunday dresses and then helped Marta get dressed as Maria attended to herself.

"Mama used to let me take one of her good handkerchiefs to church. May I take one this morning?" Maria asked.

"Of course. Do you know where they are?"

"Yes, they are in the drawer of the glass cupboard."

"Why don't you go and pick the one you want while I make your bed?"

With a contented smile, Maria skipped out of the bedroom. As Ellie made the bed she mulled over in her mind Maria's obvious pleasure in choosing one of her mother's handkerchiefs. Such a simple request, yet it seemed to be very important to the sensitive little girl. She still considered the "Remembrance Trunk," as she thought of it, a good idea, but perhaps the girls also needed something they could have constantly close as well.

Hearing John come in, she quickly went to the kitchen. By the time he was washed up, the breakfast was ready on the table and the girls sat waiting in their chairs. The family joined their hands in prayer as John asked a blessing on their food as well as this day set apart for worship. This morning there was no time to linger over the meal. Ellie quickly cleaned up the dishes and just barely had enough time to ask John about the jewelry chest before he was ready to get the horse and buggy.

Ellie donned her Sunday dress. Her stomach fluttered a bit, thinking of going to church as a new family. She knew that all eyes would be on them. Most people understood John's need for a new wife, but there were always those whose tongues would wag at the unusual. Ellie's decision to cut off her own engagement and the speed of her and John's courtship and marriage, she knew, were already the subjects of many neighborhood gatherings. She lifted her chin as she reached for her good hat and coat from the front hall closet. She and John knew why they did what they did. It was their business, not their neighbors'! *Keep your head held high!* she told herself as she helped the girls out the door and down the walk to where John was waiting.

As she had surmised, heads turned as they entered the small country church. People watched as they sat in the pew occupied such a short time ago with Regina as a part of the family. John set Marta on his knee and moved his leg to press against Ellie. Furtively, she glanced at him. She knew he was aware of her discomfort and wished to reassure her. Release came as the first song was announced and people's attention shifted to their hymnbooks. Unconsciously, Ellie breathed deeply in relief, then joined in the singing.

Sunday services were usually a delight to Ellie. The pastor at John's church was not much older than John. John had often spoken of how much he enjoyed their pastor's sermons. Ellie had looked forward to hearing them, but this morning it was a little hard to concentrate. Everything felt so new. The added pressure of being so closely observed kept her from fully absorbing the message. However, the repeated rendering of the scripture settled into her heart by the end. *"Be content with such things as ye have: for he hath said, I will never leave you, nor forsake you."* From these verses she surmised that she should be thankful for what she and John had at the present and be assured that, if the Lord would never leave or forsake them, they could safely trust Him for the future. She couldn't help but hope that their love would deepen. They still felt more like tentative friends. It wasn't the same as the exciting love she had felt for Gerhard. She tried to ignore the thud in the pit of her stomach that always accompanied her thoughts of the love she and Gerhard had shared and the contrast between that and her present relationship with John. If John noticed the sudden lift of her chin, he didn't let on. Maybe he didn't know her well enough yet. Her family knew that, when her chin lifted like that, it was a sign that she was determined to accomplish something, no matter how hard.

After the close of the service, it seemed everyone wanted to come to talk to them. Ellie hurt for Maria when several people asked her, "So how do you like your new mama?"

Maria, each time, just shrugged her shoulders and tried to hide behind her papa. Although she was sure they meant well, Ellie wished people would be a little more discreet and kind in their approach.

Finally, they reached the safety of the buggy and headed home. The purple-lined autumn clouds to the west turned darker to the north. The bright sun illuminated the yellow and red of the leaves so that they stood out in brilliant contrast against the lavender-blue clouds. Occasionally leaves fluttered to the ground.

At home, John stoked up the fire for Ellie as she prepared the pan for frying the potatoes and opened the jar of beans. He supervised the girls in setting the table, then sat down on the settee to read a book to them.

"Would you get the slaw from the cellar, John?" Ellie asked after awhile. "By that time things should be pretty well ready."

In short order, the family was seated at the table enjoying the food and happy conversation.

"I'll do the dishes, John, if you would like to put Marta down for a nap. When she wakes up, we can go on with our plans."

"All right, Marta!" said John as he lifted her from the chair, "Let's go have a rest!"

"I'm not sleepy!" protested the little girl.

"Well then, missy, would you lay down with your Papa while he has a rest, so he doesn't feel lonely?"

"Yes! I will!"

Maria looked at Ellie. "What shall I do?"

"Why don't you color a picture in your coloring book? Marta won't sleep long. Then we'll do the something special I told you about."

"What is it?"

"I think it is something you will really like, and you'll find out very soon."

Maria got out her coloring book and crayons and set to work neatly outlining each part of the picture before filling it with color. Deciding which color to use took just as much meticulous care as the actual coloring. Ellie casually observed the process as she washed and dried the dishes. Maria was a very organized and conscientious little girl, who took a lot of care in doing things right. She seemed to be very anxious to please. While this was a good trait, Ellie thought, she could see that trying so intensely to be perfect could be hard on the little girl. She hoped Maria could learn that doing her best was good enough, and that there was no sin in making mistakes if one learned from them.

She smiled to herself. "Look who's talking!" she said, under her breath. She knew that she, herself, hated making mistakes. She, too, liked to do things right the first time. *Maybe we can learn together!*

After putting away the last dish, Ellie sat down beside Maria.

"You do very nice work, Maria!

John and Marta came yawning from the bedroom.

"Was the sleep not long enough?" Ellie asked.

"Marta seemed to think it was."

"Cause I want to do our special thing. Papa said we could when I wake up!"

"And so we can! Shall we go upstairs?"

"Upstairs?" chimed the girls together.

"Yes," Ellie said, "up to the spare room."

Together, they went up the stairs. John opened the door, and seeing the pile of things on the bed, suggested. "Why don't you girls and I sit on the mat in front of this trunk. I want to tell you something first, then I will let your new mama tell you some stories."

They settled down on the mat and Ellie sat on a small footstool beside the bed. John took Marta on his knee, and Maria leaned close to him with her father's arm around her. "Your new mama had a good idea," John began. "You know that she is your first mama's sister, and you know that sisters love each other very much—just like you, Maria and Marta, do—so she wants you to remember all about your first mama, and how much she loved you. Now I'm going to let her tell you the plan she thought of to make it easier for you to remember all about her."

"When I was a little girl," Ellie began, "Aunt Matilda used to take us to her room to show us some things which her parents and grandparents had given her. These were kept in her bureau. The other day, when I was emptying my trunk, I thought, perhaps, we could make this a 'Remembrance Trunk' for you girls. Each thing in Aunt Matilda's bureau had a story. The things in this trunk, too, will have stories. Some I will tell you, some Papa will tell you, and for some things you may have your own stories. You may even think of some things you want to add to the trunk. First, I want to show you this," Ellie reached for the silver cup and spoon.

"Your mama was the first great-grandchild my mother's grandma had. She was so pleased to have this new baby in the family that she bought this little silver cup and spoon and had your mother's name, Regina, engraved on it. It also says the day she was born. Do you remember seeing this?"

"I do," said Maria, quietly. "She used to let me hold it when she cleaned out the glass cupboard. It was way up on the top shelf."

"Yes, it was!" Ellie agreed. "Do you think the Remembrance Trunk would be a good place to keep it? We can come here as often as we like to look at it and remember Mama," she suggested.

Maria nodded her head in agreement. "Could we put the little china doggie in the trunk too? Mama used to let me hold that, too, when she cleaned out the cupboard. She told me it was a gift from Aunt Grace."

"Sure we can, Maria. That is a good idea," her father said.

Ellie lifted the lid of the trunk. "Would you like to put the cup in now, Maria? Maybe you would like to put it up here in the little sliding tray. We'll add the little dog when we have everything else in."

Maria gently held the cup and spoon for a moment before carefully placing it in the tray.

"Next, I want to show you these quilts that your mama made. This one is called a 'Dresden Plate.' It is made of many different prints with yellow in the center. Most of the prints are from dresses or aprons that your mama or grandma wore. Someday I'll tell you about the others, but I do want to show you this one today," Ellie pointed to a white print with tiny blue and pink flowers.

"This is the dress your mama wore on the first day she went to school. Oh! This green print with yellow flowers, over here, is a piece of material that our grandma sent. There was enough that both your mama and I had dresses from the same material. It made me feel very proud to have a dress just like my big sister. She was very special to me. Marta, do you want to help Papa put this in the trunk?"

"How old was Mama when she started going to school?" Maria asked.

"She was six-and-a-half," Ellie replied. You will be just a little older than that when you start next spring. You could have started this fall, but Papa thought you might like to wait since there have been so many changes in your life."

"I'm glad I can wait," Maria whispered. "I think I will be scared to go."

"That's all right," Ellie assured her, "I think everyone is a little scared on the first day of school, but it's exciting, too, to make new friends, and then it isn't scary anymore."

Ellie reached for the next quilt. "This one is called 'Log Cabin.' See the red square in the middle, and then the pieces that keep going around the square, like logs in a house? The red squares are like the warmth at the center of a good home. On two sides the pieces are darker colors, and the other two are lighter, for in every home there are happy times and sad or difficult times. In this quilt, too, are many pieces of material with stories. Many of the darker materials came from Grandma and Great-grandma's dresses. This was the first quilt your mama made. Her grandma helped her make it when she came to visit. It took her quite awhile to get all the squares made before she could put it together and quilt it. Your mama got the red material for Christmas when she was twelve years old and she started making the quilt after Christmas. All of the piecing on this one was done by hand. Your great-grandma thought that was the only way to properly make a quilt, even though your grandma had a sewing machine by that time. See, here is a piece of that same dress that your mother wore the first day of school. In a log cabin quilt you can use up some very small scraps of fabric."

Refolding the quilt, Ellie suggested, "Maria, you can put this one in the trunk." Maria stood to place the large bundle in the bottom of the trunk, on top of the Dresden Plate.

Ellie reached toward the bed again. "I think both of you will remember these," she said, tenderness in her voice.

"Mama's aprons!" Maria exclaimed. She reached for them and held them to her face. A tear trickled down her cheek, and a sob caught in her throat. "They still smell like Mama!"

John held her close, and Ellie laid a hand on her shoulder. There were tears in her eyes as well, as she softly said. "It's all right to cry, Maria. You loved your mama, and it's good to remember how it felt to be held close in her arms. She liked giving you hugs, didn't she?"

Maria nodded.

"Mama used to kiss me on my tummy, just like you did last night!" Marta pitched in.

"Good! That's nice to remember." Ellie commented. "Maria, why don't you just keep holding those aprons until I tell you the story about this dresser set?" She reached for the three-piece set of runners.

"These," she said, "were made of the material that was left from making Uncle Willie's first baby dress. Aren't they nice fine cotton?" Ellie held them out so they could see. "Your mother embroidered the light blue flowers on them, then grandma showed her how to crochet the lace around them. Do you know something?"

"What?" the girls wondered.

"Your mama got so discouraged trying to make this lace! She tried and tried to get it right, but kept making mistakes, and grandma would tell her to do it over again. Each time she had to take out the stitches and do it over again she would say, 'I'll never learn!'" Ellie paused. "Do you know what Grandma told your mama?" she asked.

"What?" asked Maria.

"Grandma told her, 'That is exactly how we learn—by trying, making mistakes and learning from them. Every time we make a mistake, we find out one way not to do something!'" Ellie smiled, "What do you think about that? We really don't need to be afraid of trying."

Ellie reached for another from the bed. "You can see by this other runner that your mama did learn how to crochet beautifully."

She reached for the jewelry chest and handed it to John. "I think Papa will tell you about some of the things in here."

Carefully, John opened the lid. From the chest he drew out the locket on its fine chain. "This you will remember Mama wearing. It was my first Christmas gift to Mama." John seemed lost in memory.

"Did Mama like it?" Marta queried.

John roused. "Yes, Marta, Mama did like it! She wore it every day. Sometimes it was under her dress, but she always had it on. See, on the back it has our initials, J and R, and if we open it up, there are pictures of Mama and me."

"Please, may I see it?" Maria asked.

John put the locket into Maria's hand and watched as she longingly looked at the tiny picture.

"Mama had dimples like me, didn't she?" she whispered.

"Yes, she did, Maria. You look very much like your mama! Someday you will probably look very much like that picture."

"I want to see too!" Marta begged.

"When Maria is finished, she will let you look too!"

He reached into the chest again for the wedding ring. "This is the wedding ring I gave your mama when we got married. It, too, has our initials on the inside. Someday, perhaps one of you will wear it. Until then, we will leave it in the jewelry chest, which will go into the Remembrance Trunk."

Ellie reached over to pick up the ring with Regina's birthstone. "When your Mama turned sixteen, she got this ring with her birthstone in it. It is opal because she was born in October. Each of us got a ring on our sixteenth birthday. Mine is emerald because I was born in May. The rings made us feel very grown-up."

Ellie handed the little knitted outfits to her husband.

John began, "This is the sweater and little bonnet that Grandma made for Mama when she was a baby. She kept it safe all these years. Now we will put it in the trunk as a remembrance of Mama."

He paused as Ellie handed him the next outfit. "When we knew God was going to send us a little baby to add to our family, Mama began knitting this little white outfit. We didn't know whether it would be a boy or a girl. When our little girl was born with a tiny round face and dark curly hair, she looked as cute as a button in her new outfit. We thought Maria Regina would be a good name for her."

"It was me, wasn't it, Papa?" Maria stated. "I was your first baby."

"Yes, you were!" said John. "And oh, how we loved you. Your Aunt Ellie came to help look after you and Mama when you were born."

Maria looked at her Papa and then at Ellie. "Now she will be our new mama!"

John gave her an extra hug before lifting up the soft yellow sweater set.

"When Maria was almost three, another baby came along. This time, the baby had reddish blond curls and a cute turned-up nose. We thought Marta Anne was a good name for this new little one."

"That was me! That was me! Wasn't it, Papa?" cried Marta. "And you and Mama loved me too, didn't you?"

"My, oh, my! Yes, we did! Then, just soon after Marta was two, we knew another baby was coming. Again Mama started another outfit. This time she knit it in white again. Mama and John Junior both went to heaven, but we are going to keep this little outfit to remember both him and Mama who had so much love that there would have been lots of love for all of you."

"Maybe that is enough for now," Ellie said as she packed the last of the things into the trunk.

Quietly Maria handed over the aprons to add to the collection. "There are some pillowcases on the bed yet," she observed.

"You are right," Ellie said, "See the flowers your mama embroidered on them? The crocheted lace she did too. Doesn't it match the flowers nicely? I thought it might feel good for you to have these on your pillows, so that every night when you go to bed it will be a little like having Mama's arms under your head."

She gave one to each of the girls. They held them close to their chests. John closed the lid.

"We'll look through our Remembrance Trunk as often as you wish. Perhaps we'll find other things we want to put into it. Mama will help you add the little dog. You just ask if you would like to see the things again. Both Mama and I will tell you the stories again and again, if you like."

Marta put her arms around John's neck. "I liked hearing stories about our Mama!" she said.

"So did I!" Maria added heartily.

"Let's go downstairs now. Maybe you and Mama would like to come to the barn to see the calves. We still have one that needs a name!"

"Can we get the doggie and put our pillowcases on first?" asked Maria.

"Sure," said Ellie. "Come, and I'll help you do it right away!" When the little china dog was safely in the sliding shelf and the pillowcases were on the girls' pillows, Ellie helped them into older dresses. "Now I have to change my dress yet, then we'll be ready to go to the barn. Have you thought of names for the new calf?" she asked.

"We have to see it, first," Maria told her. "Sometimes the spots on the calf look like something that makes a good name for it."

"Oh!" replied Ellie, "I hadn't thought of that."

The calf was lying down in the stall when Ellie and the girls got there. They watched awhile, then went to watch Papa milking the other cows. The cats watched too, very intently.

"Give the cats some milk, Papa," urged the girls.

"All right!" he replied, "Stand aside in case I miss!"

Instead of squirting the milk into the pail, he aimed it at the cats. With their mouths open wide, they caught the most of the stream, and then licked their faces for what they had missed. The girls and Ellie laughed.

"Good shot!" she commented. "Oh, I see the calf is up! Shall we go and have a better look?"

The girls ran to the box stall. Marta stuck her fingers between the slats of the pen, rousing the calf's curiosity. It came over and licked Marta's finger, making her giggle.

"Her tongue is rough!"

"Look!" Maria said, "There is a spot on her side that looks like a flower. Could we call her Rosy?"

"I think that would be a good name for her," Ellie agreed. "See if your papa thinks so!"

While Marta continued to pet the calf, Maria ran to ask her father.

"Papa said that was a good name for the calf. Come here, Rosy!" she urged.

When the girls tired of playing with the calf, Ellie suggested they go into the house and make some popcorn to have after supper.

"There is one more thing I'd like to do before supper," said Ellie when all was ready. "See, I have two small boxes here. Haven't they got pretty lids?"

The girls came to look. "I like this one with the cutter and horses and the people going for a ride in the snow best!" Maria said.

"I like the one with the pretty flowers," Marta said.

"Good! You can each have the one you like best. I thought maybe you would like to divide Mama's good handkerchiefs and keep them in these boxes in your top dresser drawers. That way, they will be your own and you can always choose one each Sunday morning and look at them as often as you wish."

"Can we, really?" asked Maria, in awe.

"Yes," assured Ellie. "I'll put them here at the end of the table, and you can look at them and decide which ones each of you likes best. Make two piles, one for Maria and one for Marta."

With much discussion, the girls set about dividing the handkerchiefs. Ellie was pleased that they were able to do so without any big arguments. She could also see the pleasure they felt as they opened each one before choosing the pile to which it should go.

Later that evening, with the girls tucked in bed, Ellie lay in John's protective arm and mused, "I think today was a good day for us all, don't you think, John?"

"It was, indeed, Ellie" John replied. "Your idea was a good one. I think it helped Maria, especially, but I think, over the years, that trunk will come to mean a lot to both girls. It will be a good way to keep their mother's memory alive. The stories you told were good for them to hear. Maria is such a little perfectionist. It was also good for her to be able to cry a bit. I know what she meant about the smell of those aprons.

That is why I couldn't face taking Regina's clothes out of the closet for so long."

Wordlessly, Ellie stroked his arm. After a moment, John sighed and held her close. "I'm glad you are here now, and that you understand both me and my girls!" he murmured into her hair.

Chapter Six

As life relaxed into a familiar schedule, Ellie sensed an aura of unreality in the daily routine. The first few weeks had been an all-out effort at a new beginning, but it often seemed as though John was going through the motions of what was expected while his heart still grieved for what he had lost. At times Ellie felt as though he acted the part of patient teacher and saw her as a younger pupil. On those days, the memories of the love she and Gerhard had shared would creep into her mind and she would find herself making comparisons to her present situation. Then, suddenly, guilt would wash over her—married to one man yet yearning for another. She longed to tell John her frustration, yet did not wish to add to his load of grief. Often, she cried out to God for patience and wisdom.

On other days, John's kindness and vulnerability and his obvious efforts to please her tugged at her heart and made her ashamed of her impatience to reach a deeper plane of comfort and companionship.

After one of his gloomy, downhearted days, she waited until the girls were asleep, then drew up a chair beside the rocker in which John sat with his eyes closed.

"John, you seem so sad tonight."

There was a moment of silence before he sighed deeply.

"I'm sorry, Ellie!"

"Oh John! I wasn't asking for an apology. I just want you to share your sorrow with me. I can't change the way things are, but I can listen. Sometimes talking about it helps."

"I suppose, Ellie, but I don't want to burden you with my sadness when you have given up so much to be a part of this family. It doesn't seem fair to you."

"John, I promised to be your wife. In that vow I promised to be with you in sickness and in health, in trials and adversity. If you keep your sorrow and grief to yourself, I can't share it. If we are to truly be husband and wife, we need to walk together through good times and bad." She reached out and held his hand in both of hers. "Please let me in."

"Oh Ellie!" John laid his other hand on top of hers. "You are right. Sometimes I still feel as though I am walking in a fog—or a dream—and nothing seems quite real. Much as I appreciate you and your understanding, there is part of me that wants to go back to having Regina here and you as her little sister."

He untangled their hands and put his arm around her. "You are right, though, it is you and me now. I need to let you be my wife as you promised. It just seems as though there have been too many changes all at once."

Ellie put her hand up to his cheek, but stayed silent.

"I know that you, too, have made big changes. I have really appreciated your understanding and help. We will learn to love each other more deeply. I hope you can be patient with me for a little longer, Ellie."

"Of course, John. Just, please, keep talking about it. When you withdraw, it adds to my struggle to know that I did the right thing. I truly want to be a helpmate to you, but I can't if you shut me out or treat me as a guest in your family."

"Oh Ellie, is that how you feel?"

"Not always, but in the last few weeks it felt as though you were withdrawing, and I want us to walk together through whatever comes. I need that too!"

John rose and pulled Ellie to her feet. As he drew her into his arms, she saw tears in his eyes.

"I'm sorry, Ellie. I will do my best to be more open with you. You have been a real support to me and have found so many ways to help the girls feel comfortable. Let's try again!"

Ellie stood on her toes and pulled his head down and kissed him. He responded with tenderness. Ellie's eyes sparkled.

"I'm quite willing to do that! Thank you, John. I feel better already, just talking about it."

"So do I, Ellie. I guess you've proved your point. It does help to talk."

As each week went by their comfort level did increase. John was always kind to her. Sometimes she was still suspicious that he was feeling sorry for her, for what she had given up to marry him and for the sadness which had permeated the beginning of their marriage. As time went on she realized that he was truly just trying his best to care for her and make her as happy as he could. She began, more and more, to appreciate his gentleness and tender qualities. When he suffered bouts of melancholy, she tried to be patient and understanding, knowing his grief still haunted him. Gently, she would encourage him to share it with her. In that understanding, she sensed the seeds of love were being sown and had begun sprouting.

Christmas was less than a week away. This Sunday they were to go to Ellie's parents' for dinner, and then on Christmas Day itself, to John's parents'. Even though in the last few months they had been able to visit with most of the family, she still did not know them well. Since it was almost ten miles, they would leave right after chores, and then it would probably be late for evening chores when they got back.

Ellie had been busy baking Christmas cookies and candy to take to both places. Maria and Marta had been included in the fun, and Ellie had enjoyed letting them help. Maria could cut some of the fruit while Marta became the official stirrer. They each took turns with the cookie cutters. The part they liked best was when Ellie would inquire, "I wonder who should taste these to make sure they are good enough for Christmas?"

Usually Ellie would suggest they keep a sample for Papa, too, so that he could give his expert opinion. Now the shelves in the pantry held tins full of their efforts.

Ellie smiled as she remembered the first time Maria had called her "Mama." It had come only about a week ago, when they were talking about making decorations for Christmas.

Maria had excitedly asked, "Can we string popcorn, Mama?"

Suddenly a look of consternation crossed her face, followed by a look of relief when Ellie just calmly replied, "That would be lots of fun!"

In her heart, though, Ellie rejoiced that Maria was beginning to think of her and accept her as a mother.

Love, mixed with sympathy, flooded her heart. *Poor little girl!* she thought, *she shouldn't have to go through this loss so early in life.* Now, as she tucked some pieces of cedar behind the clock on the mantle, she hummed the strains of "Silent Night" and wondered what more she could do to both honor their memories of Regina and make this a memorable first Christmas for their present family. Perhaps they could make a few pomanders from cloves and the oranges she had got in town. She did have a few extras, and the girls would enjoy pressing the cloves through the rinds if she poked them with a needle first. Finished with a bit of lace, they would be pretty hung in some cedar branches above the door where they could shed their fragrance into the room. She had found a Yule log Regina had made to hold candles on the table. This they would give a place of honor.

She and John had decided together that new fur hats and muffs would be suitable Christmas gifts for the girls. Although it might be hard for Marta to keep her hands tucked inside, she would be pleased to be thought of as a big girl— big enough to have a muff like her sister!

She had taken some of the money she had saved before her marriage and bought a pocket watch for John. To her, it was special, for it told him what she had begun to feel in her heart. Love for John was still only a seedling, but it held possibility, and for that she was thankful. On the lid she'd had engraved "To John, with love from Ellie." She would have liked to get a chain and fob to go with it, but she thought perhaps she would get that later, for his birthday or next Christmas. It was safely put away in the back of her drawer. She didn't think he had any idea of its presence, but she was anxious to share both the gift and the sentiment that was growing day by day.

"I'd better get a meal on the table," she told herself. "The men will be ready for some good hot food after another day in the bush."

John's cousin Jake had been staying with them for over a week, helping John cut a supply of wood for next winter before the snow got too deep. The first day they brought the big stone from the back field and put it at the end of the lane. The cedars would have to wait until the frost was out of the ground.

Jake was good for John. His joking and repartee were enough to keep everyone in good humor. Maria and Marta enjoyed his fun and banter as well. Often, after supper, Jake could be found on his stomach on the floor, intent on playing a game with Maria, or on his hands and knees, giving horseback rides to Marta. The girls would often be in gales of laughter as they tried to get their "horse" to obey their commands while he took unexpected turns and bent his head for food, sending Marta sliding to the floor, then neighing with glee as he "galloped" off. Even now, the girls were probably enjoying his teasing, for they had accompanied the men to the barn for chore time.

Ellie was just taking the scalloped potatoes out of the oven when she heard them all come in the back door. "Mmm-mmm! Something smells good to a hungry bushwhacker!" remarked Jake as he sniffed the air.

"Sure does!" John agreed. "It's been a long day—a long week—but there's a lot of wood piled and ready to bring to the woodshed next summer. It's nice working in the woods, though."

He went to wash the day's grime from his face.

"Could have had rabbit suppers for a week if we'd have taken our guns!" commented Jake. "Every time you turned around another fluffy tail disappeared behind a tree!"

Jake took his turn at the washbasin. Then, as he toweled dry, John motioned for the girls. "Come," he said, "you need to wash up too, even if Rosy licked your hands clean! Mama has supper on the table and we want to get there before Jake eats all the food! Just see how hungry he looks!"

No doubt remained regarding the tastiness of the food, for it disappeared quickly. As Jake polished off the last of his apple dumpling, he laughingly told John, "I hope you realize what a fortunate man you are to have married such a good cook!"

"Nothing to worry about there!" John assured Jake, "I'm well aware of my good fortune."

"I'm sure there are lots of young women who would be glad to show you their culinary skills and provide you with good meals," Ellie teased.

"That's right!" John agreed, "If you don't watch out, you'll be a confirmed bachelor!"

"Maybe I've realized that all the good ones are already taken!" he winked at Ellie, making her blush.

"Maybe you're too afraid to look!" she retorted.

All of a sudden, the subject changed. "You sure have this place looking like Christmas!" Jake remarked. "Do you think there will be gifts in your stockings, girls, or do you think you'll get only be a lump of coal?" he teased.

"Oh Cousin Jake!" Maria remonstrated, "We have been good girls! I'm sure we'll both get presents!"

"I'm going to hang the biggest stocking I can find!" Marta added in smug confidence.

"The apple dumplings may have slowed the horse down a bit, but is anyone up for a slower ride?"

"Me! I am!" Marta enthusiastically crowed.

"You'd better hurry!" John told her, "It's almost bed time. I'll get my violin, and as soon as you've had a ride, we'll have our little music time. Then it's off to bed. Cousin Jake and I have only tomorrow left to work at the wood before he goes home on Saturday."

"Then we go to Grandpa Kessler's on Sunday!" Maria happily exclaimed. "I think Grandma will have gifts for us, too! And that will be before Christmas! Come on, Marta! Get on the horsey! Get-up, horsey, gett-ee up!" Off went the horse at a slow trot, swaying his back, to the delight of the girls.

Ellie finished the dishes, they tucked the girls in bed, and Jake retired upstairs as well. When they returned to the kitchen, John held his arms out to his wife.

"Come here, Ellie."

"What is it, John?" Ellie put her arms around his neck and looked into his face.

"I just need to hold you close; I need you so!"

Ellie pressed him to herself. When she felt a sob in John's throat, she quietly asked, "John, did something happen today?"

John didn't speak for a moment. Then he gently led her into the bedroom. "Let's get into bed, then I'll tell you."

John got ready and sank into the bed. Ellie climbed in and put her arm around him. "What is it, John?" she whispered.

"Oh Ellie!" again John sighed. "You may not understand—I hardly do myself. Today, when we were trimming the branches off one of the trees we had felled, Jake said something about it being the shortest day of the year. Like a flash, I suddenly realized that it was December 21—the day I asked Regina to marry me. I felt like I was frozen for a minute, then I felt sobs coming from way down inside me. I told Jake I had to go back to the sleigh for something, and I went down over the hill so he couldn't see me. My grief welled up from a place so deep I thought I couldn't stand it! I thought I would never stop crying."

A shudder ran through him.

"Oh John!" Ellie's heart cried, "It's all right to cry."

"I had thought the worst was over," John whispered, "It came like such a surprise. All of a sudden it was just there, I couldn't help it."

He paused, "It's not that I don't care for you, Ellie. I do! I don't know what I would do without you!"

"Shh-hh, John! You don't need to feel that you are hurting me by grieving for Regina! There may be more times like today. If there are, let yourself feel them, and know that I am here for you. I share your grief."

It was Ellie's turn to pause. "I love you, John!"

John turned to her, "Do you really, Ellie?"

"Yes I do, John!" Ellie exclaimed. "I have felt my love for you growing, but tonight I had to tell you!"

John rose on his elbow and almost reverently kissed her. "Thank you for that wonderful gift!"

Eagerly she responded, pulling his head closer as she showered him with her own kisses until John lost all reserve. When they had sealed their love, they lay in quiet content. There was something new between them—something tender and precious.

"Goodnight, my dear, dear wife!" John whispered with a sleepy sigh.

"Goodnight, my love!" was Ellie's gentle reply. Quietly she let John's words reverberate in her mind and heart—"Goodnight, my dear, dear wife!"

Chapter Seven

On Sunday morning they went to Ellie's parents' church, then on to their farm for dinner. Aunt Matilda and Willy and Mary and their little Frederick were also there. The goose had been roasting in the oven since morning and the table was already set. The men and children settled down in the parlor while the women prepared the vegetables.

As they worked, Aunt Matilda asked Ellie, "Did you hear about Gerhard?"

"No." Involuntarily, Ellie's heart did a bit of a flip, but she replied with a forced calm, "I haven't heard anything of him for some time now. What about him?"

"He and Rowena Elliott have announced their engagement. They are to have a big wedding in February! The Elliotts have rented the Hotel in Bolton for the reception."

"My!" Ellie responded, "That should be quite a do!" Inwardly she thought *Well, well! Gerhard! That should give you a big boost up the social ladder!*

For a few moments Ellie's mind was filled with thoughts and emotions akin to jealousy and resentment, perhaps even inferiority. She realized that she could not have given Rowena Elliott's kind of prestige to Gerhard, to whom such things were so important in his quest for success. *Stop it, Ellie!* she cautioned herself. *Would you really rather have that kind of prestige and financial success than the love of a good man like John?*

Thinking back to the last few days, Ellie's heart responded confidently with a negative answer to the question her mind had presented. Even then, it was a bit of a struggle to let go of that initial reaction. To win a moment away from the women, she carried some dishes to the dining room table. Through the door to the parlor she caught John's eye and his almost imperceptible wink. Her heart responded with love and she smiled back at him with her eyes and soul. With a glad heart she helped in the final preparations for the festive meal.

True to Maria's expectations, after dishes were done and everyone went and found a seat in the parlor, Grandma and Aunt Matilda began to distribute small gifts to each of the family members. Aunt Matilda had dainty handkerchiefs for each of the girls, and from Grandma and Grandpa, Maria and Marta each received a beautiful book of stories.

"Thank you, Grandma and Grandpa!" the girls chorused.

"Maybe Papa can read some of these stories at bedtime!" Maria added. Quietly, she sat looking at the pictures in her book.

"It won't be long," her grandma told her, "until you can read these stories all by yourself!"

"I know," Maria replied, "I am going to start primary class after Easter."

"My," Grandma said, her eyes full of love, "our granddaughter is getting to be a big girl!"

"Come, Grandma," Grandpa called. "Come to the piano and we'll gather 'round and sing some Christmas Carols."

The next half hour passed quickly as the family lifted their voices in the harmonious melodies of the season. Then John suggested they had better start for home or the animals in the barn would wonder where they were. Everyone got bundled up and goodbyes were said. John got the horses from the barn and the family waved goodbye as they went out the lane.

"Frederick is so tiny, isn't he, Mama and Papa?" Marta commented. "But he's so cute when he smiles. When will he be big enough to play with us?"

John chuckled. "By next year you will probably be trying to keep him out of your things! He probably will be crawling around by then, and perhaps, even walking!"

Ellie's thoughts slipped back to the news about Gerhard and Rowena. It had been she who had broken the engagement. It was Gerhard who had expressed hurt and even anger. She had made the decision on her own, even though it was her parents who had really urged her to do so. It was difficult for her to believe that this news had brought such an unsettled feeling in her heart. Was it hurt, that Gerhard had found a replacement so soon? Was it jealousy, because Rowena, perhaps, could provide some of Gerhard's wants and needs better than she? Wasn't that awfully selfish of her, when she was really finding so much happiness with John?

The changes had come so fast. The course of her life had taken a real twist in a matter of months. She glanced at John and then at the girls. These past months had brought her a lot of joy. Her heart had responded to her growing understanding of John and the strong yet sensitive nature that was his. She thought again of Thursday night and the change that had taken place in their relationship with the declaration of her love. Her life sure was different than she had anticipated a year ago. She smiled to herself as she thought—*Different isn't necessarily bad! In fact, it has turned out to hold some unexpected delights!*

Ellie looked over the girls' heads to John. "Did you hear that Gerhard is engaged to Rowena Elliott?" she asked.

"Yes, your dad told me. Any regrets?"

"No. No regrets!"

For some time they traveled on, each absorbed in their own thoughts. Suddenly Maria broke the silence.

"Would John Junior have been walking yet?" she asked quietly.

Ellie hugged the girl. "No, Maria, probably not quite yet, but he would have been sitting up by now and throwing his toys on the floor for you to pick up! Did Frederick make you think of the little brother you could have had?"

"Yes, he did, Mama. I think I'd like to have a little brother!"

Ellie held Maria close. This young girl's thoughts ran deep, she realized. For her age, she was so serious and responsible. Ellie realized that John was struggling with his emotions, roused by his daughter's query. Marta had fallen asleep after the big day. After some time, in order to lift the sadness they all felt, Ellie asked, "Maria, only one day left until Christmas! Do you think we can get ready? "

"Papa," Maria asked, "Could we have a Christmas tree like Grandpa's? Could you get one tomorrow? Please? I could string some more popcorn and we could make a paper chain for it, and maybe we could make some paper snowflakes like Mama used to make for us."

John smiled at her as they turned in their lane. "I think there is a small cedar down in the swamp that would like to be a Christmas tree. You can get busy making the decorations first thing in the morning and I will get the tree before dinner. That way, it should be ready to welcome Father Christmas when he comes to fill your stockings!"

John pulled up close to the stand. "All right, little girl, can you wake up? Just a minute, Ellie, I'll let the horses stand here while I carry Marta in."

John jumped from the cutter. "Whoa, boys!" he cautioned the horses, which were ready to get back to their stalls.

Marta rubbed her eyes as she sat in the rocking chair where John had left her. When Maria saw she was awake, she told her little sister, "Marta! We're going to have a Christmas tree like Grandpa's! Papa said he would get it tomorrow!"

"Really?"

"Yes! Really! We'll have to get the decorations made tomorrow morning."

The next day was a busy one for everyone. Ellie popped some corn and got Maria started stringing it. Marta sat patiently, handing Maria a fluffy kernel each time she was ready for another.

While the girls were busy with that, Ellie folded a pile of square papers ready for cutting snowflakes. She cut strips of green and red paper for the paper chains. *That should keep the girls busy and the tree well trimmed,* she thought.

Quickly, while the girls still worked on the popcorn strings, Ellie prepared coleslaw and got a selection of cookies and goodies ready to take along on the morrow.

By that time the dishpan was full of popcorn strings, so she showed Maria how to carefully cut the snowflakes before she hurried to get the dinner on the table.

It wasn't long before John appeared with a little cedar he had found. He had already fastened some pieces of wood to the bottom of the tree so it would stand nicely in the corner of their parlor. The girls could hardly content themselves to eat before the decorating started. Excitedly, they chattered throughout the meal.

"So, do you think you would like to have a nap before decorating the tree?" John asked, with a twinkle in his eyes.

"No, Papa!" they cried in alarm. "We want to do it now! Please, Papa? We can't wait!"

"Well then, Mama!" John said in mock gravity, "do you think we should let them do it now?"

"I guess since Father Christmas can't come until little girls are fast asleep, maybe they can go to bed earlier tonight if they stay awake now," Ellie thoughtfully replied.

"Yes! Yes!" The girls agreed. "We'll go to bed early tonight!"

"Do you think we should have a star for the top of the tree?" Ellie asked.

"Yes, that would be nice, wouldn't it, girls?"

"Where are we going to get it?" Marta asked.

"I have some shiny gold paper," Ellie replied. "If we cut out two big stars, we can paste the top points and the side ones together, and then we can slip the tip top of the tree inside."

"Oh, that will be pretty!" enthused Maria.

"Here, Maria, you carry in the dishpan with the popcorn string in it. Do you think you can manage? Marta, I'll give you this basket of snowflakes. Papa will help you with those things while I make the star. We didn't get the paper chain done, but we will do that afterward and Papa can put it on right after supper."

Within an hour the tree was brightly decorated and the girls sat before it in rapt wonderment. John put on his thick winter jacket and hat. "I'm going to take Max and gallop into town quick before chores," he told Ellie. "Did you need anything?"

"No, I don't think so," she replied quizzically. "What do you need in town?"

"Now, now," he cautioned. "No questions so close to Christmas!"

"All right, then! You'll be back for chores, I suppose. Is that question allowed?"

"Yes, I'll be back." He tipped his hat and waved as he went out the door.

True to his word, John came back in good time, the chores were done, supper enjoyed amidst excited chatter, the last trimmings were put on the tree and the stockings hung on the mantle.

The girls had no objections to being tucked into bed early. The day had been full of excitement and fun. John and Ellie went together to put them to bed. John told them the story of that first Christmas night and how the shepherds had been the first to hear the good news of Jesus' birth. Prayers and goodnights were said, and now, all was quiet.

John and Ellie started the stockings with an orange in the toe, and then candy and nuts and a hat in each filled them over the top. The fur muffs were wrapped in gay paper and placed under the tree. The snack left for Father Christmas had been dutifully consumed.

"Ellie, I would like to give you my gift tonight, while we are alone. Is that all right with you?"

"Why, yes! I think that would be very nice! I shall get mine for you as well!"

"Let's go into the parlor, on the sofa beside the Christmas tree. I'll wait for you there."

Ellie raised her eyebrows as she went to the bedroom. "Apparently," she thought, full of curiosity, "it must be small enough that he already has it with him!"

Quickly, she got the pocket watch from its hiding place in the drawer and tucked it deep into the pocket of her full skirt. She picked the atomizer up from the dresser and gave herself a small misting of perfume. With one last look in the mirror and a pat on her hair, she went into the parlor to sit beside John. He looked quizzically at her when she came into the room with nothing in her hands, but said nothing.

When she was seated, he put his arm around her. "Before I give you my gift," he began, "I want to tell you something. I hope you can bear with me, because some of it may be hard for me to express." He paused. Ellie quietly reached for his hand.

"When Regina and I met, I felt very soon that I had found the love of my life. The more I got to know her, the more sure I was that my first inclination was right. The first days of marriage were a heady delight. The coming of our babies just cemented our relationship. We were so happy." John paused awhile before continuing his story.

"When Regina died part of me died with her. I thought I would never feel whole again." Again he paused.

"When your parents came, only two months later, asking me to consider marrying you, I was horrified, at first, by their audacity! I couldn't imagine letting someone else into Regina's place in my heart and life. But they kept urging me to think about it."

He was silent for a moment. Ellie laid her head against his shoulder.

"Ellie, everything seemed so unreal. As I've said before, it felt as though I was walking in a fog—or a dream. Surely, I would wake up and find everything as it had been! Gradually,

I knew in my heart that something had to be done for the children's sake. Life was too fragmented for them. That is when I asked to see you and get to know you—you, whom I had always looked at as a little sister.

"Please don't be hurt by this, Ellie, but at that time in my life, it felt as though I was just going down the path of least resistance." He swallowed hard. "Those few Sundays we spent together, I began to see you as an adult. I could see real strength of character, and yes, some of the familiar family traits that I had loved in Regina. I began to feel that I could commit myself to learning to love you as time passed. I have done that. I set my course to learn to love you.

"Those first weeks of marriage, I saw more and more in you to love and appreciate. I hit a rough spot when I started to feel it wasn't fair to burden you with my sorrow. Then you gently drew me out of that pit, so that I began to trust you with my feelings. I began to see you in a new light. There still were, and probably will be, times that I feel torn between grief and newfound peace. Sometimes I wondered if you could ever love me as you had a right to love a man, because I know you did what you did because of your parents' request. But Ellie, last Thursday, when the grief seemed to spill out of the very depth of me, I shared that with you—and you not only heard and understood, but made me feel safe in telling you…"

He lifted her face and looked into her eyes, "Then, from your heart, and of your own free will, you gave me the gift of your love! Somehow, Ellie, that sincere and unsolicited expression of your love brought such a release and healing—I can't put it into words!"

He gave her a long, ardent kiss.

"That night, I found I could love you for being you. That love is a new—and still small—plant, but one that holds promise of better things to come. I believe it will grow. Regina I will always love in my memories, but I have found there is lots of room in my heart to love you too. I wanted to signify this in some way, so when I took Jake home on Saturday, I stopped in town to order you a Christmas gift. That is what I had to pick up today."

He withdrew a package from his pocket. "With this, I give my heart to you, dear Ellie."

Reverently, she accepted the gift and opened the small box.

"Oh John!" she cried.

From the box, she drew a heart-shaped locket. On the back was inscribed "J. & E." She opened the locket to find pictures of her and John. "Where did you get this picture of me?" she asked.

"I asked your mother for one on Sunday," he replied. "Here, let me fasten it around your neck."

The locket fell into place on her chest.

"John, thank you so much for sharing so honestly. I feel so honored to receive the gifts you have given me—the gift of your love, and this gift that I'll always wear and treasure. I do love you."

They held each other close until, suddenly, Ellie exclaimed. "You touched me so with your gift and your words of love, I almost forgot!" From her pocket, she withdrew John's gift. "It was supposed to be my means of telling you that I love you, but I guess I couldn't wait that long," she laughed.

John opened the box and took out the watch. "What a nice watch!" he remarked as he pushed the latch to open the lid. When he saw the inscription, tears glistened in his eyes.

"Thank you, Ellie!" he sighed. "That is one message I shall never tire of hearing! It will be a beautiful surprise whenever you tell me, and always when I look at the time!"

"I shall never tire of telling you that I love you, my dear husband!" Ellie replied.

Resting his cheek on her head, he whispered, "Just look out that window!"

There lay the world, under a fresh blanket of snow, sparkling in the light of the full moon. "It's almost too romantic a night to be indoors!" remarked John. "If it wasn't for having to get up early to get the chores done before going to my folks', I'd suggest a little walk."

"Let's just blow out the lamp and enjoy it from here for a bit before we go to bed," Ellie suggested.

So, for awhile they sat in quiet comfort, reveling in the new love they had discovered, remembering the eve so long ago when Love itself was born, knowing that Love would guide their love and their lives.

In the mellow mood that enveloped them, John once more whispered, “Ellie, let’s pray.”

“Sure!”

John began, “Heavenly Father, on this eve, when we remember the Love you sent into the world to redeem and heal and make us whole, we lift to you our thanks for the love you have brought to Ellie and me. Our grief-filled days have been in need of your redemption and our broken lives have needed your wholeness.

“Into my life you have brought Ellie to administer healing and love more than I could have thought possible. You know the difficulties and struggles we may still face, but we are assured that, with the love you have given us for each other, you will grant us, also, what we need to surmount whatever we face.

“For tonight, this special night, we rest in your love and in this gift of love for each other, and we give you all thanks and praise, for the glory of your name. Amen.”

Ellie squeezed John’s hand and added her own prayer.

“Dear Lord Jesus, you who came as a babe this night so long ago, the love you have given us for each other seems like a precious new bundle from heaven too.

“Lord, help us to nourish this new gift, so that it may grow and flourish in all the ways that you know it can. May we and our love bring you honor and glory forever. Amen.”

“Ellie…what a beautiful thought and prayer!”

By the light of the moon, arm in arm, they found their way to their bed.

Chapter Eight

It wasn't long after John had gone to the barn Christmas morning that Ellie heard the girls getting out of bed.

"Put your slippers and robes on before you come out!" she called.

"Come on, Marta," she heard Maria say, "Hurry, hurry, get your slippers on. I'll help you with your robe. Hurry! We want to see what is in our stockings!"

"I *am* hurrying!" she heard Marta protest. It wasn't long before they came running, faces aglow.

"The cookies and milk are all gone!" Marta exclaimed.

"And our stockings are all bulged out and full!" Maria's excited voice added.

"Do you want me to help you get them off the hooks?" Ellie asked.

"I can reach mine!" Maria assured her.

Ellie went to retrieve Marta's. "Why don't you sit on the rug to empty them and see what is inside?"

Ellie smiled as she saw the difference in how the girls went about the joyful task. Maria was carefully removing the hat from the top of the stocking. Marta held her stocking upside down, shaking with all her might, trying to spill the contents all at once.

"Oooh! What a fuzzy, warm hat!" Maria exclaimed as she put the white fur on her head. "It feels so warm and cozy!"

"It looks pretty too!" said Ellie. "Your black curls and rosy cheeks set off the white of your hat. One pretty little lady you are!"

"Look at all the candy and nuts!" was Marta's first happy cry as she shook the stocking, "and there is still something in the toe, but I can't get it out."

"Why don't you reach in with your hand and see if that works?" asked Ellie. She watched Maria carefully sorting her candy and nuts into little piles.

"I really like maple buds!" she said. "But I like the peppermint sticks too—only they are sometimes a little burny!"

Marta had rescued her orange from the toe of the stocking and she smelled it with anticipation.

"Do you want to try on your hat?" asked Ellie.

Marta nodded, "Yes, but I don't know which way it goes."

"Come," said Ellie, "I'll help you!"

The soft brown fur of the hat, from which escaped a few reddish gold curls, framed the round, red-cheeked face.

"Oh!" cried Ellie, "You look sweet enough to eat!" she told her as she gave her a big hug.

"Where did you get the locket, Mama?" asked Marta.

"Your papa gave it to me for Christmas. Isn't it pretty?"

Maria came to look at the gift. "It's almost the same as our mama's, except it is the shape of a heart instead of an oval, and it's gold instead of silver."

"You are right!" Ellie commented. "Perhaps tomorrow we can look at the things in the Remembrance Trunk again. Then you could hold your first mama's locket again. Would you like that?"

"Yes!" the girls answered together. "Will you tell us more stories about Mama then?"

"Sure, I will," answered Ellie. "I'll tell you some of the ones I did before, and perhaps some new ones."

"Goody, goody!" exclaimed Marta. "I can't wait!"

"Well, right now I think we'd better get breakfast ready, because we have a long trip to Grandma and Grandpa Kurtz's today." Arising from the floor, Ellie added, "If you bring your oranges to me, I will fix them into pretty flowers for breakfast."

"I want to eat mine!" Marta objected.

"Oh, don't worry, you can still eat it." Ellie assured her. "Come, I will fix Papa's into a flower, then if you like what you see, I will do yours that way too."

Intently, they watched as Ellie carefully scored the rind in perfect eighths from the top to near the bottom of the orange. She loosened each section of peel to the end of the cut, then curved the top point of the peel down to tuck it in where the rind was still fastened to the orange. Then she separated the sections of the orange, giving them the appearance of inner petals. Finally, she tucked a big fat date in the center. "What do you think of that?" she asked.

"That is pretty!" said Maria, with admiration.

"Do mine now!" begged Marta.

Soon there were four oranges, each neatly centered on a small plate, one at each place at the table.

"Papa will be so surprised, won't he?" said Marta, with sparkling eyes.

Suddenly, Maria looked appalled. "Oh Mama!" she cried. "We should have made something for Papa for Christmas! He is the only one without a gift!"

"That is very nice of you to think of him! Next year, we will remember to either make something or buy something for you to give to him. However, he did get something this year too. I gave him a pocket watch. When he comes in he will show it to you."

"Oh," Maria said, with relief in her voice. "I'm glad you got something for him."

"Here comes Papa now," Marta excitedly announced. "Papa, Papa! Look at the table!"

"Oh, what a pretty sight! They are too nice to eat, aren't they?"

"No, they aren't!" objected Marta, fearfully, "Mama said we could eat them."

"Yes, yes, little one. I only meant that they are really nice to look at. Mama can sure make pretty things, can't she?"

Still holding the towel, he asked, "Was there anything in your stockings this morning?"

"Oh, yes!" the girls cried together. They ran to get their hats.

"And look at all the candy and nuts and things we got," Marta added.

"And the oranges were in the very bottom, at the toes!" Maria informed him.

"Was there anything under the tree?"

"We didn't look!" they said in surprise.

Ellie looked at John as the girls ran to the parlor.

"I thought it would be nice for you to be in on some of the excitement."

They went to join the girls beside the tree.

"There are two parcels here with tags on them," Maria said, "Who are they for?"

John looked at the tags.

"This one says 'To Marta, from Papa and Mama' and this one says, 'To Maria from Papa and Mama.' So you can each open your own."

While Maria carefully opened the paper wrapping, Marta tore into her parcel.

"Oh-hh! This is just like my hat!" she cried. "But what is it?"

By this time Maria had retrieved hers.

"Mine matches my hat too! It's a muff. Marta, look! You put your hands into it like this. It keeps your hands all cozy and warm. I've seen the big girls and ladies at church wear them."

She ran to get her hat and came back wearing them both.

"Thank you, Papa and Mama. They are beautiful!"

"My girls look beautiful in them. I think we'd better get our breakfast, though, and get started for Grandma and Grandpa Kurtz's! Come let's get to the table and see if we can eat our oranges."

"There are 'Eggs in the Nest' in the oven as well," Ellie said.

"What are those?" asked Maria.

"Come, I will show you,"

Ellie opened the oven door. There were pieces of toast with a little hole in the center. The yokes of the eggs rested in the holes and the whites spread around them. Over this Ellie had grated a bit of cheese.

"Oh! We are having a pretty breakfast!" Maria exclaimed.

"Well, it is Christmas!" Ellie commented. "I thought it was a good time to use some of our precious eggs since it is such a special day we are celebrating."

Seated around the table, the family, as usual, reached to hold hands to pray.

"Heavenly Father," John prayed, "This is indeed a special day we celebrate! Even as we rejoice in the gifts we give to each other, we know that you have given us the best gift of all. Thank you for our Lord and Saviour, Jesus Christ. Help us, throughout this day and every day of our lives, to keep in mind your great love for us and the gift you have bestowed on us. Be with us as we gather with our family, and may we all have traveling mercies. Bless the food you have given and which Ellie has so lovingly prepared. Strengthen and nourish us that we may use our energies in your service and for your praise! Amen."

As they enjoyed the special meal, Maria spoke.

"Papa, I thought you were going to be the only one that didn't get a gift for Christmas, but Mama said she gave you a watch. Will you show us before we go to Grandpa's?"

"I think we can take time for that," John smiled. "It is a very special watch!"

His eyes met Ellie's and there was an exchange of delight in their deepening love. Ellie's heart fluttered in wonder and in thankfulness.

Everything for the trip to Grandpa's was loaded in the cutter. The horses were eager to be off. John slapped the reigns and clicked his tongue to give them the signal to go.

"Grandpa Kurtz's, here we come!"

Ellie tucked the robe around their legs. "It's a cold wind, so you'll be glad for your new hats and muffs. Keep your scarves up over your noses so you don't get too much cold air."

The biting north wind hit the sides of their faces as they headed east. It was too cold for conversation, so Ellie's thoughts wandered. This seemed like another milestone in her new life. It would be the first time she would be with John's whole family. She hoped she could keep everyone straight.

She went through the list: Albert, John's older brother, married to Gerda—four children. Warner, Heidi, Erik and one-year-old Lottie; Isaac was the next youngest to John—wife Emma—their three children, Blanche, Walter and Adrianna; Rosa, married to Theo and their three—Louis, Gisela and Magdalena; Elda, John's youngest sister, just a little younger than Ellie herself, had been married to Joseph only since February. They were expecting their first in April. Ellie had met Elda on several occasions when the young people of the churches had gotten together in her youth. Joseph was from the church where she had attended before her marriage, so that had provided other occasions for them to be together. What a lot of people to remember!

Driving through the little town of Monkville, she admired the red ribbons bedecking the gateposts and the garlands of cedar on stores and homes. She wondered what it would be like living in a town. She had always lived in the country, and couldn't imagine what it would be like to have such close neighbors.

Several times groups of people arriving at a house along the way would wave at them and shout, "Merry Christmas!"

John would return the greeting as the family nodded their heads and smiled behind their scarves. The wind was not quite so strong here in town. The bricks Ellie had heated and wrapped to put at their feet were cooling by now, and they still had some miles to go.

As they left the town behind, John once more slapped the reigns to urge the horses on. The farms in this area had bigger houses than where Ellie grew up. Here most of them were brick. Although the house where she and John lived was also brick, it wasn't as common in their area.

The roads, for the most part, were lined with tall maples. She knew from John's telling that, in the spring, most of the trees would be tapped to gather sap for making syrup. The barns, too, seemed to be bigger in this area. Many of them were hip-roofed.

It was good that the Kurtz's had a large house. With twenty-three in the family, the table would need to be stretched from the kitchen right through the archway to the living room. Albert and Gerda farmed right across the road from their parents, so she was sure that Gerda had helped with the hot dishes that were needed.

Of course, she thought to herself, *Mom Kurtz will have been busy for weeks, getting things ready for her big family. She always bakes wonderful breads and rolls.*

John lowered his scarf a bit to tell the girls, "Look up ahead! See the weather vane on Grandpa's barn? The rooster on top is facing right into the northwest wind! We're almost there!"

They had barely alighted when Grandpa Kurtz came to the door, calling out, "Merry Christmas! Merry Christmas!"

"Merry Christmas!" they called back.

There were already three other cutters and sleighs lined up at the barn as John went to add theirs. He put the horses in the barn for the day.

Ellie and the girls hurried in to Grandpa's hearty welcome. There were hellos and greetings all around, repeated again when John entered the house. Ellie smiled. What an exuberant family! She supposed that even the numbers made it seem so, but there was something that happened in large families that was absent in smaller ones. She was amazed at how everyone was pitching in to do something, seemingly knowing what was his or hers to do without having to ask or be told.

"Is there something you would like me to do, Mother Kurtz?" she asked.

"Let me see, you were bringing the coleslaw, weren't you? You can set that on the table if you like. Did you bring it in one dish or two?"

"In one."

"Perhaps you'd like to get two smaller dishes from the glass cupboard and divide it between the two. With twenty or so at the table, it takes one dish awhile to make the rounds," she laughed.

It wasn't long before everything was ready. Amid much laughing and joking everyone found a spot at the long table. The chatter abruptly stopped, as all eyes turned to Grandpa Kurtz. "Let us pray!" he announced.

"Heavenly Father, it is with grateful hearts that we bring you praise this day. We praise you most of all for the gift that you sent in the Lord Jesus Christ. We give you praise for this day to celebrate his coming to earth to bring us salvation and freedom from the sin that would bind us and keep us alienated from you. We give you praise that we can be together as a family around this table so amply laden with the good gifts you have given. We give you thanks that, even though there have been difficult times in the past year, you have brought healing and new blessings that have begun to fill our emptiness. Thank you for each one at this table. May we be mindful that we are all gifts to each other and treat each other as such, and in the doing of this, may we bring all glory to you, our Saviour and Redeemer. Amen"

His eyes glistened as he raised his head. "Now pass the food and help yourselves," he added.

Ellie noted those unshed tears and thought, *I see the same sensitivity and depth of love in his dad as I see in John.*

By the time John's mom served the steamed pudding and sauce, there was scarcely room to enjoy the delicacy. In this family, even the men helped clear the dishes and take out the extra table leaves to give more space for the afternoon activities. The summer kitchen at the back of the house had been pressed into duty. The big stove out there had cooked some of the food, so it was still warm enough to do the cooking dishes away from the crowd. As Ellie and Elda shared in the clean-up, Ellie asked how Elda was feeling and if she was getting excited about the coming of their little one.

"I'm feeling fine now. The first three months were difficult because I found it hard to keep anything in my stomach. I was afraid Joe would get tired of having this sickly wife around. It's better now, though. I am busy sewing little outfits and getting everything ready." She paused. "How about you? How is it going with you and John? It's good for the girls, because I know they have always felt you were a special aunt, but I've often wondered how you really feel about it!"

"Well, Elda…" Ellie paused to think how to respond. "I'd be less than honest if I didn't say that it required a lot of adjusting on both our parts. John is not through grieving for Regina and little John, but then, neither am I. As time goes by, there is so much I admire about John. I thought today, after the prayer at dinner, that I could see where he gets some of his traits. I think it was harder for Maria than Marta to think of me as her new mom. At first she seemed resentful of me taking her mother's place. In her quiet way she resisted thinking of me as a mother, but gradually she is changing. Especially in the last few weeks, she seems to have become more comfortable. We are developing a good relationship."

"Maybe I'm being too nosy," Elda continued. "If I am, you don't need to answer." She paused. "When I heard about Gerhard and Rowena's engagement, I wondered if it might hurt you."

Ellie was quiet. She felt a little uncomfortable talking about this with John's sister, even if she had something of a friendship with her.

Elda, probably sensing her discomfort, hurried on, "I mean, I just keep thinking how it would have been to give up Joe six months before we planned to get married, and then to marry someone else a few months later. I just can't imagine being able to stop loving one person and start loving another—if you really could love another one—and then to have that one still grieving for his wife, how can that be for you?" She rambled on, faster and faster, "—Oh, I'm sorry! I shouldn't even have asked. I really am sorry!"

She looked so repentant that Ellie smiled in spite of her former discomfort.

"Elda, I'm sure you asked out of concern for me and probably for your brother." She took a deep breath. "I feel rather uncomfortable talking about it, but just let me say that it wasn't easy breaking up with Gerhard, but my parents really wanted this. I have always admired John as a brother-in-law and I already loved the girls." She paused again and chose her words carefully. "As for being able to love each other, we're coming along very well in that department. The news about Gerhard helped me realize I have no regrets." She looked up at Elda and smiled, "Does that set your mind at ease?"

"Oh Ellie! I really had no right to ask," Elda lamented, "but John is my big brother, and I felt so sad for him when Regina and little John died! And I felt sorry for you too, because Gerhard was a good catch!"

"So is John." Ellie assured her quietly.

Grandma Kurtz had knitted thirteen pairs of mittens for her grandchildren. There was a lot of merriment and much giving of thanks as they were distributed. After the gift-giving they sang Christmas carols, the sound filling the room as all the voices were raised in harmony. Then John said that, if they were going to get home at all, they had better get on the way.

"It's good I brought the lanterns along, for it will be dark before we get home."

After passing through Monkville, they encountered drifts across the road in some places, and John had to be careful not to upset the cutter. It took longer to get home than anticipated. At least the wind had subsided, and the stars twinkled brightly in the dark winter sky and the world brightened again as the moon rose. Marta had gone to sleep soon after Monkville, and by the time they turned into their own curving lane, Maria had been asleep for some time as well. John tied the reigns to the post, helped Ellie get the girls and the dishes into the house and quickly changed his clothes before going to the barn to do the necessary chores.

It was late when John finally came in from the barn. The girls had already been in bed for for a while, and Ellie sat reading her Bible.

"It's been a long day for you, John! I've fixed a sandwich for you and the tea is hot. Do you want more than that?"

"That will be fine. I'm still quite full from the big dinner and all the candy, popcorn balls and goodies from this afternoon."

John washed up and came to sit at the table. "Why don't you read to me while I eat? What were you reading?"

Ellie looked at John, "I was reading from the first chapter of John and thinking about gifts and gift-giving—how we give and how we can receive. Listen to this," she began to read: "In the beginning was the Word, and the Word was with God, and the Word was God. The same was in the beginning with God. All things were made by him; and without him was not any thing made that was made. In him was life; and the life was the light of men. And the light shineth in darkness; and the darkness comprehended it not." Then down a few verses, "He came unto his own, and his own received him not. But as many as received him, to them gave he power to become the sons of God, even to them that believe on his name...

"You know, as I read that, I know that when it says 'the light shineth in darkness and the darkness comprehendeth it not,' it is talking about Jesus as the light, but I had to think about the light of our growing love that is shining on the darkness of our grief. It took awhile for the light to get through to our darkness too. It's maybe not proper theology, but I think, just as it says, 'as many as receive him, to them gave he power to become the sons of God, even to them that believe on his name,' it's sort of like that in other parts of life. If we are open to receiving the lessons and the blessings he has for us, he gives us so much more than we expect. He can only give gifts to open hands and hearts. If we refuse to put out our hands and open our hearts to receive, he can't place it in our closed fists." Ellie paused, "Does that make any sense at all?"

"Sure it does!" John laid his unfinished sandwich on his plate. "I think the pain of grief, at first, makes us withdraw and close ourselves, probably for self protection." He reached for her hand.

"You, Ellie, have helped me open my hands and my heart again." He opened her hand so that it was resting, open palm up, on his own open hand. "Let's try to keep our hands open to all that God has for us. Like this we can hold a lot," he moved her hand then so that their fingers were interlocked, "like this, they can hold even more. This is how I hope our relationship can work. Interlocked, but each of us with open hands to receive and share." He reached forward to kiss her before picking up his sandwich to finish his snack.

Ellie's eyes glistened with tears. "John," she said, resting her hand on his knee. "That is so beautiful and contains such wisdom!"

A peaceful glow seemed to surround them as John finished up his meal and they headed off to bed. It had been a good Christmas.

The peace was broken early in the new year when Maria began coughing. In spite of Ellie's remedies, the cough only worsened. An ominous dread fell with a thud in Ellie's heart when, three weeks after it began, Maria's coughing left no doubt. The next morning the doctor was called and it was confirmed—Maria had contracted whooping cough. A sign was affixed to their door proclaiming their home in quarantine because of the dreaded disease.

It was not long until Marta, too, began with what appeared to be a cold, which then turned into a cough as well. It got much worse than Maria's had been. There were times she turned blue when she was in the midst of an outburst. Ellie mixed honey with ginger and lemon to try to ease the cough that shook Marta's little body until she appeared entirely worn. They tried all the home remedies they knew as well as those that were recommended by others. The doctor made visits and gave advice, but admitted that there was only so much he could do. They first propped her up with pillows, then began to take turns sitting up with her, holding her in the rocking chair to make sure they were there when they were needed.

One night, just after Ellie had relieved John, Marta began to cough and after one big whoop, she stopped breathing.

"John!" Ellie screamed. John came running, and seeing the situation, held her upside-down, clapping her on the back. It seemed like hours before Marta gave another big cough. John held her to himself and began to sob. "My poor little girl!" he comforted, between his tears. Marta lay listless against his shoulder.

In the morning, after John went to do chores, Marta seemed to be sleeping comfortably. Ellie's arms ached and tiredness enveloped her body.

"Dear Lord," she prayed, "Please keep Marta safe. There has been enough death in this family. I have been trying to do my best, but I feel so inadequate. I see the fear and despair in John's eyes and I don't know what more I can do....and... oh Lord, I am so scared and tired myself, I don't know how I can go on."

The tears streamed down her face.

"Please, Heavenly Father, hold me and John and Marta in your arms and give us the strength we need."

She sat quietly, rocking and letting the tension ooze out of her.

"Lord, you have said when we are weak, you are strong. I feel completely empty of strength. Just be my strength, Lord, please be my strength."

Through the window and through her tears she saw the first rays of the sun coloring the sky a soft pink. The frosty branches of the trees took on a tone of silver gray, turning the whole world into a muted fairyland.

"Thank you, God!" she breathed.

A warm glow settled on Ellie, for she took the scene to be an affirmation that her prayer had been heard. She reached to draw the footstool closer, so she could put her feet up and make Marta's weight more comfortable. She placed a cushion under the arm that held Marta's head. Leaning back, she breathed a prayer of thanks for the new day, the beauty of the sky and the assurance she felt in her heart. She closed her eyes.

It wasn't until John gently touched her shoulder that she awoke.

"Let me try Marta on the couch," he whispered.

Ellie blinked her eyes to shake away the sleep. She nodded, and then whispered back, "I'll put some pillows down so she won't be laying flat."

Ellie rose, feeling awkward with stiffness from holding Marta so long. Her one foot felt numb and began to tingle as she walked to the couch.

Marta stirred momentarily when her father laid her down, but then slept on. John reached for Ellie and drew her into his arms.

“Do you want to lay down and rest awhile?” he asked. “I can watch Marta.”

“You are just as tired as I am. Let’s have some breakfast. She has at least slept longer than she has for a while. She only coughed twice since that bad one… I was so scared, John.”

“So was I, Ellie. When I saw her so blue and not breathing, I thought we had lost her.”

“How did you know what to do?”

“I didn’t! I just had to do something. I’m just glad it worked.” John gave her an extra hug. “You are getting tried as by fire in this parenting role, aren’t you?”

“I felt so tired before I had that little sleep, but I remembered that God said when we are weak, He is strong. The sunrise was so beautiful. It was as though He was assuring me that He would watch over us. I guess it was then that I shut my eyes and just let myself rest in Him.”

As it turned out, that had been the worst night. Although Marta remained pale and weak for some time, and both girls coughed for weeks afterward, there was gradual improvement.

Chapter Nine

1887

Ellie hung the last of the clothes on the line. What a bright sunny day! There was a soft breeze blowing, so the clothes would dry quickly and gather a fresh smell. She still had strawberries to pick. The patch that John and Regina had planted three years ago was lush with fruit this year. Even three years and more since her death, Ellie sometimes missed her older sister. Before she went to the house to exchange her wash basket for bowls in which to pick the strawberries, Ellie went to see if there might be enough peas ripe to have some for dinner. She taste-tested a few plump pods that she found. *Yes*, she thought, *there will be enough for a meal*. She would bring a basket in which to pick those too. She went back to the clothesline and picked up the clothesbasket. Usually the girls would have been there to help her, but they were staying with her folks for a few days.

As she returned to the garden her thoughts were on her family. Two years at school had made such a difference in Maria. Ellie remembered with what trepidation Maria had faced that first day in the spring. It took a week, at least, for her to feel comfortable and know what was expected of her. *Change does not come easily for Maria,* Ellie smiled as she thought, *I hope the next adjustment is easier for her!* She was glad that she and John would have this evening alone. She was anxious to share the news with him.

The strawberries still hung thick on the stems. They were a little smaller than the first ones, but they would make lovely preserves. Strawberry jam was one of Marta's favorite foods. How insulted she had been that she would not be allowed to go to school, too, when Maria began. Ellie remembered how she sweetened the prospect of time alone with her by giving Marta toast and strawberry jam for afternoon "tea" some days. It became their special treat on occasional afternoons that were not too busy. Ellie would get out the small teapot and some tiny cups she had left from her childhood. Mint tea and the tiny triangles of toast with jam served on the front porch in the summer and in the parlor in the winter were the epitome of grandeur and opulence to the little girl.

The row of zinnias, marigolds and bachelor's buttons were coming up nicely. The nasturtiums, too, would soon be blooming. She enjoyed the flowers so much, and loved keeping several vases filled with whatever was in bloom. Sometimes wildflowers substituted for what was unavailable in her gardens. As she stood to relieve her back and legs, she looked out the lane to where the huge bolder was backed by the small cedars flanked by the forsythia. These were still quite small, but they had bloomed this spring. Now the red geraniums were taking over for the yellows and reds that the daffodils and tulips had provided earlier. John was right. It was a nice welcome to visitors as well as to themselves when they returned home after being away.

She remembered the day she had first come in the lane as John's wife. She had wondered if it would ever seem like her home, or if it always would feel as though she were living in Regina's home. *What a difference a few years and a lot of living can make*, she thought. *Just a few more months until our third wedding anniversary.* Their love had grown a lot over that time until now they felt they belonged to one another. She was sure that John still had times of sadness when he thought of Regina. She sometimes sensed his melancholy. At such times she had to be careful to not slip into wondering whether or not she measured up to her big sister. More and more, though, she felt secure in their love for each other.

Maria and Marta, most of the time, seemed to be quite at ease. They still frequently asked to see the things in the Remembrance Trunk and enjoyed hearing the stories of their mother and her love for them, but it had blended into life as it had become instead of the wish that things could have continued as they had been. She thought that, for Marta especially, it had kept alive memories of her mother that would have otherwise been nonexistent. They now slept upstairs in the room next to the trunk, and she had often seen them peeking into the room on their way past.

Ellie hurried to the house with her small basket of peas and big bowl of strawberries. John had taken the girls to her folks' this morning and had some business out that direction, so he wouldn't be back until chore time. Ellie would have the afternoon to make the jam. The clothes were drying so nicely; she would get the things that needed ironing off the line while they were still damp and do that this afternoon too.

She wanted supper to be special tonight. They would have fresh strawberries and cream to eat with the leftover coffee cake from last night. She would add the peas to the small potatoes, for which she had forfeited one hill of what could have been bigger ones. With some green onions in a cream sauce served with cold sliced beef and pickles, it would make a good meal.

The afternoon passed quickly. John came home just in time for a cup of tea before chore-time. Ellie was almost bursting with the news, but forced herself to wait. When supper was ready, except for the things that would have to be done at the last minute, she went to put on a clean dress. Carefully, she chose one that had drawn a compliment from John. She fixed her hair and patted on a bit of perfume.

To put in some time while she awaited supper, she went to find some of the first blooms on the climbing rose along with a few wild daisies to put in a vase on the table. She snipped a few fronds from the parlor fern to accent the arrangement. She set the table with the good dishes, and put napkins in the silver napkin rings that had once belonged to her grandmother. She stepped back to survey the table, and nodded in satisfaction. Just then, she heard John coming in the back door.

John whistled when he saw the unusual setting. "I would ask if we're having company, but I only see two places set! What is the occasion?"

"It's not often that we get to dine alone! That, in itself, is cause enough for a special celebration, isn't it?"

"You are right, Ellie! I'll wash up and change into clean clothes. It somehow doesn't seem fitting to sit down for such a lovely meal with clothes smelling like the barn!"

"That would be nice! I'll get things on the table."

When John came back to the kitchen, with clean shirt and trousers, he came to give her a hug. "I just never know how my dear wife will surprise and delight me! You truly are special!"

"Thanks, but I'm doing it for someone who has found a very special place in my heart, so it's a joy." Ellie smiled and lifted her face for his kiss. "Let's sit down and eat."

Ellie tried to take pleasure in her carefully prepared meal and to allow John to enjoy his, but she was eager for the meal to be done. Finally, John pushed his chair slightly back from the table.

"That was truly a delicious meal, all the better because it was made by and shared with such a beautiful, loving wife, my dear!"

"I'm glad you enjoyed it, John. It was special having a meal with just the two of us again." Ellie reached out for his hand. "I have something else yet, though!"

"Oh, Ellie!" John protested, "I am so full, I don't think I can eat another bite!"

"No, no! This is not to eat! I just wanted to tell you that—well, that I think I am going to need some time this winter to knit little sweaters and booties and things like that!"

John raised his eyebrows, "Ellie, do you mean— Ellie do you really mean that?" He looked disbelieving.

"Yes, John, dear, it looks like we're going to have a baby!"

John pulled Ellie from her chair onto his lap and held her close. "Ellie, oh Ellie!" he whispered, "My dear Ellie! You make me so happy! A new baby with you will be wonderful! But—but you will be careful, won't you? I don't think I could stand losing you!"

"Oh John! I hadn't thought that it might scare you!" She put her arms around his neck and kissed his forehead. "I am healthy, and many women have babies and don't die. I know Regina did with her third, but those were special circumstances. I promise I will see the doctor regularly and do everything I can to keep healthy and well. John, we have to trust God too!"

"You are right, Ellie!" John softly replied. "I'm sorry I reacted that way! I guess my first thoughts were about the way it turned out the last time I got news like this. I really am happy, and I know chances are that all will go well. It would be nice to have another baby in the house. The girls will be so pleased. Every time they see one of their little cousins, they long to have a little sister or brother."

He stood and gently drew Ellie into his arms again. "You truly have been such a blessing to me! I love you so much!" He held her for a moment then lifted her face to kiss her. Looking deep into her eyes, he asked, "Do you know, beautiful *frau*, how much I love you?"

Ellie's eyes shone with love, "My dear John, I do know that you love me deeply, and I will always be so thankful for that love! I guess that is one reason I am so happy about this baby. He or she will be the tangible fruit of our love. To be able to share in making a new life that will be part of both of us feels like such a miracle, just as our love is to me!"

"Ellie, can we stack the dishes and go for a walk before dark to celebrate this news? It stays light quite late these evenings. I'd like to walk back to our Dining Glade in the hemlocks. It won't take more than a half hour to get there." He paused, "That is, if you are up to it!"

"Sure, I'm up to it!" Ellie assured him. "I think that would be a lovely thing to do!"

Quickly, she put away the little food that was left while John stacked the dishes. Hand in hand, they walked through the summer evening to the woods where they had begun exploring their relationship and where they had returned on numerous occasions, although usually with the girls. As they walked, they talked of that first day and how their love had grown in the time since then. When they arrived at the little haven, John put his jacket on the ground and sat on the soft needles. Patting his jacket, he asked Ellie to join him.

"Ellie," John began, "that first day we came here, I think I was still walking in a haze, as it were. I had committed myself to loving you, but everything still felt rather unreal. Looking back now, that day, even more than our wedding day, seemed like the true beginning for the two of us." He paused in deep thought. "There have been some other significant days—mileposts—since then. Today is another one. I just wanted to come back here and make another commitment to each other and to God. Is it all right with you if we pray?"

"I would like that very much, John!" Ellie agreed.

With one arm around her and his other hand on hers, John began, "Gracious and most loving God, it is with awe and thanksgiving that we come to you this evening, here in this secluded sanctuary. It is a hallowed place and a special day for us, for you are blessing us again with new evidence of the love that has been growing in our hearts. Cast all fear from our hearts, Lord, and help us to have perfect trust in you. As this fruit of our love, as Ellie has called it, grows within her body, we will put our trust in you to keep both her and the baby safe. As a sign of this trust we want to commit both ourselves and this new little life to your service for your pleasure and your glory. Accept, we pray, the song of praise and thanksgiving our hearts are raising to you. In Jesus' name, Amen."

Ellie laid her head on his shoulder. "Amen!" she whispered before a sob shuddered in her breast.

"What's the matter, Ellie?" John asked as he raised her face and saw the tears streaming down her cheeks. "Is it something I said?"

"No, no, John!" she cried. "Well, maybe it is something you said. It's just that...that you pray so beautifully and so sincerely...right from the heart! I love you so, and I am so thankful for the sensitive, godly man who is my husband."

John kissed her and smiled. "I thought I said something that hurt you, but a statement like that—well it's something I don't mind hearing!"

He kissed her again, and they sat in silence for a while.

"Look, Ellie," whispered John without moving. "See that woodcock over under that far hemlock tree?"

Together they watched the unique bird scratch for food. It took only a small movement of John's foot to send the shy creature scurrying away.

"It takes some waiting and patience and maybe a lot of luck to see woodcocks. They are quite reluctant to let themselves be seen. We'd better get started back to the house, or it will be dark before we get there. "

Arm in arm, they returned to the house, sometimes talking and laughing, sometimes in comfortable silence, but always in the knowledge of the love that was theirs. By the time they reached the house, the sky was ablaze with deep oranges and reds and the trees were silhouettes against the horizon like sentries standing guard over their abode, assuring them of a peaceful night.

In those first months Ellie found herself reacting emotionally to many situations. It seemed that it took nothing at all to bring the tears to her eyes. It was upsetting to her until she confided her concern to John's sister Rosa at the Kurtz family picnic in August.

"Oh Ellie! That is quite common in pregnancy!" Rosa consoled her; "You will feel better in a little while. I know for several of my pregnancies I felt as though I was crying the first three months. Anything—happy or sad, frustrating or joyous—could bring tears to my eyes faster than you could blink an eye! I think I'd rather have that, though, than feeling sick those first months. With our second I felt nauseous in the mornings and I couldn't wait until that was over."

Ellie heaved a big sigh. "I'll have to tell John. He'll be relieved. I can't tell you how often he has thought he said something that hurt me! I've felt like such a baby. It's a relief to know that others have felt like this too. I'm glad I confided in you."

"So am I, Ellie. We women aren't the only ones who have to suffer some of the discomforts of pregnancy! I guess that is all right though. We're in this parenting business together."

Later that fall, when Ellie felt the babe stirring within her, she felt the urge to begin sewing and knitting in readiness for the birth of their little one. One night she asked John, "Do you think it is about time we told the girls that there is a baby on the way?"

"Yes, it probably is," John replied, "Otherwise they will be wondering what all your sewing and knitting is about! Let's tell them tomorrow morning. It's Saturday, so they will have the weekend to absorb the news before Maria goes back to school."

The next morning, as they were finishing breakfast, John casually told the girls, "We have some good news we'd like to share with you, Maria and Marta. Would you like to hear what it is?"

"Yes!" Maria and Marta replied together. "Are we going to Grandma's?"

"Or are we going to town to go to the stores?" Marta tried to guess.

"Whoa, Marta!" John cautioned, "Why don't you slow down and let Mama tell you?"

The girls both turned to look expectantly at Ellie. She looked first at Maria, then at Marta. "You know how every time you are with your cousins you enjoy playing with the little ones?" The girls nodded. "How would you like to have a baby at our house?"

The girls' eyes widened. "Really?" whispered Maria.

"Whose?" asked Marta, always the practical one.

"Yes, really, Maria!" Ellie promised, "The baby will be our very own, Marta. The baby will be ready to be born in March, so it won't be right away. We thought you would like to know and help to get ready for a brother or a sister. I think we will have some good helpers to lend a hand in caring for the little one, don't you, Papa?"

"I will!" Marta volunteered, "I can make him smile and I can hold him sometimes."

"It might be a sister!" Maria interjected, "But I think I would like a brother."

"For that, we will have to wait and see." John told them, "but I'm sure we will love the baby, no matter whether it's a sister or a brother."

"I'm going to be doing some knitting to get ready for the baby. Perhaps you girls would like to learn to knit this winter as well. We'll have to get out the cradle you girls slept in when you were little and decide where to put it. We have to make sure there is lots of bedding for it and there will be many other things to decide. We can do that together, can't we?"

The girls left the breakfast table happily planning what they could do with a baby in the house. Ellie went about her work with a light heart. As a young girl, she had looked forward to the time she would have a little one in her arms. When she married John, her first attention, of necessity, had been the two daughters that had come with the marriage.

Turning nieces into daughters, as it were, and making the leap into a marriage that she had not foreseen six months before were both gigantic tasks that had left no room for anything else.

For almost a year now, she had thought perhaps the day would come when she would have this joy, but as the months went by, she wondered if it was actually going to come to pass. She and John had shared the secret for those first months, and during that time, it still felt like a dream. Telling the girls and feeling the movements of the baby within her had finally lent reality to the occasion.

She thought of John's solicitous care for her. She knew that he still struggled at times with fear for her safety because of the outcome of the last pregnancy in his house. She sensed in him a real tension between fear and joy.

They had been in bed for a while that night and John was already asleep when Ellie heard someone outside their bedroom door. She rose up on her elbow, “Who is it?” she asked.

“What?” asked John, roused from his sleep.

“There is someone outside our bedroom door.”

John threw back the blankets and was out of bed in one action. He slowly opened the door. The moon cast enough light to see that it was Maria.

“What is it, Maria? What is the matter?”

“I couldn’t sleep, Papa.”

“You’re going to get cold, Maria. Why don’t you go and get your slippers and robe and I’ll go and get mine, then we’ll talk.”

When Maria came again, John reached out to take her hand. “Come, let us sit on the settee, closer to the stove.”

The stove still shed some warmth, but John picked up the afghan and wrapped it around both of them. When they were seated, he put his arm around her shoulder. “Now, what is the problem? What keeps you from sleeping?”

Maria leaned against her Papa’s chest and, for a moment, sat in silence.

“Papa…I just got to thinking…how do we know…I mean, how can we be sure… Oh Papa, we thought we would have John Junior, but Papa, what if, what if…Oh Papa!”

John could hear the desperation in her voice and knew, even in the dark, that there were tears in her eyes. He drew her close.

“You are afraid of the same thing happening to your new mama and the baby, aren’t you?”

“Yes, yes!” Maria said with a sob. “What if they die?” She turned to bury her face in John’s robe and clung to him.

John held her close until she was once more quiet.

“My dearest Maria, I know how you feel. I felt scared at first too.”

“Did you really, Papa?” she seemed to sigh in relief.

“Yes, I did, Maria! That is because we remember so well what happened last time we looked forward to a new baby in the house. Maria, we can’t know for sure, but most babies are born and everything is all right. We have to trust God to keep

Mama and the baby safe. Do you think you and I can do that?"

"I don't know, Papa, I feel really scared," Maria confessed.

"We'll help each other. Why don't we pray and ask God to help us too?"

John felt Maria nod her head against his chest. He drew her close again and began to pray.

"Heavenly Father, here in this shadowy night, we come to you to tell you about the dark fears that have found their way into our hearts and minds. We want to be joyful when we think of the baby that is on the way, but our memories of loss and grief snuff out our joy like a strong wind blows out the light of a candle. We thank you that your perfect love casts out fear. So we ask you to wrap us in a protecting blanket of your love, so that we can truly rejoice in the thought of welcoming a new member to our family. Help us to think of the smiles and cute ways that babies bring the delight we find in caring for little ones. Lord, we ask, too, for your protection and care for the baby and the dear new mama that you brought into our lives. Help us to put our trust in you and to know that you love us far more than we can think or imagine. Be with Maria as she goes to bed, and help her to feel your everlasting arms about her. Amen."

"Thank you, Papa!" Maria whispered. "That helped me feel better. I think I can go to sleep now. Your prayer helped me feel God's blanket of love."

"I'll come and tuck you in," John said, getting up, "I'm glad we had this little time together. You just let me know if there are times you feel like this again."

"I will," whispered Maria as they reached the bedroom door. "And Papa, I hope God helps me keep my candle of joy burning."

John gave her a kiss as he tucked her in. "I believe he will, my dear one!"

As John returned to Ellie, she whispered, with deep concern in her voice, "Is Maria all right?"

John got into bed and turned to put his arm around Ellie.

"I think she is feeling better now. She still has some vivid memories of her mother and little brother dying. She was old enough that she remembers the anticipation, then the deep disappointment and trauma in her young life." He paused. "I guess she's like her father; she's almost afraid to feel anticipation and joy because of the outcome of the last time she experienced this."

Again there was a moment of silence.

"I prayed with her and she said it helped. In fact, it was a good reminder for me, too, to trust God for the safety of you and the baby."

"I thought that was what you were doing. I guess that's the best thing we can do. We know that God loves us. I hope Maria can feel that deep enough to take care of her fears, poor little girl!"

"It's often through difficulties that we can grow. If we can give Maria the understanding and guidance she needs through this, it'll make her a more understanding woman. Dad always said that difficulties in our lives could become either stumbling blocks or stepping-stones. I hope that Maria can make this a stepping-stone. It just might strengthen her faith. She's such a sensitive young girl, but she thinks things through carefully." He paused. "I think she'll work things out and mature in the process. Of course, we will need to support her while she's doing that."

"I'll surely try to do what I can," Ellie assured him.

"I know you will, and you'll do it well," John said with certainty. "But don't you go worrying about it. We want you take care of yourself right now."

"Like father, like daughter," Ellie quipped, "Go to sleep, and don't you worry!"

John chuckled, then, with a sigh, rolled over and was soon sleeping soundly.

Christmas took on special meaning to Ellie that year. The coming of her own baby created a kinship with Mary, the mother of Jesus. Although Mary's baby was the Son of God and the implications of His birth had had worldwide effect on every generation since, Ellie, too, pondered in her heart just what a difference the child within her could make on the world. She acknowledged that he or she might not become known world-wide, but she prayed that this child would live to its true potential and let God direct his or her life and thoughts and actions. As they decorated the tree and gathered around to open their gifts on Christmas morning, Ellie's thoughts drifted to how it could be next year and imagined watching a nine month-old participating in Christmas.

It was in the wee hours of March 10, 1879, that Ellie shook John's shoulder.

"John! John!" she whispered. "John! I think it's time you went for the doctor."

"What?" John fought to shake the sleep from his brain. Suddenly the reality of what Ellie had said hit him.

"I'm not leaving you alone for long! I made arrangements for Cy Miller to go for the doctor when the time came. I want to stay here with you. I'll go over to the Millers and let them know the time is here! He will also do the chores and take the girls to your parents when they wake up."

He was already dressing, quickly pulling his pants on over his nightwear. He lit the lamp.

"Are you sure you will be all right until I get back?"

"Well, I think so. It's my first experience, but first babies usually take awhile, or so I'm told. The pains are just beginning to come quite regularly, but they are still quite far apart. Dr Mitchell will bring Mrs. Dunkirk with him, he said."

"I shouldn't be gone more than twenty minutes or so. You are sure you'll be all right?"

"Yes, John, just go!"

John hurried from the room. She wondered if he'd had time to put his coat on by the time she heard the back door close. She felt another pain beginning in the small of her back. She breathed deeply, waiting for it to pass.

Lord, keep your hand over me and help me to rest in you! she silently prayed.

True to his word, John was back within twenty minutes. "How are you doing, my darling?" he asked as he came to sit on the side of the bed.

"I'm doing all right," she answered. "Do you want to get the bedding and towels and things that I got ready? They are in the wardrobe, in the box just to the right of the door. We should get those on the bed now, I think."

When all was ready, John insisted that Ellie lie down again. It was almost two hours before they heard the Doctor and Mrs. Dunkirk at the door. Dr. Mitchell came into the room to examine Ellie and inquire as to the progress. He assured her that all looked normal.

"I have another call I need to make just a few miles down the road. Mrs. Dunkirk will, of course, be here with you, and I will be back in two or three hours. I'm quite sure that will be lots of time."

In fact, John did his own chores, the Millers took the girls to their grandparents' when they awoke, and even breakfast and dinner were over when at last, at about 2:30, an infant's cries heralded the arrival of George James Kurtz.

As Dr. Mitchell prepared to leave, he said, "I need to go past Ellie's parents' place before I return to the office. Do you want me to stop in and tell them the news?"

"That would be helpful," John gratefully replied. "Tell them the girls can come home any time."

Ellie cradled their new son in her arms and wept tears of joy.

"Oh John," she said, looking up at her husbands tearful eyes, "Isn't he a handsome wee man?"

John bent to kiss them both. "He is, indeed, dear, sweet Ellie! You've had some hard work! Thank you for this son!" He wiped his eyes with the back of his hand. "I'm so glad you are both all right!"

Ellie reached to lay her hand on top of John's, which was resting on his new son's head.

"God is good! He has answered our prayers! Maria will be happy to see that all is well."

It was almost dark when their grandparents brought the girls back home. Mrs. Dunkirk met them at the door. Maria's face mirrored concern, whereas Marta's was full of expectancy.

"Can we see the baby?" she asked.

"Why don't you take your coats off, first," Mrs. Dunkirk suggested, "then perhaps it would be a good idea to stand in front of the oven for a moment so you don't take the cold air into the room where your mother and little brother are waiting for you."

When they were sufficiently warmed up, Mrs. Dunkirk led the girls and their grandparents toward the bedroom door.

"Mama will be tired, so our first visit should be short. You can see them again tomorrow morning."

The door opened. There was the cradle, just where they had decided it would be best. But it was empty. Mama was in the bed, and there in her arms, all bundled in one of the blankets they had helped to prepare, was a round-faced, dark-haired little baby!

"Hello, girls," Ellie gently welcomed them. "Come meet your new brother."

Shyly, they moved to the bedside. "See his tiny nose and how his mouth is like a little bow?" Ellie asked. "Here, I'll undo his blanket a bit, so you can see his little hands and his long fingers. I think they are pretty big hands for such a small baby. Do you think they will get as big as Papa's someday? Go ahead— touch him!"

Marta reached out her hand and softly brushed her finger over the tiny, open hand. The little fingers closed around hers. "Look, Mama, he's holding my finger!"

"He must be saying hello to his big sister," Ellie smiled.

Maria, too, stroked little George's head, but then she looked at Ellie.

"Are you sick?" she asked.

"Oh no, Maria!" Ellie reassured her. "I am just fine. The Doctor says both of us are fine. I just need to rest a few days to get used to being a mama, then I will be up and about. Mrs. Dunkirk will stay for a few days to help care for the baby, and Tina Miller is going to come and fix meals and do the washing just as we had planned, you know. Everything is just fine. You don't need to worry. In fact, you can say thank you to God in your prayers tonight."

By the time George was three months old, Maria and Marta had become accustomed to caring for their little brother. It was Marta's crowning achievement when her sweet singing and gentle rocking of the cradle could soothe the baby into restful sleep. After her days at school, Maria had the privilege of holding him if he was fussy.

John sometimes teased the girls that they were doing everything for their brother and that he deserved a turn too! What a proud Papa he was when, just after George turned one year old, he took his first step into his father's outstretched arms.

"Just look at that, Mama!" John called. "Our little boy isn't going to let the grass grow under his feet!"

"Oh dear!" Ellie exclaimed, "I'm really going to need my nurse-maids now! How am I going to keep track of him? He's already been getting into enough things by crawling on his hands and knees!" she laughed.

It was true; George had an inquisitive mind and seemed bound to explore the very limits of his world. *It may keep us busy, but that's the kind of child I like,* she thought to herself. *They are the kind that are apt to figure things out and be a real contribution to the world.*

There were times over the next few years when she would wonder if George was going to live to make that contribution. He was a delightful, but daring little fellow, climbing anything on which he could possibly get a foothold, following the cats on their mouse hunts in the fields. She was forever bandaging up his cuts, bumps and bruises.

Once, she caught him going out the lane and heading for the deep ditch that held some water from the recent rains. No matter what his escapade, when reprimanded, his sweet smile and chubby arms would go around her neck as he proclaimed, "I sowee Mama!"—and always, her heart melted.

By the time he was three, he seemed to have figured out, at least a little more, what some of the dangers of life were, and began to be a bit more discerning in his exploration.

John was such a proud Papa. Whenever he could, he would take George along for the ride or let him play at the edge of a field or in the garden as he hoed. When George would plead, "Papa, me help you!" John would always try his best to find a way to allow him to come along if it was at all possible.

When the time for George's first day of school approached, he had absolutely no fear. He looked forward to going to school with his big sisters. He only balked on the days John was doing something that was especially interesting to him. Learning came easy for him, so it was hard to keep him challenged. He was a voracious reader and it was difficult to keep good reading available to him.

In the next four years, Ellie suffered three miscarriages, always in the first trimester of the pregnancy, and each time there was a period of grief for both her and John. Then she no longer even became pregnant. She saw other couples welcoming new babies, and it always filled her heart with longing for another wee one for her own family. Although the longing never went away, after awhile Ellie accepted the fact that there seemed to be no more children destined to be part of their family. She resolved that she would try to settle into enjoying those she was privileged to mother.

Chapter Ten

1895

As their tenth anniversary was approaching, John asked Ellie one night, "Do you think your parents would come to stay with the children for a few days?"

"What did you have in mind, John?" Ellie asked, full of curiosity.

"I have been saving up a bit of money, thinking I might like to take my wife to Toronto for a day or so. We never did have a wedding trip of any kind and I have never been to the big city. Now that the children are all in school, I just felt it would be nice for you and me to take a day or two for us again. I thought we could take the train. We could afford at least one night in an inn, I think."

"Oh, that would be lovely!" was Ellie's enthusiastic reply. "My Uncle Eli and Aunt Grace live in Thornhill and Aunt Mattie and Uncle Ralph live near Concord. Now that they have the electric railway up Yonge Street, it would make it easy to go up there. I'm sure they would be glad to have us visit. We can ask Mama and Papa when we go to their place for dinner on Sunday."

Within a few weeks all was arranged. Ellie's parents would take them to the train station and stay with the children while they were away. Uncle Eli and Aunt Grace would give them supper one day and they would stay for that night at Uncle Ralph's. John had insisted they stay in a hotel in Toronto for the first night. Ellie felt like a schoolgirl, or at least like a young bride, as she prepared for the trip. She quickly sewed up another dress with piped edges around the stand-up collar and down the front of the bodice. Tiny buttons marched down the front and up the wide cuffs. This particular shade of dark green was chosen to set off the chestnut highlights in her hair. The tight bodice and long, gored skirt emphasized her waist. Since she was sewing anyway, she also made a new nightgown of filmy white with little sprigs of tiny pink roses. *After all, if this is going to be the wedding trip we never had, I want to be dressed for it!* She hoped her planning would give John some pleasure. The dress he had seen—the nightgown would be a surprise.

Sitting side by side on the train, observing not only the passing scenery but seeing each other with renewed love in undisturbed peace, made the ride to Toronto a good beginning to their time away. By the time they reached Union Station, they felt almost carefree and definitely ready to explore the city.

Unbeknownst to Ellie, John had arranged to go to a photography studio to have their portrait taken. She was glad, then, that she had made the new dress. With John in his good suit and Ellie in the new dress, they made a striking couple, or so the photographer told them.

After checking in at the hotel and leaving their baggage in their room, they walked about to see the sights. They then found a restaurant and had a leisurely meal before going back to their hotel.

"What luxury!" Ellie exclaimed.

"Nothing is too good for my wonderful wife!" John remarked as he took her in his arms in a loving embrace.

They stayed in bed a little later than usual the next morning to prolong the luxury of the room and the privacy so unfamiliar to them. Eventually, they decided that they really should see some of the sights of downtown Toronto. They embarked upon a leisurely walk to University Avenue and went to see the Ontario Legislature buildings. They explored several big churches and stopped in to see the Timothy Eaton store before catching the Yonge Street trolley to Thornhill.

Uncle Eli met them at the stop. Ellie saw him from the trolley before it came to a halt. His hair, parted in the middle, was a little whiter than she remembered, but the handlebar mustache was the same as every time she had seen him. He had always taken pride in his appearance, and today was no exception. His pants were pressed and his vest buttoned neatly. As she stepped onto the sidewalk, she noted the watch chain and fob that were so much a part of Uncle Eli. He hurried to them with outstretched arms and a beaming smile.

"My, my, Ellie," he remarked as he embraced her, "It is a long time since we have seen you! Marriage must be agreeing with you. You look well and so much more mature than the sixteen-year-old I remember. This must be John," he said as he extended his hand toward John in welcome.

"Oh, yes! Uncle Eli, this is my husband, John. John this is Uncle Eli, my mother's one and only brother."

"Glad to finally meet you, Uncle Eli! I have heard so much about you and the treat that the Thornhill visits were to Ellie and her family."

"We'd better hurry back home," Uncle Eli advised. "Grace has dinner ready to serve the minute we get there. She was hoping for a good visit with you before Ralph and Mattie come to pick you up. We live down this street," he said as he turned off Yonge Street. It was a short but pleasant walk along the tree-lined street. They turned in at a large white frame house with a wide verandah and pretty gingerbread trim. As Uncle Eli opened the screen door, Aunt Grace came down the hall, wiping her hands on her apron. Carefully waved hair framed her round face and her eyes sparkled through her round wire-framed glasses.

"Hello! Hello! Come right in! We're so honored to have you come to visit us. Come right in! Here, Ellie, let me give you a hug! It's so good to have you here."

Without a pause, she hugged Ellie and then turned to John.

"John! We finally get to meet you. We never did get to see you when you and Regina were together. We were so sorry when Regina and little John died. Our hearts were with you even if we couldn't make it to the funeral. But Ellie is a precious girl. I'm glad she could step in and be a help to you. And now you have a little boy of your own! George, isn't it? Well, come in and sit down. Just make yourselves at home. Dinner is ready. I'll get it on the table."

John shot an amused glance at Ellie. Would Grace stop talking long enough for anyone to reply? Ellie managed to ask, "Can I help?"

"Oh no, my dear. Eli, you just take them into the dining room and get them settled. It will only take me a jiffy."

With that, she took off towards the region of the kitchen. "Now, let's see, I need to get the potatoes in a dish yet..." they heard her telling herself.

"We'd better do as we are bid," said Eli as he motioned the way to the dining room. "John, you can sit at the end of the table, and Ellie, you sit on this side. Grace will want the place closest to the kitchen. She loves an excuse to cook for company. Edith is the only one of our children to live close enough for frequent visits. She and Peter live in Langstaff. The others live in Delhi, Goderich and Kingston, so we don't get to see them very often."

The table was soon laden with fried chicken, gravy, corn and lima beans, and a dish mounded with mashed potatoes. Small dishes of gherkins, pickled watermelon rinds, pickled beans and sliced tomatoes filled up any available spaces. All this was done with a running commentary from Aunt Grace. Finally, she hung her apron on the hook beside the kitchen door and settled on the remaining chair. She paused and looked expectantly at Eli—Eli took the cue.

"Let us ask a blessing on the food..."

No more had the "Amen" been said before Aunt Grace began once more.

"Pass the food and help yourselves! I had hoped that Edith and Peter and the children could come to join us and meet you, but Peter had to work late. Take all the chicken you want, there is more in the kitchen. They may be able to drop in yet before Uncle Ralph and Aunt Mattie come to get you, but of course, Ralph and Mattie will have to be here before too late, because Concord is a little ways to go. Eli, pass the gravy. Edith is pretty busy having three children under the age of five, but she still teaches some piano students. Make sure you try that watermelon pickle, Ellie. I got the recipe from my neighbor last summer. I'd had some of hers and I thought it was real good!"

Taking advantage of Aunt Grace's short stop for a breath, Ellie quickly responded, "It would be nice to see Edith again. We used to have a lot of fun together when we came to visit. Looking back, I guess it wasn't that often, but as a child those times were special and they live in my memory as a big part of my childhood experiences."

"I'm sure Edith would like to see you too, so I do hope they make it. You girls always had a great time. Remember how you used to giggle at simply anything? Uncle Eli used to call you Giggling Gerties. Now John, you just help yourself to more any time you want. We always did enjoy when your family came to visit. Being so far, we didn't get to see enough of each other. Oh my! I do believe I forgot the beet pickle. I'll just go and get it yet."

During the meal, Ellie was amazed how Aunt Grace could keep up the conversation and still manage to devour a good portion of the food. *She must work it off in nervous energy,* Ellie thought. *She sure doesn't look like a person who eats that much.* Occasionally, Grace would ask a question about the family and would actually wait for an answer. Her constant chatter, however, dominated the meal. Glancing to her right, Ellie caught a twinkle of merriment in John's eyes.

After they were finished eating, Ellie offered to help with the dishes while the men went to visit on the verandah. Again, Grace kept up a relentless stream of information about family, memories and life in general. They were no more than half done with the dishes when they heard children's voices through the screen door.

"Oh, that must be Edith and Peter and the children!" Grace said, just as Edith entered the kitchen. "Glad you're here, Edith! Why don't you take Ellie out back and show her the lawn swing your father made? I'll finish the dishes and that will give you girls some time to get caught up! Ellie just lay the dishtowel down—I will finish up. You just go on with Edith!"

Edith reached for Ellie's hand and shook it.

"Come on, Ellie, let's do what Mom said!" As she shut the back door, Edith asked, "Has she been talking your ear off? I think she has gotten worse with age! She was used to having the family around all those years, and now, with just her and Dad, I think she tries to make up for lost time whenever she has a new listening ear. It is good to see you, Ellie!"

"It's good to see you too, Edith! Don't worry about your mom. She sure welcomed us and helped us catch up with your family in a hurry, which is what I wanted to do with this visit. I have a lot of good memories of times spent here and I'm glad John is getting to meet more of my family. He has such a large family. It was hard at first to remember who was who."

The two young women had a good conversation as they took advantage of the rustic lawn swing and compared notes on parenting. It wasn't long, though, until they heard the arrival of Aunt Mattie and Uncle Ralph. Reluctantly, they left the back yard to join the others on the porch.

Uncle Ralph was such a tall, slender man, but he had the kindest eyes Ellie had ever seen. His interest in people came from a genuine love of others. Even though they were invited to come in, Uncle Ralph said they had better be on their way. Before long, good-byes had been said, and John sat in the front with Uncle Ralph while Ellie sat in the back with Aunt Mattie. Ellie felt so comfortable with her. It was almost like being with her mother. Aunt Mattie wanted to know all about her sister and the family. John and Ralph were soon immersed in conversation about farming. The conversation was pleasant and the trip didn't seem long.

When Ellie and John were safely in their bedroom with the door shut, John let out a low chuckle. "What's that about?" Ellie asked.

John's eyes were alive with mirth. "I've wanted to do that ever since the first few moments with Aunt Grace. There was no doubting our welcome, but my goodness—there was hardly a chance in her presence to get a word in edgewise! I wonder if Uncle Eli's vocal chords ever get a chance to be exercised?!"

"I must admit I had forgotten what a talker she is. But Edith says she thinks Aunt Grace is getting worse with age. One thing about it, I got caught up with the happenings in their lives and those of their children, relatives, friends and neighbors in a hurry!"

Even after they were in bed and Ellie was almost asleep, she felt the bed vibrate and discovered John shaking with silent laughter.

"John?"

"I'm sorry, Ellie— it's Aunt Grace. I was just wondering if she stops talking to sleep. Even after you and Edith went to the back yard, I could hear her talking to herself out there in the kitchen! I don't know if I have ever heard anyone talk so much! She went straight from 'Concord is a little ways' to 'pass the gravy' to 'Edith's pretty busy' without so much as a catch of breath!"

By this time Ellie was laughing as well. A more audible titter escaped from her.

"Oh John! If we're not careful, Uncle Ralph and Aunt Mattie are going to hear us and wonder if we're laughing at them!"

"All right, my love, I'll have to retain the rest of my mirth until we are safely at home! Good night, Ellie."

"Good-night John."

A moment later, Ellie again felt the bed quiver.

"John!" she gave him a playful poke. "Stop it, or you'll get me going again!"

The next morning, before Ralph and Mattie took them back to catch the trolley, they were well nourished with a real farmer's breakfast. They left carrying a basket of Damson plums Mattie wanted to send home for Ellie's mother. Both Ralph and Mattie expressed appreciation for the visit and urged John and Ellie to come again and bring the children along.

On the train ride home, John and Ellie basked in their remaining time alone. They sat, holding hands and reliving the pleasures they had experienced.

"I can hardly wait to see the pictures. They will be a wonderful remembrance of a splendid time together. I'm glad we ordered enough for all our families. They will make nice Christmas presents. Thank you so much, John, for this time. I will always cherish it."

"I'm glad you enjoyed it, Ellie. It sure was a treasured time for me too. I have wanted to do this for some time. Our marriage began during great difficulty, and it wasn't really fair to you. You have become so precious to me, and I wanted to do something to let you know that, even though Regina and I shared a wonderful love, my relationship with you has achieved an even greater depth. That is probably partly due to the deep valley you and I have traveled, but my heart is so thankful for what we have together."

John laid an arm across her shoulder and glanced around. No one seemed to be looking, so he tipped up her chin and planted a kiss on her lips.

Ellie's eyes shone with love. "Dear, dear John! You are such a good husband. You find the nicest ways to show and voice your love. I love you so!"

As they approached the train station, John and Ellie saw her parents and the children waiting on the bench. Before the train came to a halt, George made a dash for the train. Thankfully, his grandfather caught his coattail and made him wait until the train came to a full stop and his parents came down the steps before he was released.

"Can I get on the train?" was George's first question.

"No, son, not today. We will try to plan a trip for you very soon."

"I want to take a big long trip and go far, far away!" said George as he watched the train move, once more, out of the station. "I'd like to be the engineer and blow the whistle."

The last of the garden produce needed Ellie's attention upon her return home, but the joy the trip had brought gave her a deep contentment even in her busy days. When she and John, after work-filled days, retired to their room, they reveled in their love for each other.

One morning John informed Ellie that he was going over to help Cy Miller for about an hour or so. He said he should be back by noon, at the latest. Ellie gave him a kiss.

"Take care! And don't forget I love you!" she added.

"I carry that thought in my heart always," he assured her as he gave her a quick kiss and a hug before going out the door.

Ellie had finished the dishes and was getting ready to go to work on the flowerbeds when she saw Ben Miller coming in the lane, the dust flying behind the buggy. A sudden sense of foreboding washed over her and she dashed out to the lane.

"You'd better come, Ellie!" Ben's eyes were wide with fear.

"What is it?" Ellie almost screamed.

"It's John! The bull unexpectedly charged and caught him. Thankfully he threw him out of the pen, but he's hurt bad!"

Ellie's knees went weak and she almost sank to the ground.

"Ellie! You've got to come with me. We have sent for the doctor, but you should be there."

Ellie didn't know if her legs would carry her, but she couldn't wait to be with John. She climbed into the buggy and Ben took off. When they reached the Miller barn, she ran to the door, wondering what she would find.

"Oh please, God! Don't let him die!" she implored as she ran.

Through the open door she could see John on a bed of straw. His eyes were closed. His shirt and pants were bloodied. Cy held a towel on the open wound.

"William went for the doctor. I am so sorry!" he said with ragged breath.

Ellie dropped to her knees beside John. Her hand caressed the side of his face.

"Oh, my dear, dear John!" she murmured.

"Ellie!" he whispered. "Oh Ellie!"

"The doctor is coming and I am here. I love you!"

She bent over to kiss his forehead. Someone came to the door, and Ellie looked up, surprised to see Dr Mitchell.

"As luck would have it, I was on my way to a call close by and met William less than a mile from here." He was already examining the wound. "See if there is any boiled water in the house," he ordered, "and get some clean cloths."

Cy rose to his feet. "Ben told Martha to get some ready before he went for Ellie. I'll go get them."

Finally, Dr. Mitchell had done all he could. "Normally I don't like to move someone with such injuries very far. However, since your place is so close, he may just as well be in his own bed. I have stitched things up quite well, but there may be some internal bleeding and I am not sure that his kidney hasn't been damaged. Get some straw and a quilt on the wagon, and if we drive carefully, I think we can move him home."

Ben went to rally the help of a few more neighbors while William and Cy readied the wagon. Most of the time John was unconscious, but occasionally he opened his eyes and whispered, "Ellie?"

She always squeezed his hand and assured him, "I'm right here, John."

Obeying Dr. Mitchell's instructions, many hands helped to carefully lift John, keeping his body as straight as possible, as they placed him gently on the wagon. With great care, the wagon slowly moved toward John and Ellie's place. Praying all the way, Ellie hurried home to ready the bed for John.

When John was laid on his bed and the doctor had once more checked him, he motioned for Ellie to come to the kitchen.

"Ellie, I wish I could give you better news, but to be honest, I really don't know what the outcome will be. The bull's horn went quite deep. I did my best to cleanse the wound and suture all that I could. Perhaps he will come along well. There is always the risk of infection, and as I said before,

I am concerned about his kidney. I gave him a bit of a sedative that will deal with the pain and help him sleep. Keep a watch on him. Get him to drink as much as he can. If his fever goes up, have someone come for me. I will stop in again tonight and in the morning."

He laid a hand on her shoulder. "I'm so sorry. This family has already experienced more than its share of troubles. I have my other call to make, but if you wish, I can stop to speak with your parents on the way home."

"Thank you! Dr. Mitchell, I would appreciate that. I suppose I should have someone tell John's parents as well."

"Rosa and Theo live in town, so I will let them know and they can take care of that," Dr. Mitchell assured her. He patted her back as he left.

Cy came to the back door. His face reflected the pain he felt. "If I would have had any idea this could happen...I just didn't expect...I'm so sorry..." his voice trailed away.

"I know you meant no harm to come to John. I just hope he makes it!" Tears welled in her eyes. "I don't know how I could live without him."

"Don't you worry about the chores and the farm work. The neighbors are all willing to pitch in to keep it up. I'll see to organizing it. Martha will be over in a little while and she'll stay until someone else comes. "

"Thank you! I'd like that. Right now I want to get back to John."

"You do that. Martha will come. You shouldn't be alone. The children will be home from school soon too."

Ellie's face blanched. "How am I going to tell the girls what happened? They already lost their mother!"

Cy's eyes were downcast. "I wish I hadn't asked John to come and help!" he burst out. "I am so sorry to have caused your family this added pain. I do hope John will recover."

"Yes, yes! I hope so too. And Mr. Miller, I don't blame you. You had no way of knowing this would happen. But I must get in to John again."

Cy left, and Ellie hurried to the bedroom. John lay so still with his eyes closed. His breathing was heavy, but even. She went to find a comfortable chair to put beside the bed. She wanted to be right there if he should awaken. She sat down and held his hand in hers.

"Dear God," she prayed, "I am numb with fear right now. Help me to deal with it before the children come home. They are going to need me to be strong for them. The girls have already gone through too much grief in their young lives."

Into her mind popped the verse she had read to John soon after they were married. They had repeated it to each other often in those days. *Give ear, O Lord, unto my prayer; and attend to the voice of my supplications. In the day of my trouble I will call upon you: for you will answer me.*

"Please, oh Lord, hear my supplications, for I call unto you."

There didn't seem to be adequate words to voice what she was feeling and what she needed for herself, John, and the dear children. She hoped that it was right that the Spirit would make sense of her groaning and present her needs before the Throne. The thought didn't bring perfect peace, but it did still her somewhat. Momentarily, her thoughts went back ten-and-a-half years. Surely she hadn't given up her plans with Gerhard only to lose John after such a short time! God wouldn't do this to her, would He?

These thoughts startled and disturbed her. *Ellie Kurtz! How can you think that after all the good things you and John have shared? He isn't dead yet! How can you be thinking of Gerhard now?* She reached to stroke John's face. He had become so dear to her. Silently she entreated, *Please, John, keep fighting. Don't leave me now!*

An hour or so later, she heard the children gaily chattering as they came up the lane. Her heart filled with dread. She took a deep breath and prayed, "Lord, give me the wisdom and the words that I need."

She rose and went to the door to greet the girls. Maria stopped mid-sentence.

"Mama! What is the matter?" she asked with alarm.

Ellie put an arm around each of the girls. She sat down and pulled George onto her lap.

"Maria and Marta, George, something bad happened this morning." She quickly drew a deep breath. "Your papa went over to help Cy Miller with his bull. Unexpectedly, the bull charged and caught your papa. He is hurt quite badly, but is resting in bed. Dr Mitchell will come to see him again tonight and Mrs. Miller will be here soon too."

Maria's eyes filled with fear, but she remained quiet.

"Is he going to die?" Marta asked.

George's eyes opened wide.

"Oh children, I hope not. He is very badly hurt, though, so we need to face that possibility. Hard as it is to believe it right now, we know that God loves us and he has told us that he won't ask us to go through more than we can bear. He has promised to be with us."

"Can we see him?" Maria asked.

"He is sleeping, but you can go and touch his hand and tell him you love him. I'll go with you."

It was Marta who reached the bed first. She reached for his hand and whispered, "I love you, Papa!"

At the sound of her voice, John's eyes opened.

"Marta!"

"I love you, Papa!" she repeated.

"And my love will always be with you, Marta," he whispered. "Maria?"

"Yes, Papa."

"Remember, no matter what happens, my love will always be with you too."

"Yes, Papa," tears clouded her eyes, "I will always love you too! Please get better, Papa!"

"I will try, girls—for all my girls," he said, looking at Ellie. "Where is George?"

"He is still just outside the door."

John winced in pain. "Bring him in too, will you?"

"I will, but John, don't talk too much. The doctor said you should rest as much as possible. Come, George, Papa wants to see you too."

An unusually subdued George peeked around the corner.

"Come," said Ellie, "Tell Papa how much you love him."

"George," John said, "You are my little man, aren't you?"

"Yes, Papa."

"Try to remember the good times we have had working together and always remember that I love you."

"I love you, Papa!" Looking at Ellie, he asked, "Can I give him a kiss?"

"Here, I'll lift you up so you can kiss him, but be careful not to bump the bed."

"We'll go and watch for Mrs. Miller," Maria quietly said, "You can stay here with Papa." Ellie nodded and smiled gratefully.

When the children were out of the room, John looked Ellie in the eyes and said, “Ellie, in case I don’t make it, I want you to know some things. Most of our money is in the bank at Monkville, but I do have an account in Malden with some extra. It should cover funeral costs and keep you going for a bit.” He winced again and paused a moment.

“Oh, please, John!” Ellie pleaded, “Don’t wear yourself out talking. I hope you get better.”

“I hope so too, Ellie. I don’t want our life together to end yet, and I sure don’t want to leave you, but I want to tell you this, in case. Perhaps you should sell the farm. Joseph is hoping to buy a farm. He may be interested.”

He paused for a moment, and Ellie thought he was falling asleep again.

“Ellie, Jake is a barrister-solicitor; he can help you handle the legal stuff, and he’ll give you good advice about anything you need. He has my will.” Again he was silent, his eyes shut.

“What about chores tonight?” he suddenly asked.

“Don’t worry about that,” Ellie assured him. “Cy Miller said the neighbors will look after that as long as it is needed. Now why don’t you go to sleep again?”

“Ellie, I love you. Thank you for being such a good wife. I truly have been blessed.”

“I love you too, John. I, too, have been blessed. Remember our verse, ‘Give ear, O Lord, unto my prayer; and attend to the voice of my supplications. In the day of my trouble I will call upon you: for you will answer me.’”

“Oh yes, Ellie. He will!” John whispered before he fell asleep.

After a while Ellie heard Martha Miller come in the door. Ellie hated to disturb John right away, so she sat quietly for some time.

“Here come Grandma and Grandpa!” she heard George exclaim.

Ellie arose and left the bedroom, quietly shutting the door behind her. She crossed the room as her mother came through the door, and then she was enfolded in her warm arms.

“Oh Ellie!” her mother sobbed. “We came as soon as we heard. How is John?”

"Not good, Mama. He was awake a while ago, but all he wanted to talk about is what I should do if he would die. Oh Mama, I don't know what I would do if he did!"

Her dad moved to put his arms around her. "Let's hope he doesn't!"

Ellie leaned against him. "I'm so glad you are here, Papa. I should check on John again."

"You go and stay with him. We'll look after things out here."

Her mother was already taking an apron from her purse. Martha Miller moved toward her.

"Ellie—I don't know what to say. I brought a pie over with me, and some cold beef. Since your parents are here now, I will go home again, but if you need anything, just let us know. We'll come over now and then to see if you need anything, and of course, the neighbors will be looking after the chores and farm work. We're so sorry!"

"I know, Mrs. Miller. Thank you for coming and bringing food. We will let you know if you can help." Ellie wearily wiped her hand over her brow as if to clear the heaviness from her mind. "I just can't think what our needs may be right now."

"There, there, of course you can't," soothed Martha Miller, "You go on in to John and I'll just let myself out."

Quietly, Ellie returned to the bedroom. John's face looked so pale against the pillow. His breathing was labored. Again, her heart twisted in fear. If John should die, it would leave her alone, responsible for three children. She knew it might be premature thinking, but the many different issues she would face began to march through her mind with eerie precision and growing doom until her mind screamed, "Stop! Stop!"

"Oh God!" She groaned within herself. "This would be more than I can handle. I can't do it, Lord! Please don't let him die!"

My grace is sufficient for you.

Ellie raised her head to see from whence the words came. There was no one there. Instead of comfort, the words that had sounded audible in her mind deepened the desperation in her heart. Did that mean that God knew she would need His grace for what may lie ahead?

"No, no, no! Lord! Please don't make me face this. Don't let John die! Please, oh please!"

Outwardly she may have looked calm, but in the depth of her soul she writhed in fear and tumult. The battle raged on as she watched John's labored breath and the grimace of pain that often crossed his face. Oh, if she could only cry! She mustn't do it here, anyway, but there seemed to be a wall of steel around her heart that kept her tear ducts dry. Her mind was a frenzy of irrational thoughts. It was all too much. She felt like literally screaming. She might burst if she did not, she thought. Suddenly, she felt drained, the fight gone out of her.

"I just can't do it, Lord!" she quietly whispered.

I will never leave you or forsake you.

Again the words came so clearly she didn't know if she had actually heard them or not.

Just then John opened his eyes slightly. "Ellie?"

"I'm right here, John, my darling," Ellie reached to hold his hand, but his eyes were closed again.

"Ellie?"

"Yes, John, I'm here."

It seemed to take almost more effort than he had strength for to get the words out.

"You are a strong woman…you have been such a …strength to me…so strong! …you will not be alone…God will walk with you."

"Oh! John!"

Ellie didn't trust herself to say more, but enfolded his hand in both of hers. She hoped the doctor would come again very soon. He seemed to be slipping.

Her mother opened the door.

"Ellie, do you want to come and eat?" she whispered. Ellie shook her head. "Dad can come and sit with John."

"I'm not hungry. I don't think I could eat. Anyway, I want to stay here, with John." Ellie said in hushed tones.

"You've got to keep up your strength, Ellie. I'll bring you a plate to eat here, then."

When her mother brought the plate, Ellie told her to set it on the dresser.

"You make sure you eat it, though," her mother admonished.

"I'll try!"

"There are several of the neighbors out in the barn doing chores," her mother informed her. "Now you try to eat something!"

An hour later, when Ellie's mother came to get her plate, it was still largely untouched.

"Ellie," she whispered, "you didn't eat very much."

"I ate all I could, Mom. I hope the doctor comes soon. John seems to be in a lot of pain and his breathing is more labored. Are the children all right? "

"They've eaten and now they are in the living room. Maria is reading a story to keep George occupied."

"It's almost bedtime. If the doctor doesn't come soon, perhaps Papa can come and sit with John so I can at least tuck George in and say goodnight to the girls."

But the doctor did come, and while he examined John, Ellie took the children upstairs. Even Maria, at fifteen, always liked having her say goodnight. This time Ellie suggested they get together in one room to pray for Papa's healing before going to bed. She heard the fear in their voices and saw it in their eyes, but it was hard to reassure them when she, herself, was so afraid of what the outcome could be. Instead, she acknowledged the fear and their need to trust God whatever happened.

When she came back downstairs, Dr. Mitchell was waiting in the kitchen. Her eyes sought his and asked the question she could not voice.

"Ellie, it doesn't look good right now. However, bodies are wonderfully made, and it sometimes surprises us how they heal themselves. I've done all I can. I gave him more sedative; try to keep him as comfortable as you can. If you can get him to sip water now and then it would be good. I'll be back early in the morning. John's parents are coming then. Ben Miller said he would sleep on your couch down here in case you need me through the night," he paused. "Try to keep strong, Ellie."

Wordless, she nodded. As he strode to the door, she managed, "Thank you, Dr Mitchell."

As the door shut, Ellie's mother put her arms around her.

"Ellie, you need to get some rest too. Why don't you lay down for awhile?"

"No, Mama, I'll stay on the chair beside John. I'll put a pillow behind me so I can rest a bit, but I want to stay with him. If he is better in the morning, I will lay down then. You and Papa can sleep in the spare room."

"Your father and I will take turns to check on you through the night, but call us if you need us."

Her father moved toward them and put his arms around both his wife and daughter. "May the Good Lord watch over us this night!"

Chapter Eleven

Ellie wrapped herself in a blanket from the chest, tucked a pillow behind her head and settled in the chair beside John. She reached for his hand and tenderly held it in her own. How she had come to love those hands. They were large strong hands with long fingers. She loved the way she felt when he held her own hand in his. His caress made her feel so loved and treasured. Cherished—that was the word! The way he touched her made her feel cherished! She felt safe and comfortable in his love. Unconsciously, she stroked his fingers.

"Ellie?" John almost startled her with his whisper. "We're good together, aren't we?"

"We sure are, John. Now all you have to do is get well again."

"I'll try…but right now I don't know…if I can...Ellie…" his voice was even softer now, "If I don't make it…I'm sorry…but you will be all right...Be strong…but let people help you."

"Oh John, I hope I don't have to. But I will remember what you said. I love you so! I don't want our life together to be over yet."

"Neither do I…my dear Ellie." John's eyes closed. "Make sure the children...know how much…I love them"

"They know, John, and even if you don't make it, I will be sure to remind them often. Don't talk more than you should. Try to rest. Do you want another sip of water?"

"Not now. Are you…going to…stay here, Ellie?"

"Yes, I've wrapped myself in a quilt and have a pillow here. I will be right beside you all night."

"Thank you, Ellie…Goodnight."

Ellie dozed off and on. Her parents came to check on her several times. It was almost six o'clock when she awoke to hear John's voice.

"The music, Ellie. Do you hear the music?"

"Do you hear music, John?" she asked.

"Oh yes! It's lovely!"

She felt his forehead. It was quite warm. Perhaps he was delirious. She hated to leave him, but maybe she should get a cool washcloth. Suddenly, he struggled to get up.

"Yes! Yes! I'm coming!" he said with enthusiasm.

She rose in alarm and gently urged him back to his pillow.

"John, just lay down!"

"I'm coming!" he happily sighed as he settled back on his pillow. A smile crossed his face, he breathed a few more times, and then he was gone.

Ellie buried her face in his chest.

"Oh John! John!"

Tears spilled down her cheeks. A strange mixture of grief and awe filled her. A loss too deep for words fueled her grief. But the awe at witnessing John's delight in the passage from life on earth made the room feel like holy ground. Even though he was no longer in his body, she felt his comforting presence in the room all around her. The moment felt too sacred to end it.

"Oh, dear God, heaven is not so far away! I can feel your presence here too. But oh, how I'm going to miss John in his earthly form."

She kissed John's cheek once more and stroked his hair back from his face and closed his eyes. She reached for a handkerchief to dry the tears from her eyes. As quickly as she dried those, more appeared. She let herself cry for a while, and then she said to herself, *All right Ellie, John believed in you, now prove him right!* She pinned some lose strands of her hair in place, tucked the blouse into her skirt and went to waken Ben. She gently shook his shoulder.

"Ben!"

Startled, he sat upright. "What is it? Is John worse?"

"Ben, you'd better go for Dr, Mitchell. John died about ten minutes ago."

"Oh no! Ellie!" he groaned.

"Ben, you tell Dr. Mitchell to do whatever has to be done. I guess we'll need the undertaker too."

"I'll go right away. Do you need my mother to come?"

"My parents are here and John's parents are coming." Ellie looked dismayed. "Oh! Now they will wish they had come last night! They won't get to say their good-byes!" she paused. "Anyway, I will be all right for now. You just go for Dr. Mitchell."

When Ben left, Ellie went upstairs quietly, so as not to wake the children. She gently opened the door to her parents' room.

"Mama, Papa," she whispered. "Do you want to come downstairs?"

"What is it, Ellie?" her father asked in alarm.

"John just died," she told them, "Ben has gone for Dr. Mitchell. I thought we'd let the children sleep awhile yet. "

"We'll be right down."

Ellie went downstairs and put the teakettle on the stove. She felt as though she was walking around in a dream. She couldn't believe how calm she felt. When her parents came down she asked, "Do you want to see him? He looks so peaceful."

Together, they went to the bedroom.

"Mama and Papa, I want to tell you how it went."

She paused and took a deep breath.

"Our bedroom literally became Holy Ground. He awoke and asked me if I heard the music. He said it was really lovely. Then he said, 'Yes! Yes! I'm coming!' and he tried to get up. I thought maybe he was delirious, so I tried to gently get him to lie down again. He sighed happily and said once more with such delight, 'I'm coming!' He took a few more breaths and then he was gone, but I could still feel his presence in the room. It was a sacred moment. But oh, I'm going to miss him. It's going to be so hard to tell the children."

"Mama?" Maria said from the door. "What is going on?"

Ellie hurried to the door and took Maria into her arms.

"Maria, my dear daughter, I don't know how to tell you this. I wish it weren't so, but your papa left us to go to heaven this morning."

She felt Maria stiffen in her arms.

"No! Mama!" she said in an unbelieving whisper. "No!"

She stood as if frozen on the spot. Then suddenly, a strangled cry came from the depths of her being.

"Papa!"

She rushed to the bed where John's body lay. She fell on her knees and buried her head in the covers, reaching for his hand.

"Oh Papa! Don't leave us now! Please don't leave us! Papa!"

Sobs shook her body. Ellie's heart felt as though it was being torn out of her body as she moved to stroke Maria's head. Tears ran down her cheeks as she tried to comfort this child who was so dear to her. Child, yes, but she was as tall as Ellie herself, and was on the verge of becoming a woman. The memory of her mother's death was still vivid to Maria. It didn't seem fair that she should lose her father, too, while still so young.

Finally, she lifted Maria to her feet, and once more embraced her.

"My dear, sweet Maria!" she whispered, "We must be brave! We will miss your papa so, but he would want us to go on. I'm here and we will go through this together. Do you want to come out with me to sit on the settee?"

Sobs still shook Maria's body.

"Mama, can I be alone with Papa for a little while?"

"Are you sure you want to do that?" Ellie asked with concern.

"Yes, Mama, I do. Please! Just for a little bit. I will be all right. Please, Mama."

"All right, Maria. Grandma and Grandpa and I will be right in the kitchen. Come there when you are finished."

"I will," promised Maria.

When Ellie got to the kitchen, her parents were sitting at the table.

"Come, Ellie, have a cup of tea. The doctor and undertaker will be here in a while. Would you have a piece of toast too?"

"Perhaps a cup of tea."

Ellie listened to the sounds of Maria's low voice in the bedroom.

"I hope she is all right," she said, pressing her hand to her forehead. "She has always been the quieter type, keeping her emotions more hidden. This will be so hard on her!"

"There is a lot of depth and maturity there too, Ellie," her father commented. "She will be all right."

"Papa, Mama, do you think I should waken Marta and George, or should we wait until John is laid out? It's a little after seven now and they are usually awake by seven-thirty."

"Perhaps it would be just as well to let them sleep as long as they can," Mama suggested. "Maybe we could take them to our place until after noon. By that time the undertaker should be done. Are you going to have the coffin in the parlor?"

"I suppose. I hadn't really thought about it. We'll have to think about funeral arrangements too." Ellie heaved a big sigh. "Oh dear! There is so much to think about and I'd rather not think at all."

The bedroom door opened, and Maria came toward the kitchen. Her eyes were swollen, but she seemed calmer. Ellie motioned for her to sit beside her.

"Oh Mama!" she sighed as she laid her head on Ellie's shoulder, "It's going to be so hard to live without Papa!"

Someone was coming in the lane. "That is probably Dr. Mitchell," Papa said as he opened the door. "No, it isn't!" he said in surprise, "It is Abe and Sarah Kurtz!"

Ellie joined her papa at the door as they came up the walk. "We woke early and couldn't get back to sleep. We felt anxious, so we decided to come. How is he doing?"

"Oh, Mom and Pop Kurtz!" Ellie said in anguish. How could she tell them?

"Is he that bad?" asked Sarah.

Daniel Kessler laid his hand on Abe's shoulder. "Abe and Sarah, come in and sit down. It is hard to tell you this, but John left his earthly body about an hour ago."

It looked as if the news knocked the wind out of the older couple. They sank into chairs and stared at Ellie with unbelief.

"We should have come last night," Abe finally said. "Mother wanted to, but I thought this morning was soon enough."

"Do you want to see him?" Ellie asked.

"Could we?" Sarah asked. As she rose, she seemed to be suddenly conscious of her granddaughter sitting there with swollen eyes.

"Oh Maria!" she cried as she held her to her ample bosom. "My poor dear!"

The day passed as if it were in slow motion. Ellie almost felt more like an observer than a participant. Doctor Mitchell came, then the undertaker. When Marta and George awoke, Ellie, as lovingly as she could, explained what had happened. They once more cried together. George had a lot of questions he wanted answered and she tried her best. She explained that they would go with Grandma and Grandpa Kessler for dinner. When they came back the undertaker would have John's body ready. Maria pled to stay with Ellie, so her parents left with Marta and George.

Neighbors began to arrive, bearing food and condolences. Pastor Moyer came to talk about funeral plans. Visitation was set for that evening and the next day. The funeral would be on Thursday. Albert and Gerda came to see if they could help. They moved the furniture in the parlor to make room for the casket. When that was situated in its place, Gerda went to change the bed linens and air out the bedroom. Things seemed to be organized without Ellie's help.

A fog of unreality settled around Ellie's numb heart. Willy and Mary brought Marta and George back home mid-afternoon. For a while a semblance of reality returned as she comforted Marta and tried to answer George's questions. With all three of the children gathered around her, she told them of the last moments she had shared with their father. She tried to emphasize that, although Papa didn't want to leave them yet, what he saw as he was dying must have been a happy surprise for him—it sounded as though he was seeing something more beautiful than anything they could imagine. It was hard for George to understand.

"Why doesn't Papa wake up?" he asked over and over.

Ellie tried to explain how the body is just a house for the soul, and that John's soul had gone to be with Jesus.

"But can't his soul come back so he can wake up?" he wanted to know.

"No, son," Ellie told him, "but some day we can go to see him."

"He is with my first mama now, isn't he, Mama?" commented Marta.

"That's right, Marta."

"I wish Papa could come back. I don't think I want to go to see him if I have to die and can't come back," declared George. "I want to be with you and Marta and Maria and my grandmas and grandpas too. I don't want to lay in a wooden bed like Papa and leave my body!"

"It's hard to understand everything, George. I don't think you need to worry about dying until you are much older."

She gathered them into her arms and held them, drawing strength and comfort as much as giving it.

Neighbors and friends brought in their supper. It seemed as though it would be sufficient to feed more than those who were there. After their meal buggies began to come in the lane, and soon became a steady stream as more neighbors, friends and relatives came to pay their last respects.

By the time the last people were leaving, Ellie longed to go to her bedroom and close the door—to just have some time alone to shut out some of the activity and noise. She needed to have some time to think and to try to let her mind catch up with reality. She felt so out of control—as though events were carrying her downstream in a boat without a paddle.

Before Elda and Joseph left, Elda came to Ellie to say, "I made a fresh pot of peppermint tea. It's on the back of the stove. Have some of that before you go to bed. It will help relax you," she gave her a hug, "We'll be back in the morning."

Wearily, Ellie thought, "If John was here, he would gather us around him for a prayer before we go to bed, but I don't know if I can pray. There are no words adequate to express what I feel—especially when I hardly know what I feel!"

When the door was shut for the last time, Ellie took one last look at John's body lying there, so bereft of the life that had brought such joy to her. She turned to her children and John's parents, who were staying for the night.

"Elda left us a pot of peppermint tea. Let's go to the kitchen and have some."

Elda had even set cups out on the cupboard. Ellie poured the tea and set the cups on the table. The last one for George she diluted with a bit of hot water from the teakettle. With a sigh, she settled her weary body on the remaining chair. She looked at Abe Kurtz. How much he looked like an older version of John! "Pop," she suddenly asked, "would you say a prayer before we have our tea?"

"Why, of course, Ellie!" he agreed. "Let's come to our Heavenly Father.

"Gracious and Loving God, Holy Comforter, we come to you tonight with aching hearts and weary minds and bodies. We surely do need your comfort. You know that it is hard for John's mother and I to say goodbye to a dear son. Your heart and your care reach out to Ellie as she is faced with responsibilities greater than she should have to bear and loneliness that must envelope her very soul. You know that Maria and Marta have already had to cope with the loss of their mother and that it seems to us that George needed his father to guide him to manhood."

Abe paused for a moment. "We thank you for the gladness that John expressed as you came to bear him away and for those sacred moments that Ellie shared with him. May this be a beacon of light in our present gloom. Carry us through the darkness and set our feet on an upward path that will bring us to the sunshine of your love. Be with us now that the night may bring our bodies rest and renewal for what faces us on the morrow. In confidence we ask these things, for we ask in Jesus' precious name. Amen."

Ellie's eyes glistened with tears. "Thank you, Pop. John must have learned to pray by listening to your prayers. You both find such beautiful, touching ways to express the prayers of your hearts."

"The Father listens even to the wordless groaning and glad cries of our hearts, Ellie, but I'm thankful if the words of our prayers helped you!" Abe said, with a sad smile.

They drank their tea mostly in silence, then Ellie went upstairs to see the children to bed. When she came downstairs, John's parents were waiting. "Are you going to be all right, Ellie? Are you sure you want to sleep in your bedroom?" asked his mother.

"Yes, Mom—to both questions. I still feel numb, but very tired. Tonight our bedroom feels like a sanctuary. Both because of the precious moments John and I shared there, and because it will be good to be away from all the hustle and bustle of the day. Thank you so much for being here and staying for the night!"

In spite of her tired body, it took some time for Ellie's mind to slow down enough to let her sleep. She sensed John's presence there, though his side of the bed was empty. The events of the past few days paraded again and again through her mind. Even though she finally slept, many times through the night she awakened and, once more, with incredulous disbelief, her mind would process the happenings of the last two days before sleep would come again.

Chapter Twelve

The next few days passed in a dizzying round of visitation and then the funeral. John's body was laid to rest beside Regina's and it seemed like a multitude of people came back to the house for refreshments afterward. So many expressed their condolences that everything started blending into one hazy mass. When people finally left, Ellie couldn't remember if she had eaten anything or not.

Even yesterday there was family around, cleaning up and setting things to right. Today there were still mounds of food, so that she didn't think she would have to cook for a week or more, but the house felt strangely empty. There were only she and the children there. Even though just one was missing, the hole seemed larger than that. It felt as though the anchor post was gone and the whole fence that delineated their family was leaning at a crazy angle. She felt no sense of direction and couldn't think what she should do or where she should begin.

Jake had told her at Wednesday's visitation that he would come out to the farm on Monday to go over the will and the legal papers that needed to be signed. He suggested that they could also talk about her options.

Sunday seemed too soon to be out in public, so they stayed at home. Ellie tried to read a few Psalms to the children, but her voice got choked up and she was afraid she was going to cry again. Instead, since it was such a nice day for mid-October, she suggested they go for a walk to the bush at the back of the farm. As they walked, they spoke about how much John loved nature and the lessons he derived from watching God at work in the world. They visited the old oak tree and sat in the hemlock glade for a while. Ellie thought back to her first visit there. Her situation then, too, had felt so new and uncertain as to the outcome. That time it was John who was in the greatest pain. She had tried to appreciate what he was experiencing then, but now she wondered how she could have really empathized. She realized, now, the difference between losing a sister and losing a mate. She let the quietness of this hallowed place soak into her soul. As they returned to the house, she felt more comforted than at any time in all the flurry of the last few days.

By ten Monday morning, Jake was at the door. The will basically left everything to Ellie, but there were a lot of papers to sign. "I know you haven't had time to think about the future," Jake ventured, "but maybe we could talk about a few options for you to start thinking about."

"The night before he died," Ellie interjected, "John suggested that Joseph and Elda may want to buy the farm. Right now it's hard to think about leaving it. I know I can't farm it on my own, but we had so many dreams for this place."

"I know, Ellie! You don't have to decide anything right now. The neighbors will continue to do chores for a few weeks anyway. I was talking to John's dad and brothers. We came up with a suggestion that would tide you over the winter, if you like. Albert and Isaac thought they could each take a few of your better cows into their herds. Theo could finish off the pigs and you could sell a few. You and the children can look after the chickens. That way, in the spring, if you do want to sell the farm there will be animals to go with it. We would need to talk with Joseph and Elda, but perhaps you could work something out that you could trade the farm for their house in Malden— as long as that is all right with you. Of course, the farm is worth more, so you could invest that part or take the mortgage and have the interest as income. It's just an idea for you to think about."

Ellie was quiet for a moment. "There may be some added benefit to that idea. Maria is taking ninth grade work this year, and we had thought she would have to board in town next year if she went on to high school. If we lived in town, she wouldn't have to leave home. It would be nice to stay here at least until spring, though."

Jake reached across the table and laid his hand on Ellie's. "I know this is hard for you, Ellie. Why don't you let me make the arrangements for the livestock with John's family? That will give you the winter to decide about further changes."

Ellie nodded her head, "Thank you, Jake, I think that is what I should do. It would be very kind of you to look after that for me. John said you would help me."

"Even though John was quite a bit older than me, we always got along well together. I always enjoyed coming to help him with cutting wood and doing other projects here on the farm. I chose to get into law, but getting back on the farm now and then has always been a nice change. By the way, I will still come and get your woodshed filled for the winter, just like I usually do."

"Oh, would you?" Ellie's relief and gratitude sounded in her voice. "The children and I can help stack it in the woodshed."

Jake rose to his feet. "I think I have everything that I need for right now. There will still be some details to which I need to attend later."

"Don't leave without dinner, Jake! We have enough food left over to feed an army. The girls and I will have something on the table in a few minutes. "

"Well – if you are sure…"

"Oh yes! I'm sure."

"Perhaps, while you get the meal on, George and I can go out and check the barn and make sure everything is in order," Jake suggested. "George!" he called out to the kitchen, "Do you want to go with me to see if everything is all right in the barn?"

George came running.

"Sure, Jake!"

He was obviously pleased to have Jake's attention.

"Come, then, little fellow," Jake said affectionately. He tousled George's hair. "We men have to look after things, don't we?"

Sharing the meal with Jake seemed like a little reprieve from all the newness they were facing. Although Jake was sensitive to their grief, his irrepressible humor still came through several times. It was good to know they all could still smile. He even had them laughing at the memory of several hilarious times with John. When he left Ellie and the girls all remarked that it was beneficial to remember the good times their family had shared.

That evening, as she was getting ready for bed, she opened John's dresser drawer. There, beside the stack of neatly ironed handkerchiefs, in its special box, lay the pocket watch attached to its chain and fob. She opened the lid again to look at the inscription, 'To John, with love from Ellie.' Her heart wrenched again in unbelief.

"I just can't believe it's over! I can't believe we won't share any more precious moments! Oh, dear John," she whispered as tears welled again in her eyes, "our love could have lasted for many years yet—lasted, and even kept growing deeper and stronger!"

The first few months seemed to last forever. Time crawled on relentlessly and yet seemed suspended in unreality. She made meals for the sake of the children, but with John's empty place at the table so evident, the food seemed tasteless to her. She did the washing and ironing, but the absence of John's clothes made it seem like an incomplete task. She cleaned the house regularly, but there was no one to comment on the difference it made. Every time Ellie opened the wardrobe door, John's clothes hanging there were sharp reminders of his absence, yet she couldn't bear to take them out and put them away. She knew that eventually they would have to go, but she couldn't part with them yet. At bedtime she would sink into bed bone-tired, but the place that had for so long been a haven at the end of the day, was now another reminder of the emptiness of her life. She still woke often through the night. It seemed the minute she was awake, those last hours with John would immediately parade through her mind as if to ensure she believed the reality of it all. Yet the fog of unreality would not dissipate. She could not believe that her present life was real.

There were so many unexpected confrontations with her loss—finding a note in his handwriting or seeing his winter boots in the woodshed standing there as though they were awaiting the feet of their owner. John had fashioned a unique walking stick from a young sapling and its root. He always took it to the pasture when he went for the cows and it stood beside the woodshed door. Whenever Ellie went by, she would stroke it with her fingers and press it into her palm. It seemed to still retain the warmth of his hand.

The sympathy cards and letters had dwindled to a stop, yet Ellie still visited the post office with the hope of some letter or note of understanding and acknowledgement that someone else was missing John. With the children back in school, her days sometimes felt empty and long. She often began a task, then was distracted by her thoughts and memories or her feelings of inadequacies and fears. Blindly, she would stumble on to another task, or sit and wallow in her misery. At the end of the day, there would be several unfinished chores.

One day, toward the end of November, feeling the need of fresh air, she slowly walked out the lane, noting the bleak, bare trees. They reflected, she thought, the state of her life. The bare branches of her life were still there, but the foliage that gave life to the limbs was gone. She paused for a while to sit on the large stone in front of the sign they had fashioned together to fulfill John's dream. The black "Maple Lane Farm" letters were neatly painted on the white sign. It stood between the stone and the cedars. It did give a lovely welcome to the farm. Now it might be someone else's. *John, oh John, am I doing the right thing? Can I bear to let go of our dreams?* She shivered from the cold. Her heart felt almost as cold as the granite on which she sat.

Ellie gave a big sigh and rose to continue walking out to the road. She was about to turn back toward the house when she saw Cy Miller approaching with his team pulling a wagon. He waved as though to stop her. When he got closer he called to her.

"I was in town and picked up your mail for you." He pulled on the reins. "Whoa! Whoa, there!"

The wagon came to a stop. Cy handed her several letters, then reached for a parcel.

"How is it going, Ellie?"

The Millers had been so helpful since John's death. They often dropped in to see if there was anything she needed or if they could help with some of the heavier tasks. Ellie reached for the parcel without looking at it. She found it so hard to answer that question when people asked. Did they want to know the grim reality, or a softened version of it; or would they rather she would say something inane as *I'm doing as well as can be expected*; or were they hoping for *Quite well, thank you?* At least, with Cy, she was sure that he asked out of genuine care.

"Thank you for your concern, Cy. I am trying to adjust to living without John and the possibility of leaving the farm. It hasn't been easy, but I'm not the only one who has had to make such adjustments."

"Those changes are big ones, I know, Ellie. We want to help you in any way we can."

The pain in his eyes spoke of the guilt and sorrow he still felt in the part his need for help had played in John's death.

"Thanks, Cy. You have been very good to me."

"It's the least we could do. Take care now!"

Waving goodbye, she started back toward the house and glanced down at the parcel in her arms. When she saw the return address, *Merton's Photography Studios. Toronto, Ontario,* Ellie thought a knife driven through her heart couldn't have hurt more. She almost ran up the lane and into the kitchen. As if driven by a frenzied impulse, she tore at the wrappings and opened the soft gray cover of the first photo in the stack. There sat John, so handsome in his good suit, his bow tie a perfect accent to his white pleated shirt, his arm resting casually on the table beside him. Ellie stood to his right, in the dress she had made especially for the occasion, her left arm on his shoulder. She could almost feel the cloth of his suit and the smell of his shaving cream. She clasped the photo to her breast. From the very depth of her soul arose an anguished cry, and she began to weep with utter abandon. Her grief rolled over her in huge, angry waves; the crest of each wave brought a new outburst that erupted with a loud wail. She was thankful they had no close neighbors, for she was powerless to stop or even tone down the volume. She felt as though her insides were literally being torn out. Tears ran down her cheeks and wet the front of her dress. She reached for a second handkerchief to blow her nose and wipe her eyes.

It was in vain, for there seemed no end to the tears. She wept on until her ribs hurt from the effort. When finally the fury of the storm had somewhat subsided, she walked, forlorn, through the house, fully recognizing each little thing connected with John and wholly sensing the loss of his presence, weeping all the way.

Finally she was spent. She sat on the couch feeling completely exhausted, yet somehow cleansed as well. She felt as though she had been on a long journey. She tried to get her bearings. Several hours had passed, and she hadn't eaten any lunch, but now the children would be coming home before long. She got a washcloth and went out to the pump. She pumped and pumped as if to wash away the grief.

When the water was as cold as it would get, she wet the washcloth and held it against her face. Several times she repeated this, then, with a shuddering sigh and a shiver from the cold air, she went inside.

She felt as though she had been dumped at another station on the journey through her grief. She didn't want to be there any more than she had wanted to start the journey in the first place. It still didn't seem real, but she was there. She knew there would be more of the journey ahead; this was just a brief stopover. She sighed.

Ellie went back to the parcel and picked up one of the photos. She set it up on the sideboard. The rest she put away. She supposed their families would still appreciate having one, but no longer did it feel like the perfect Christmas gift for them.

Even though her energy was drained, she thought she must plan supper for the family. Again, she was drawn to the photo on the sideboard. How glad she was for that trip to Toronto. She had known then, that it was a time she would always treasure, but thankfully she hadn't realized just how much, nor that the possibilities for such times would be over so soon. Slowly, once more she set the photo down and headed to the kitchen.

True to his word, Jake came several times to split wood and bring it to the woodshed. A number of those times, Joseph and Elda accompanied him. She and Elda would supervise the children in making neat piles in the woodshed. She was glad for the help, but she felt all the more alone. The winter was turning out to be a cold one, so Ellie was glad for the bounteous piles of fuel to keep them warm.

Even though Ellie's heart was not in it, because of the children, she made some preparations for Christmas. She was going through the motions, but the spirit was gone. She felt like one horse in a team hitch—and the load was not pulling evenly. When George started to ask questions about who was going to help him get the Christmas tree, Ellie asked Jake, on one of his visits close to Christmas, if he would take George and get one. Jake made it a real adventure. When they returned triumphantly with a tall spruce, George's cheeks were red and his eyes were shining. Jake stayed for supper and helped with the trimming, joking and teasing the children. While Ellie was reaching to put a bauble on the tree, he winked at the children. Coming up behind Ellie, he gently deposited some tinsel in her hair. The children burst out in laughter. It took some time before Ellie found the cause and joined the merriment.

The Saturday before Christmas, the children had gone to bed, and Ellie sat for a moment to read and pray before going to her lonely bedroom. She was startled at the sound of the stair door. There stood Maria and Marta, with such uncertain and cautious looks in their eyes. "What is it, girls?"

"Mama…" Maria began, but then hesitated and looked at Marta.

"Mama, you know how we have some of our first mama's things in the Remembrance Trunk? Well…Maria and I were just talking…we were just thinking…do you think we could put a few of Papa's things in there too? Then, when we tell our stories about Mama, we would have some things there to remind us of Papa, too, and we could tell stories that we remember about him. Could we, Mama?"

Tears glistened in Ellie's eyes as she reached to put an arm around each of the girls.

"I think that would be a marvelous idea. What do you think of doing it on Christmas Day after we have opened our gifts? I will get some things ready, then we will have a good time of remembering as we put them in the trunk. Are there any things that you would especially like to put in the trunk?"

"I would like that wool vest that he wore in the winter," said Marta. "It always felt so warm when you leaned against him. It just made him look…well, I don't know how to say it. I guess it just made him look like a warm, loving Papa!"

"I thought perhaps the pen that he always used to do his books, and maybe the ink well, unless you still want to use that," Maria said thoughtfully. "I remember him sitting there at the desk with the lamp shining on his face. One other thing I thought would be nice to put in the trunk—you know that bank that he had when he was a little boy, the one the shape of a safe? Do you think we could put that in the Remembrance Trunk too?

"What about a few of his good handkerchiefs and—and—and the shoe horn he used to put on his good shoes?" Marta added.

"You have made some good suggestions, girls. I am so glad you thought of this. I think it can help make this first

Christmas without Papa a very special day. Now you two run along to bed. I will perhaps think of a few more things."

Christmas Eve came, the children were in bed and Ellie set about her lonely task of filling the stockings and putting the gifts she had for the children under the tree. She was surprised to see a parcel already there. It was wrapped in green tissue paper and tied with a red ribbon. She bent down to read the card. "To our good Mama, from Maria, Marta and George." Her curiosity was aroused. She wondered what it was and where and when they had gotten it. In spite of herself, she grinned at her thoughts of impatience. She had better wait until morning to find out.

In her bedroom, she looked at the basket of things she had gathered for the Remembrance Trunk.

Oh! I forgot the little bank, she thought. She knew it was in the drawer behind the handkerchiefs. She opened the drawer. Should she put the watch in the trunk too?

Tenderly she lifted it and ran her thumb over its polished cover. She clicked the lid open and read the inscription again as her thoughts wandered back to that first Christmas with John. With her other hand she fingered the locket that hung around her neck.

No, she thought, *I may add it later, but for now, I want to keep it close.*

She carefully laid it back in its accustomed place and reached to the back of the drawer for the bank. She sat on the edge of the bed. She had never seen another one like it. Someday George would get it. She turned the handle to open the little door. To her surprise, there was a little parcel inside. It was wrapped in light brown tissue and tied with a narrow ivory ribbon. Curious, she opened the tiny bow. As she opened the first fold, a little card fell out. Timothy Eaton Co., it read. She turned it over. Her heart leapt at the sight of John's handwriting.

"To my beloved Ellie, who has brought so much beauty to my life."

Tears filled her eyes as she continued unwrapping the contents. There lay the combs she had admired when they had visited Eaton's. The mother-of-pearl inlay in the brown combs radiated light from the lamp.

"Oh John! You dear, dear man! How did you manage to get them without me seeing?" she said aloud.

She could almost feel his presence and sense his delight in her surprise and joy. What a marvelous Christmas gift! She lifted them to her lips and kissed them, then laid them in the top drawer of her jewelry chest. She saw the acorns in the corner and picked them up, rubbing her thumbs over their smoothness. They were over ten years old, but they brought back the memory of that first day with John. Carefully, she put them back in place and caressed the combs again before she shut the lid. What a lot of living and loving and loss lay between the acorns and the combs. She got into bed, feeling such closeness to John and such thankfulness for the love they had shared. Getting ready to fulfill the girls' wishes and now, with this unexpected gift, the Christmas she had dreaded had brought its own warmth and healing. *Isn't that what Christmas is all about? Love came down to earth to wrap us in the knowledge of God's eternal love*, she thought as she drifted off to sleep.

Chapter Thirteen

Christmas dawned cold and bright. It had snowed through the night, giving everything a new coat of white fluff. Some clung to each branch of the trees, making it look like a picture card Christmas scene. Even though George had thought he couldn't wait until morning, Ellie was up and had the fire started before he came downstairs. He headed straight for the stockings. Ellie suggested that perhaps it would be nice to wait until the girls came, so they could do it together.

"Mama," George objected, "the girls aren't even awake yet!"

Ellie smiled at his dismay and relented.

"All right, George. You can get your stocking, but you will have to wait until Maria and Marta come before you open anything under the tree."

Happily, he raced to get his stocking. He sat on the large braided rug and began to explore its contents. He momentarily admired the pair of socks Ellie had knit for him. The next discovery was a small pocketknife on a chain.

"Oh Mama! Now I can be just like Papa. He always had a knife in his pocket."

"Yes, he did, George. You have to be very careful with it, though. I don't want you or anyone else getting hurt with it."

"I will be careful!" George vowed. "Will you show me how to open it?"

He left the stocking on the rug and came to hug Ellie.

"Thank you, Mama!"

Ellie showed him how to hold it with one hand while he used the thumbnail of his other hand to grasp the little slot and open the blade.

"What is even more important is how to shut it, George. You have to be careful not to have any fingers in the way when the blade snaps down in place again. Look, this is how you do it."

She closed the blade, then opened it again.

"Now you do it, very carefully."

She watched him follow her instructions.

"Oh, just a minute! If you close the blade now, what is going to happen? See where the knife is going to go? What is in the way?"

"Oops! It would cut the end of my finger!"

He reassessed the procedure.

"I have to hold it like this. Right, Mama?"

"That's right. Always look a second time before you close it, to make sure nothing is in the way." Ellie smiled.

The blade was really not very sharp, but she could see George was feeling quite pleased to own a knife. It was a good way to begin learning responsible use of this tool most men couldn't do without.

"Oh, I hear the girls are up and you haven't even got to the bottom of your stocking."

George returned to the rug to dig for the candy and then the orange at the bottom of the toe.

"Mama, are you going to make the orange into a fancy flower the way you always do for Christmas? Please?"

"Of course, George! Bring it to me and I will begin with yours until Maria and Marta come."

Just as she was placing the date in the center, Maria and Marta came into the room.

"Merry Christmas, girls!" Ellie greeted them. "George has already emptied his stocking. If you want to find out what is in yours, I will fix your oranges too. Then we can all sit down and open our gifts. Martin and Tina said they would stop by and take us with them to Grandpa Kessler's."

The next half hour went by quickly as they opened gifts and found delight in the contents. George was very happy with his little wooden train. Maria seemed pleased with the embroidery cotton and the stamped pillowcases, as was Marta with her stamped runner. Ellie was touched when she finally opened the green tissue wrapped parcel to find a leatherbound post-card album. "We thought it would be a good way to keep all the cards we got when Papa died," Maria told her.

"That will be lovely! Thank you so much! It was very thoughtful of you." Ellie paused, but then decided to ask. With a smile she probed, "I am very curious though, to know where and when you got it. Are you going to tell me?"

The girls looked at each other and smiled. "We wanted to get something special," Maria said, "so we talked about it for a long time. We couldn't decide what it should be, then when we were at Uncle Joseph and Aunt Elda's for Sunday dinner that time, we saw her post-card album and we thought of all the cards we got when Papa died. We thought it would be the perfect gift, so we asked Aunt Elda when she went to change Edith's diaper. She said she would get it for us and send it out with Uncle Jake next time he came to work at the wood."

"We had to sneak it in the house when you weren't looking," Marta added, with a grin. "We hid it in the upstairs of the woodshed. We didn't think you would find it there."

"I didn't know my children were such little schemers! You did a good job, though. I didn't have any idea until I saw it under the tree last night. I must confess I was very curious. I could hardly resist peeking."

"Oh Mama! You wouldn't have, would you?" asked Marta.

"No, I wouldn't, but I was tempted!" she laughed.

Ellie fixed their traditional eggs-in-the-nest. While breakfast was in the oven, they went upstairs and had a precious time as they told stories connected with the things they were placing in the trunk. She was surprised how even the memory of John working by lamplight at his accounting books gave them such a feeling of security.

One never knows what will make a child feel loved and secure, she thought.

After breakfast she told the children to get ready for going to see their grandparents. She also went to change. Carefully, she combed her hair in a style that would show off her new combs. The chestnut in her hair was perhaps fading a bit, but the combs were still perfect nestled in it, she decided, as she used her hand mirror to view them there. Her heart was filled with warmth at the thought of John getting them for her and hiding them away, anticipating the giving and the pleasure they would bring her.

Maria saw them right away. "Mama! Where did you get those combs? They are beautiful!"

"They are a surprise gift from your Papa," she told her children.

At their look of shock, she quickly told them about how she found them while looking for the bank for the Remembrance Trunk.

"It was almost as if your Papa came to visit me last night to give our family a Christmas blessing." Tears glistened in Maria's eyes, while Marta's just shone with awe and delight.

"What would have happened it you didn't find them?" George wanted to know.

"Perhaps an angel nudged Maria to want that bank in the Remembrance Trunk. It was the one thing I had forgotten to get ready until just before I went to bed last night. Maybe that same angel nudged me to remember at just the right time.

"Here come Martin and Tina. Make sure you wrap yourselves warmly. It is a cold day. Thomas and Mattie have already had a cold ride. Maria, will you get the bag with the gifts for Grandpa and Grandma?"

It wasn't long until the two families were crowded in the big sleigh along with the gifts and food. They pulled big robes up to their chins and put their feet on hot bricks to stave off the chill as they merrily set off for further festivities.

On New Year's Day they went to see John's family. There, Ellie felt John's absence with a painful poignancy, for his brothers and Pop reminded her so much of John. Although it was awkward for Ellie when she started giving out the pictures, his brothers, sisters and parents welcomed them with so much thankfulness it made Ellie's heart glad to give them this reminder of their brother and son. They all enveloped her in their love with such warm acceptance that by day's end she was again truly thankful to be part of this large, happy family.

The new year settled into a routine of dark, cold nights and long, lonely days. Jake, Elda and Joseph came several times to discuss the exchange of property, and Jake came frequently to get the paperwork all finalized—now the agreement was signed by all parties.

At the beginning of June, Elda, Joseph, and their children, Thomas and Mattie, would take over Maple Lane Farm, and Ellie and her children would move into the big, square, red brick home in Malden. It was a lovely home, set back from the street a little further than its neighbors. There were big mature trees in both front and back yards, with a little room for a garden right at the back of the lot. The big bay windows in both the parlor and the upstairs main bedroom gave the house added charm. The wide veranda invited one to sit on a rocker to relax and perhaps visit with the neighbors.

The back, too, had a large veranda, both upstairs and down. One maple tree in the back yard reached its branches very close to the upstairs veranda door.

Ellie dreaded leaving the farm. It seemed she was distancing herself from John even more. However, she was glad that she had such a nice home to which she could look forward. Even though she had never lived in town, she could already see that she would be less isolated and dependent on others by living there. The children would not have far to go to school. Maria could go on with her education while still having the support of her family. In the fall Marta, too, would be ready for that next step, for she had begun school younger than Maria had. Ellie herself could walk to the stores for her needs, and it would be easier to look for paying work in town. She needed to supplement her income some way.

Resolutely, Ellie set to sorting and packing those things that would not be needed before summer or that they could do without. She finally packed up a lot of John's clothes. She kept one shirt and a few ties with which she could not part. Otherwise it would have felt too much as though she was cutting the remnants of John out of her life.

On one of the first warmer days in late March, she had a caller. She saw the horse and rider coming down the road, but was surprised to see them turn in the lane. As they came closer to the house, she recognized Gordon McLean from the next road over. She wondered what he would want. He was a man probably in his late fifties or early sixties. He lived by himself, since his mother had died several years earlier. He was a bit of a recluse. People said his house was just getting fuller and fuller, because he never got rid of anything and never did much cleaning. His clothes looked as though he kept them on until they were worn out and then got new ones. When he knocked at the door, she opened it and said, "Hello, Mr. McLean!"

Gordon McLean took the well-worn, greasy hat off his head and turned it around several times. "Er—may I come in?" he nervously asked.

"Why, yes, do come in," Ellie offered. "Will you have a chair?" She didn't think, by the smell, that he had got his new spring clothes yet.

"S'pose I might," was his reply.

They sat in silence for a few moments. The hat kept making circles in his hands.

"Was there something you wanted?" Ellie finally asked.

"Just thought with John gone, you might be findin' it hard to do the farmin' and all. Thought mebbe I could help ya out. You know, thought mebbe we could get us married."

Ellie's first inclination after the initial shock was to burst out in laughter. She made a concerted effort to keep the sparkle out of her eyes and the laughter out of her tone.

"Why, Mr. McLean, how kind of you. However, the farm has been sold to John's sister Elda and her husband Joseph. I have bought their house in Malden and will be moving there in June."

"Oh, hadn't heard 'bout that." He paused. "Well, I s'pose I may as well go."

He rose and turned dejectedly toward the door, then, suddenly turned to face her again.

"Unless you'd like to live on my farm," he suggested hopefully.

"Thank you, Mr. McLean, but I really don't feel ready to take such a step yet," she said kindly.

"Bye then," he muttered on his way out the door.

Ellie closed the door and waited until she saw him on his way out the lane. The horse was going at a faster pace than it had on the way in. She sat down and let the laughter come.

"Of all the decisions I've had to make in the past months, that was one of the easiest," she said out loud. "Poor man, it probably took a lot of courage to come and ask, and here I sit laughing at him."

She walked over to the sideboard to look at the picture of her and John.

"I think I would have your approval on my decision, John! I still can't believe you are really gone and our life together here is over."

As she went on with her work, she thought, in spite of her sympathy for Gordon McLean, that there might be worse things than being a widow.

Her birthday fell on a Saturday in late May. She suggested to the children that they take a picnic lunch to the bush to celebrate.

"We can still walk back there sometimes when Joseph and Elda live here, but it won't be quite as convenient as it is now. What do you think?"

The children were all in agreement. As they left the house, Maria and Marta carried the picnic basket between them, Ellie carried a blanket and George was already running ahead.

"Just a minute, George!" called Ellie, "I want you to look at these trees. See how tall they have grown? They were only about three or four feet tall when Papa and Uncle Jake planted them the spring after we were married. The day after our wedding we had a picnic exactly where we are having ours today. We had gone to see the 'Grand Matriarch of the Woods,' as Papa called that big oak tree back there. We decided then to plant these here, hoping that some day they would be big enough to hang a swing on their branches."

"They aren't big enough for that yet!" observed George.

"No, they aren't," agreed Ellie, "but they are, I would say, at least fifteen feet tall. Oaks don't grow as fast as some trees, but if they keep growing perhaps Harvey or Edith's grandchildren will swing from their limbs. When we plant trees we don't always get to see their full, mature beauty, but we need to plant them for the next generation, just as our grandparents planted for us to enjoy."

The sun shone warm, the breeze blew gently and they could smell spring in the air. They took their time to fully enjoy its peace and beauty.

Keeping George quiet enough to observe some wildlife, was a bit of a challenge, but with the aid of John's bird book, which Ellie had tucked into the hamper, they were able to identify some of the birds they saw. After the first few sightings, George seemed to catch the idea. With great stealth, he ventured from tree to tree to see if he could be the first to sight a new species. Ellie smiled at his exaggerated caution. John would be pleased to see him finding enjoyment and adventure in this pastime.

"Mama," Marta asked, "do you think we could bring Uncle Joseph's and Harvey and Edith back here and show them the Grand Old Matriarch and the Dining Glade so that they know how special they are? Maybe they can have picnics here too."

"Why, yes! I think that would be a good idea. Moving day will be busy, but perhaps we can come back some day later in the summer and do that."

"I'm going to tell Harvey that we have a special surprise for him," George said. "Maybe I can show him what a downy woodpecker looks like."

"I think it's about time for us to get back to the house. We may have enough time to pick a few wild flowers on the way," said Ellie as she arose and began to fold the blanket. "Thank you for a wonderful birthday!"

They found some dogtooth violets and some blue and yellow violets. With all of them picking a few it didn't take long to make a nice little nosegay.

"Look here," Ellie called, "Can you tell me what this is, George?"

"I know," Marta said with smug superiority.

"What is it?" George asked with curiosity.

"You tell him, Marta."

"It's a jack-in-the-pulpit! See, if you lift up this petal, you can see Jack standing there, preaching his sermon!"

"Can I pick it, Mama?" George asked.

"Just take a good look at him where he is. I think we'll just leave Jack here to keep on preaching, George. We already have a nice bunch of flowers to put in our vase at home."

They continued on their way to the house, pointing out to each other more signs of a new growing season as they were noticed. Even as Ellie longed to be sharing this day with John as part of the family, she gave thanks for these children who had become hers to love and who loved her in return.

Chapter Fourteen

1896

It took Willy's, Martin's, her father's and Cy Miller's wagons to move all of their possessions to Malden. As soon as the wagons left, the women did a thorough cleaning. By that time Isaac, Albert and Theo were arriving with some of Joseph and Elda's things. Ellie had gone with the first wagonload so she could direct the men to the right rooms with the furniture and crates. Jake, who lived in a small house just a block-and-a-half away, was there to greet them. He had helped Joseph and Elda load up their wagons.

In spite of Ellie's efforts to have everything well organized, her head was in a whirl by the time everything was unloaded. Mary and Tina had corralled Jake to help set up the beds and they had found linen to get them ready to sleep in. Mama and one of Ellie's new neighbors, Moira Gilbert, were busy washing up the dishes and getting them into the cupboard. Ellie extracted a chair from the jungle of boxes and furniture. She sank into it with a sigh.

"Do you think I will ever get everything in place?" she asked.

"Yes, you will," assured Moira, "but it will take several weeks at least. It's not just a matter of unpacking—it's trying to figure out the best place for everything in a new space. You won't have to worry about supper tonight, anyway. Your new neighbors have planned to give you that as sort of a welcome. You can just leave the chaos here and go next door to the Wilson's to eat your supper."

"That sounds so good, Moira. Thank you!"

"Your beds are ready to sleep in as well," added Tina as she and Mary entered the room. "Tomorrow morning, after a good night's sleep, the mountain of work will not seem nearly as high."

Ellie had decided to take George out of school a few weeks early. Maria and Marta were going to go back, after the weekend, to stay with Elda and Joseph until their exams were done. So, the following week, she and George unpacked and began to put things in place. Elda had left some of the curtains, and Ellie hung more in the rooms that still needed them. At the end of each day she could see a difference, and bit-by-bit, this new house with hardwood floors, tall ceilings and elaborate woodwork felt more like home. There were storage cupboards built along one wall in the kitchen, which to Ellie seemed a luxury. Her kitchen cabinet looked at home beside the back door. She found it a delight to arrange things in a convenient manner.

Her bedroom upstairs had the bay window to the south and another window to the east. She had set a chair and small table and lamp in the bay. It would be a pleasant place to do some reading or write a letter. The four-poster bed, which had made their bedroom on the farm rather cramped, looked at home in this more spacious room. Even with the wardrobe, chest of drawers and large dresser, there was room to spare. It would be nice, some day, to have an area carpet in the room instead of the small mat beside the bed, but for now, this would do.

One of the first nights, as she sat at the little table in the bay window, she noticed the moon rising over the rooftops. Oh, how she wished John was here to share the view with her. Her life still felt as though there was a big chunk missing. Nothing seemed complete or completely real. She wondered if life would ever feel normal again. Much of the time she felt as though she was play-acting—going through the motions of her necessary tasks with a sense of unreality. She sighed, blew out the lamp, and went to her lonely bed in the new house.

Toward the end of the week, Ellie was doing dishes one evening when she heard voices behind the house. She thought George was outside in the yard, playing with his toys in the dirt at the end of the garden. She went to the back door to see who was there. Jake waved a ball at her.

"Thought maybe George would like to play catch. Are you going to come join us?"

"I think I'd better leave that to the men for now. I still have to finish the dishes."

Jake winked at George. "Do you think she really has dishes to do, or do you think she is afraid she can't catch the ball?"

"Oh, Mama can catch a ball real good, Jake," George protested. "She can throw it good too!"

"See, I was just trying to let you off the hook!" Ellie laughed. "I didn't want to show you up!"

"Oh-oh! That sounds like a challenge. Now you'll have to come and show me what you're made of. I can't just take George's word for it. He may be biased."

"Just let me finish the few dishes that are left and I'll be out."

True enough, Ellie did come out and Jake tossed the ball to her. She caught it and threw it back so quickly he almost missed.

"Overhand even, huh?" he said in astonishment.

Back and forth the ball flew. George cheered them both on in glee. Finally Jake caught the ball one last time and flopped down on the ground beside George.

"You were right! Your mother knows what to do with a ball! Where did she learn?"

"I guess it comes from growing up between two brothers and trying hard to keep up with them," Ellie mused.

"But you will still come back and play ball with me, won't you Jake?" George questioned. "Mama doesn't always have time, and it's—well it's a little like having Papa play with me."

"You just try to keep me away," Jake said, tousling George's hair. "This old bachelor doesn't have any boys to play with, so it's nice to have you nearby."

"Mama, can I show Jake my room?" Turning to Jake, he explained, "I've got a big room and Mama let me decide where to put things. I have the picture of Papa and Mama on my dresser and the willow whistle Papa made for me right in front of it. Mama, can I show Jake?"

"Yes, you may."

George hopped to his feet and pulled at Jake's hand. "Come on, Jake, let's go!"

Ellie lingered in the yard a bit before going to the house. Elda had put some things in the garden for her, but she still wanted to plant more, even if it was rather late. Elda hadn't planted many flowers in the beds. Next year Ellie would plant many more. She couldn't live without flowers. Most of the geraniums stayed with the farm, but she brought some slips along. If they grew well and she kept propagating them throughout the winter and spring, she should have lots to brighten things up here, as well. Slowly, she walked to the back door. She should ask Jake if he knew of any job openings that would fit in with her schedule. She hoped she wouldn't have to start work until the children were settled in at school again.

Ellie was sitting at the table with a pot of tea and a plate of cookies when Jake and George came downstairs.

"Sit down and have a cup of tea and some cookies, Jake. I have a few questions I'd like to ask."

"Maybe I should have the cookies and tea first so they're safe in my stomach in case I can't answer your questions and you want me to leave."

"Did you think I was bribing you?" she retorted. "If that's what I was doing, I wouldn't have stopped with cookies—I would have offered you a piece of strawberry pie!"

"Hmm-mm! Strawberry pie!" he said with a cunning look, "Strawberry pie, you say?" He looked at George. "How many questions do you think I would have to answer for a piece of strawberry pie?"

He blinked his eyes and licked his lips, his tongue moving in and out with incredible speed.

"You look like a hungry dog!" George laughed with glee.

"Fire the questions, Ellie! The first one costs a cookie, and anything after that will require a piece of pie! Have we a deal?"

"Oh Jake! You must be true to your namesake! Wasn't Jacob in the Bible something of a conniver?"

She laughed as she went to the cupboard.

"I might as well get you your pie. I know you won't be leaving without a piece!"

Jake gave a thumbs-up and a "Yeah!" He pulled George to his knee. "I'll even share a bite with you!" he whispered in his ear.

After the first bite Jake rolled his eyes and looked as if he was about to be transported to heavenly places.

"Mmm-MM-mm! Good!"

Suddenly, Jake changed the expression on his face. With a staid, very professional look, a stiff little bow and exaggerated dignity he said, "Now, Mrs. Kurtz—you were asking?"

Both George and Ellie roared with laughter at the sudden change. When Ellie finally caught her breath, she wiped away the tears of laughter and asked.

"You expect me to remember after that?"

"And why not, Mrs. Kurtz?" Jake continued with astonishment and the lift of an eyebrow. He looked aghast at the very thought. That just brought more laughter.

At last, Ellie stopped laughing.

"Jake, you have lived in Malden for years and know a lot of people. I was just wondering if you would keep your ear open for job opportunities for me. I might be asking for too much, but I'd like to find something that will be flexible and let me work mostly when the children are in school. I think the mortgage income will be barely enough to keep us going. A job could provide a few extras and let me save a little for a rainy day."

"Ellie!" There was genuine concern in Jake's voice. "I wish we could figure out a way so that you wouldn't have to do this. I know the mortgage money is hardly enough, but I hate to see you have to work outside the home."

"You don't need to worry. The girls are old enough that they help a lot with the regular work. With all the children in school, the days sometimes feel long anyway. It will keep me busy and that is probably a good thing— less time to think! It would probably be nice to have the summer to settle in. I think we can manage until September."

Jake's eyes were a mixture of tenderness and teasing. "Maybe you should just find some nice bachelor to help care for you!"

Startled, Ellie looked at him, then quickly looked away. What did he mean by that? When she looked back at him, he said, in even tones, "I will see what I can find out for you and let you know. I think, too, that it would be better if you could wait until September. Anyway, I will ask around."

He drank his tea in silence. It almost seemed he was avoiding her eyes.

"It looks as though you have everything pretty well in place, but if you ever need any furniture moved or heavy boxes lifted, just let me know. How long are the girls staying at Joseph and Elda's?"

"They are coming here for Saturday and Sunday, then going back for one more week. Exams will be over then. They will miss some review and probably some of the fun at the end of the school year, but I would like to have them here with me as soon as possible. I hope they can make some friends through the summer so that it won't seem so strange when they start at their new schools. It will be quite different than their one-room school in the country. "

"Maria has grown out of much of her shyness," Jake commented. "You have three sociable children, so I don't think they'll have trouble finding friends. If you go to church here in town, that will give them opportunity to meet some nice young people as well."

"Yes, you are probably right," Ellie concurred. "I'm hoping to meet some people myself. The Wilsons and Gilberts on either side of me seem like friendly people, and they are just a little older than me. Their children are mostly teenagers, except for Colin Gilbert. The Schwartzes and Winklers on the other side of the street are older couples, but very nice too. They seem interested in the children. Mrs. Winkler used to teach piano lessons and she has already suggested that she wouldn't mind teaching the children if they would like to come and use her piano."

"I think you'll settle in just fine. Your children didn't get their friendliness without a good example." Jake rose to his feet. "Thanks for the tea and cookies, and especially the pie!" he said with a grin. "There's nothing like a good, home-baked pie! I get most of my meals at the hotel, and as good as the meals are there, they all begin to taste the same after a while."

George came running in from playing with his toys. "You will come and play ball with me again, won't you?" he asked.

"Sure will! But I have to get home now."

When Jake left, Ellie got out the checkerboard and checkers.

"How would you like to learn to play checkers, George? I found the board this afternoon. I think we have time for a first lesson before bedtime."

Most of the next hour was spent teaching George the basics, but he was catching on fast. When Ellie told him it was time for bed, he begged for just one more game. When she insisted that it was bedtime and that they could play again the next night, he wailed, "But Mama, what if I forget how to play by then?"

"Then I will teach you again," Ellie told him, "but you have such a good memory, I don't think you will forget!"

Having read George his bedtime story and tucked him into bed, Ellie retreated to her own room. She sat at the small table in the bay window going over the events of the day. Jake's attention really gave George a real boost. As always, his humour brought such release from the sad feelings they lived with day by day. She thought of the uncomfortable moment after Jake's off-hand remark about a bachelor to care for her. He couldn't have been referring to himself, could he? She knew for a fact that there were several unmarried women who had tried to catch his interest, and he hadn't fallen for their charms. It was probably just empathy for her situation. Even though Jake was just a few years her elder, she had somehow always looked at him as a younger brother. That was probably because it was how John saw him. She was thankful for all the help he had been in taking care of all the details that John's death had left her to face. *Oh, Jake always has been a lot of fun, and he's good for the children. They always looked forward to the times he came to help John with the wood and other chores on the farm. They enjoy his teasing. I guess I enjoy sparring with him too. In fact, it's sometimes hard to have a serious conversation with him!*

She leaned forward, elbows on the table, and rested her forehead on her hands. "Father, let me walk step by step, day by day, not attempting to cross bridges before I even encounter them."

Over the next few months, Jake continued coming to play with George. Often the girls would be included as well. Jake brought a croquet game and set it up in the back yard. Many summer evenings they all played a few games after supper. Many of those meals included Jake. Occasionally, he made some teasing remark about becoming a permanent boarder since the meals were so good, or some other such jovial comment, but Ellie had long since set her mind at ease regarding her discomfort about his previous statement.

Ellie's parents often came during the summer for Sunday dinner. It helped to make that day less lonely and she was glad for their support. The Wilsons occasionally asked them for a Sunday evening meal. Maria and Marta enjoyed Rita

Wilson, whose age was squarely between theirs. Thomas was eighteen and sometimes joined in a board game with the girls after supper. Moira Gilbert and Ellie visited over the back fence whenever they were both outside. They often accompanied each other to the Sewing Circle with the church ladies. George liked having Colin next door and, even though Colin was a few years older, they often played together. They were settling into the community.

Chapter Fifteen

They had just finished a roast beef meal one evening in August, when Jake leaned back on his chair. As the children went outside to get the croquet out, Ellie began to rise to see to the dishes.

"Just wait a bit, Ellie, I have something to tell you," Jake said, putting his hand on her arm. "School starts in two weeks. I've been doing what you asked. Mr. Mayer at the hotel told me the other day that, with the birth of their fourth child, he was looking for someone to take some of the business responsibility his wife has been shouldering. It would mainly be working with the cook to order the supplies and supervising the maids and the cleaning. Hours could be quite flexible. The cleaning is mostly done in the mornings, and you and the cook could have your consultations a few times a week in the early afternoon. There may be the occasional evening that you would be needed to supervise additional waitresses if they are serving a group meal. The pay is quite good for a town like Malden. I told him I knew of an excellent prospect who could greatly enhance the atmosphere in his hotel," Jake added, with a significant glint in his eye. "Do you think you are interested?"

"Oh Jake! That sounds perfect! With the hotel less than a block away, it would be very handy! Thank you! When would they want me to start?" Ellie paused, "Maybe I'm running ahead of myself again. He will probably want to see if I'm suitable, first. How do I go about it?"

"When I go in for lunch tomorrow, I will tell him you are definitely interested and that you will come down to see him the following day, if that suits him. I think he is anxious to get someone quite quickly. I'll let you know if that doesn't suit him. Otherwise you can plan on going."

"Of course, I won't know until after I have seen Mr. Mayer and actually start the job, but right now, it seems as though it is a wonderful answer to my prayer. Thanks, Jake."

"I still wish it wouldn't be necessary, Ellie."

There was no teasing in his eyes as he looked at her with tenderness.

"I wish your life could have held more happy turns. I am proud of you, though, for the way you have shown such strength in going on with your life and providing such stability and security for the children. They seem to have adjusted well in spite of the changes in their lives."

"Thanks, Jake. I don't always feel so strong, I have my private moments of grief, but I do want the children to feel secure. I try to let them give expression to their grief by recalling the good times and the wisdom of their father. I think moving to town and looking forward to new schools has been good for all of them."

She rose and started to stack the dishes.

"Each of them has found friends in the church or community, and being in town, they can much more readily spend time with them. The meals and times you share with us have been good for them as well. As for happiness, although I ache at times, I do have good memories that bring me such joy even though I wish opportunities for more could have been ours. I try to find pleasure in small moments as they come."

Jake looked at her as though he was going to say more. She waited, but then all he said was, "Can I help with the dishes before we go to play croquet?"

"If you would like," Ellie agreed. "There won't be too many more of these evenings. Once the children start school, there will be homework and earlier bed times."

Ellie was a little nervous as she contemplated her interview with Mr. Mayer. Jake had stopped in to say that the appointment had been made for two o'clock. She dressed carefully in a dark brown dress that was edged in ecru lace. It was not widow's black, but she thought it nonetheless suitable. The first year was almost up. She put John's combs in her hair, but then thought better of it. Perhaps they were a bit too showy for the occasion. She switched to a plain brown pair. She wondered—gloves or no gloves? None, she decided. She slipped her feet into her good shoes and surveyed herself in the mirror. She got her small brown hat from the wardrobe and pinned it atop her head. When she reached the bottom of the stairs, she popped her head into the dining room, where the children were looking through some of the school supplies they had purchased that morning.

"Do I look like a Hotel Manager's Assistant?"

"The best ever!" Marta assured her, while George enthusiastically shouted, "Yes!"

"I think Mr. Mayer will like you!" Maria quietly added.

"You will be all right while I am gone? George, you make sure that you listen to Maria and obey her. I shouldn't be too long."

"We'll be all right, Mama!" they assured her.

As she walked toward Main Street, under the canopy of the large maple trees, she took note of the houses of her neighbors. She thought how often in late August and early September the flowerbeds looked their best. There had been sufficient rains this past month to make everything look so lush and green. The geraniums were still in full bloom. Many flowerbeds also had yellow marigolds and white or purple alyssum. One large brick house was so covered with English Ivy that you could hardly see the color of the bricks.

A house probably eventually says a lot about the owner, she thought. It had taken several years to make the farmhouse seem like hers and John's, now she was starting all over again. She neared Main Street. The Dry Goods store was right across from the hotel. If she got the job at the hotel, she would have to do some extra sewing, for she would have to dress a little differently than she did at home.

Her heart beat a little faster as she opened the hotel door. She hadn't thought to ask Jake where she should go, but she went to the front desk. There was no one there. Now what should she do? She tapped her fingers on the desk absentmindedly as she pondered what her next move should be, then she noticed a little bell with a neatly lettered sign: "Ring Bell for Service." She picked it up and gave it a small ring. Almost immediately, a man she presumed to be Mr. Mayer stuck his head out of the door from a room behind the desk. His moustache was waxed and curled neatly upward. His hair, parted in the middle and smoothed strictly back from his forehead, added an austere quality to his appearance. He peered at her over his glasses. "Mrs. Kurtz?" he queried.

"Yes, sir."

"Come on in to the office," he almost ordered.

When she entered the room he told her, "Take a chair. I'm Arthur Mayer. Now, Mrs. Kurtz, you have come highly recommended. I understand that, although you have no hotel experience, you do know how to run a well-ordered house and that you adapt well to circumstances and rise to challenges set before you."

Mr. Mayer obviously wasn't taken to beating around the bush! His direct approach took her off guard.

"Yes, Mr. Mayer, I suppose you could say that. I have had my challenges and I try to meet them to the best of my ability."

"Mrs. Mayer, at first, would work with you to familiarize you with the routines, but you would then be responsible for ordering the food and the cleaning supplies. You will consult with the chef regarding the menus for two weeks at a time and make sure you have the supplies he needs to serve the excellent meals we provide. You would supervise the maids and make sure the cleaning is done properly."

He peered at her over his glasses as if to ascertain if she were absorbing all the information.

"We try to run a first-class facility here, and we pride ourselves in our food, our cleanliness and decor. If bigger items such as linens need to be replaced, you would first consult with me, but the regular supplies would be entirely your responsibility. I do not wish to be bothered with that."

Mr. Mayer's pencil tapped twice on his desk, as if to accent his last statement.

"You should usually be able to accomplish most of your regular work between the hours of nine and three, and there could be some flexibility in those hours…"

He paused to consult what appeared to be a list.

"I believe that Mr. Jacob Kurtz informed you of the salary we are willing to pay and that you may, occasionally, be needed to help for the evening meal at times when we have larger groups coming. Very rarely we may need your help on a weekend, but that shouldn't be often."

He looked at her intently.

"Do you think you can handle this?"

"Yes, Mr. Mayer. I believe I can, especially if Mrs. Mayer shows me how she has been doing things."

"Then you do want the job?" Mr. Mayer asked.

"Yes, I do, Mr. Mayer."

"Good! I have written out a contract listing your responsibilities, your beginning salary and the possibility of a raise in six months if we are both satisfied with the arrangement at that time. You may read it over. I shall be back in five minutes or so with Mrs. Mayer so you can meet her, then we can both sign the agreement."

With that, he stepped out the door.

Ellie smiled as she began to read. He surely didn't believe in wasting words on small talk or pleasantries! She was pleased with what she read. Everything was clearly spelled out. The salary was generous to start, and with a possible raise, it should really help her financial status.

She had barely finished when Mr. Mayer was back with his wife. Mrs. Mayer was an interesting contrast to her husband. Short and petite, with a round face that looked as though it was used to smiling, she exuded a warm welcome without even speaking. Ellie stood and Mrs. Mayer extended her hand.

"Mrs. Kurtz, please meet my wife, Elise."

"So pleased to meet you, Mrs. Kurtz. We're very happy to have someone to come and help with the hotel. With four small children, it has been difficult to keep things going as Mr. Mayer—as we both wish. You have just recently moved to town?"

"Yes, we came only in June. We live just down Huron Street in the house where Joseph and Elda Wagner lived, so I won't have far to come."

"Perhaps we should get down to business," advised Mr. Mayer. "When can you start, Mrs. Kurtz?"

"I would prefer to wait until the children are in school, since they will all be in new situations this year. So, I can start the first week in September."

"That should be fine, shouldn't it Arthur?" asked Mrs. Mayer. "I will work with you for the first week, then if there are any questions after that, we live in the house just behind the hotel, so you can always come and ask."

"Have you any questions?" her prospective boss interrupted.

"Only one that I can think of right now. What am I expected to wear?"

It was Mrs. Mayer who replied. "In your position, you need not wear a costume as the maids do. Something neat and dignified, such as what you are wearing, will be just fine."

Mr. Mayer handed her a pen. "Why don't we sign the papers, then? There are still other things that I must do today."

The papers were duly signed and Mr. Mayer sat down and resumed his paperwork, making it obvious that the interview was over. Mrs. Mayer walked with her to the door.

"Arthur isn't one for much talking, Mrs. Kurtz, but he runs a good hotel and takes great pleasure in making sure that the clients' needs are well met. We will get to know one another better when we work together. I am looking forward to that. I believe you will do fine at taking over the job."

"Thank you!" said Ellie as she extended her hand. "I am so grateful for the opportunity. I look forward to beginning."

"Until the first of September, then."

With a light heart, Ellie walked toward home, anxious to share the news with her family. It would take adjustments, but they all seemed to be supporting her in this new venture. The prospect of this job gave some direction for her life and her days.

The moment she came in the door, the children jumped up to meet her. They all started to ask questions at the same time.

"How did it go?"

"Did you get the job?"

"Did Mr. Mayer hire you, Mama?"

She reached out to them all.

"It went well! I did get the job and I am to begin the first week in September. When you start your new schools, I will start something new as well. I think we will all learn. Let's sit down and I will tell you all about it."

Ellie told them about the interview and how she would be working with Mrs. Mayer for the first week to learn about the job.

"What time do you have to start in the mornings?" Maria wondered.

"Not until nine o'clock, so we'll all be leaving about the same time. I will usually be finished at three, so I should be home before you are."

"Goody!" was George's remark. "It wouldn't be fun coming home if you weren't here. I think it would be a little scary!"

"Yes, George, I can understand that it would be. However, I expect to be here, and even if I'd happen to not be home some day—if I would have to work late—the girls would be here with you. Changes can be scary, I know. If your Papa were here, he would say it is a good time to pray. Shall we do that?" she asked.

Reaching out their hands, they formed a circle. "Loving Father, our little family is faced with another change. We acknowledge to you that we feel some fear and apprehension at the adjustments we must make. We thank you that you do not change, that your love and compassion are ever the same, your promises are sure. You have promised that you will never leave us or forsake us. We take comfort in that and trust you to walk with us through this time. In Jesus' blessed name we pray. Amen."

Ellie gave each of them a hug.

They spoke then of areas in which the children could each take some responsibility, according to their ability, so that everything they needed would still be accomplished. Ellie was thankful that, at the present anyway, they seemed to be viewing this as sort of an adventure.

She hadn't expected Jake that evening, but it couldn't have been more than twenty minutes after his office closed before he was at the back of the house, knocking on the screen door.

"Yoo-hoo! Does the assistant manager of the Malden Hotel happen to be here?"

"Come in, Jake! I did get the job. I start the first week in September. My hours will be nine to three, so I will still be home when I need to be. I got the impression you gave me a good recommendation. For that I thank you."

Jake shrugged his shoulders.

"I didn't tell him anything but the truth!" His eyes twinkled again, and she knew there was a joke coming next. "Of course, as your agent, I couldn't be anything but positive, could I? You won't ruin my credibility, will you?"

"Mr. Jacob Kurtz, am I to assume that you are having second thoughts? You can't mean to say that you have any doubts?" Ellie retorted with feigned insult.

"My most humble apologies, my dear madam," Jake bowed before her with a great flourish and kissed her hand, "I would not cast any such aspersions!"

"Oh Jake, be serious! I truly am thankful for this opportunity. The children will probably have to take some added responsibility, but the girls already help with the housework and it will be good for them in the long run. I think it will be good for me as well." She paused and smiled at the remembrance, "Mr. Mayer doesn't waste any words, does he? He didn't even exchange any pleasantries. He just plunged straight into the business."

"You're right! Arthur's a good businessman and he keeps the place looking great," remarked Jake, "but I think he has always depended on his receptionist and Elise to provide the friendly personal touch!"

"Will you stay for supper, Jake?

"Not tonight, Ellie! I am to have supper with a client a little later. I just had to stop in to see if you got the job and how you are feeling about it. I'd better be on my way."

"Some nice woman trying to buy your favors with her good cooking?" Ellie teased.

Jake's eyes sparkled, "Why Ellie! Are you jealous?"

In spite of herself, Ellie blushed. Quickly she protested, "No! I was merely inquiring!"

Jake chuckled, "As it happens, I am dining with a married couple with four small children, so you can rest assured!" He winked at her with a wicked grin. "You can continue trying your cooking on me!" at which Ellie blushed the more.

Chapter Sixteen

The first week was the most difficult. She came home, her head whirling with all the new information she had to absorb. She was determined to learn quickly and do the best job possible. Mrs. Mayer was friendly and quite easy-going, although she was also explicit on details and insisted that everything be attended to properly. Mr. Mayer's curt ways made Ellie rather nervous, but by the end of the week, she began to surmise that he was more tolerant than he appeared.

After work, it seemed she barely had time to relax a few moments and try to reorient her self to home life before the children came home. They, of course, were going through adjustments of their own and needed to share their discoveries and their insecurities. Some of Maria's fears about new situations were evident as she tried to adjust to the new routines of a much larger class and Continuation School. Because she was not as quick to share her inner thoughts, Ellie tried to find moments to be with her alone so she could encourage her to voice her feelings. Marta's need, with her more outgoing personality, was time to tell her Mama about all the details of her day. George, under no great compulsion to talk about what went on at school, nevertheless, wanted an equal share of his mother's attention.

Gradually, things slipped into a routine that became a new normal in the family's life. Ellie had drawn up a chart to help equalize the tasks. The girls and Ellie took turns making supper, giving the other two free time. George was expected to set the table each night and help with the cooking when it was his mother's turn. After supper they all took turns, two at a time, to do the dishes. Homework had to be finished then before any time was taken to play, read or do other extras. Ellie was often busy ironing, mending or planning the next evening's menu. Saturdays were busy, for the washing, baking and cleaning all had to be done. Sundays were eagerly anticipated as a day of rest.

Jake often stopped by for supper on Wednesday nights, and it became usual for him to be there Sunday noon. Sometimes he would even stay for supper after playing games with them or going out for a walk or ride. He seemed to take great delight in helping George with his homework or little projects. Ellie was so thankful for this male influence on her son's life. The way he interacted with Maria and Marta—teasing them, complimenting them and encouraging them—was something she, as a mother and woman, could not do in the same way.

What would have been her and John's eleventh wedding anniversary fell on a Saturday. Ellie had gone to bed the night before poignantly aware of the empty space where John should be next to her. She longed to feel the warmth of his body, the weight of his arm around her, the delight of his caress. She dared not think of the empty years that stretched out before her. This past one, in some ways, seemed like an eternity, yet she wondered how she had been able to survive without him for a whole year. She finally fell asleep, still yearning for his comforting embrace. That night, she dreamt that she awoke to feel his arm around her holding her tightly to himself.

"John!" she exclaimed, "Oh John! You are back! It is so good to be in your arms."

She turned to run her fingers through his hair and let her fingers gently stroke the side of his face before she kissed him. He returned her kiss and drew her again to himself.

"I'm just here for a little while, my dear Ellie, I need to go back, but I just wanted to remind you of my love and that you will be all right. My love will always be with you."

Ellie explored every part of his body, trying to memorize each minute part and feature so she could remember everything. It seemed as though John was trying to give her the utmost care and delight, enveloping and filling her with his love until she was fully satisfied.

"Oh John, John, my love!" she sighed, and with that, she awoke herself, for she had said it out loud.

She made a great effort to hang on to her dream, but lost the struggle. The warmth of John's love still lingered, but the tears began to stream down her face. She hardly knew what they were about. She was full of gratitude for the dream and how real it had seemed to her. It felt as though John had actually been there. She still felt his reassurance and the calm he had imparted, but there was also sadness in the acknowledgment of reality. Gradually the sadness dissipated in the greater joy and delight his presence had brought. She drifted off to sleep again, still swathed in that love.

Throughout the next day, she was buoyed with the sense of serenity in the gift of love the dream had given her. Instead of the feeling of loss she had anticipated on this day, it was, because of the dream, a day of warm remembering. That evening, as she read and prayed at her little table, she set their picture there. She gave thanks for God's grace and mercy in giving her that dream and making this day so much easier than she had expected. Before she blew out the flickering lamp, she picked up the picture and brought it to her lips.

"We were good together, weren't we, John?"

A few Wednesday nights later, after they'd had supper, Maria and Marta took their turn to do dishes. Jake listened to George read, and Ellie was doing mending. When the girls settled at the table with their homework, Jake told George that he thought it was time for him to play on his own. Then he moved over to where Ellie sat with her mending.

"Ellie, next Tuesday will be a year since John died. I was wondering if you and the children would like to go out to visit the grave on Saturday. I thought perhaps we could plant a few spring bulbs there, then go on over to the farm and walk back to the woods, as George has wanted to since you moved—that is, if it feels right to you."

"Why Jake! I think that would be lovely! That's so thoughtful of you. I know I would enjoy it, and I am sure the children would as well. I could write a note to Elda and Joseph, so they know we are coming. Do you think we could be there in time for the noon meal?"

"That is entirely up to you, ma'am! I am foot-loose and fancy-free. Your wish is my command!" he replied, with a tip of his imaginary hat.

Ellie smiled. "I think we can work ahead enough to be ready to leave at nine. I'll get some bulbs. I was going to plant some around the house anyway, and I will ask Elda if it is all right to come for dinner. I'll take a pie along."

"Sounds as though we're all set, then. I'd better be on my way, but I will see you nine o'clock Saturday morning!"

Thursday night the whole family started the cleaning while supper was cooking. Friday was not a busy day at the hotel. She had rather dreaded asking Mr. Mayer if she might take off a little early, but as it happened, Mrs. Mayer stopped in that morning to see how Ellie was doing. As usual, she chatted on for a while. Ellie thought it was a good time to mention their plans.

"Mrs. Mayer, Tuesday will be the anniversary of John's death. We have been offered the chance to go out to visit his grave tomorrow. We thought we'd like to plant some bulbs there and go to my sister and brother-in-law's at the farm for dinner. Do you think I might be able to leave a little early today to get things ready?

"Of course," Mrs. Mayer quickly concurred. "I can't imagine what it must be like for you. It must be a sad time for you. Why don't you just go home at noon? Would you like next Tuesday off as well?"

"Thank you, Mrs. Mayer, but I don't think that will be necessary. We will have a weekend to remember. I do so appreciate your understanding."

"We are very pleased with your performance thus far, so we want to make sure that you are happy as well. Don't hesitate to let us know if there are times you need to be attending to your family or personal needs."

"That is truly generous of you, Mrs. Mayer. I will not take advantage of your kindness."

Ellie rushed home and quickly washed a few essential items, thinking they could manage that way. Then she did some baking. When George came storming in the door after school, he sniffed the air.

"M-mm! It smells good!"

He spied the cookies on the counter.

"Can I have one?"

By that time the girls were coming in the door as well.

"Why don't you all have one?" Ellie asked. "Then you can start with the rest of the cleaning while I get the last pies out of the oven and start supper."

They were all ready and waiting when Jake came the next morning. Although there was still a nip to the air, the sun shone in the blue autumn sky dotted with a scattering of purple-lined clouds. The dark evergreens in the countryside emphasized the glowing color of the maples arrayed in reds, yellows and oranges. It was a perfect day for a drive. They saw a red-tailed hawk circling high in the sky. Even the birds in the sky reminded her of John, she thought. Had it not been for him, she would have no idea what kind of hawk it was.

Their conversation flowed freely and easily all the way to the cemetery. As they neared the gate in the fenced area, a quiet descended. They turned in on the well-trodden path and Jake tied the horses to the post, then held out his hand to help first Ellie, then Maria and Marta, step down to the ground. He lifted George down and then retrieved the small basket of bulbs and the spade. Ellie reached for the girls' hands as they quietly walked to the grave where John was buried.

"You know," Ellie said in a quiet voice, "I still sometimes can hardly believe John is really gone."

"Neither can I," echoed Maria.

"At least I can remember Papa," Marta added. She rubbed her finger over her mother's name on the tombstone. "I can't clearly remember much about Mama. Sometimes I think I can remember her holding me on the rocking chair beside the kitchen window, but I'm not really sure."

"That is where she held you and rocked you, Marta." Maria assured her.

"I know, you have told me. I always imagine her wearing that apron that is in the Remembrance Trunk. That is why I'm not sure whether I really remember, or if it's just because I've heard the stories so often."

"Perhaps the story-telling just kept your faint memories alive," Ellie suggested.

"You must treasure that Remembrance Trunk," observed Jake.

"Oh, we do!" Marta quickly answered. "We have had some good times around it. Now there are some of Papa's things there too."

Ellie picked up the basket once more. "Let's plant some of the bulbs on each side of the tombstone. That way there can be some for both Papa and Mama."

Jake carefully peeled back the sod and dug some holes. Ellie directed them in planting the bulbs in clumps, varying the kinds and colors to ensure a vibrant display in the spring. When they had all been planted, Jake covered them up and replaced the sod.

"There! We can hardly tell that we have done anything, but there will be a happy surprise in the spring." Jake leaned on the spade. "Maybe there is a parallel to our lives," he continued, "We live our lives often in quite ordinary ways. The surface of life doesn't seem to change that much. Then we die and for a time everything seems quite empty. After awhile, in the lives of those we have touched, the effect we have had on them begins to bloom in their lives. I know that, since John's death, I have tried consciously to carry on some of the traits and wisdom that I had admired in him. I think I can see that same thing happening in you children and you, too, Ellie. So part of John is blooming in us."

Ellie listened with growing surprise. Jake was much more inclined to humor. It was not often that he was so contemplative or perceptive.

"Why Jake, that is a beautiful insight. It expresses well what I've felt in this past year. At first, my grief was too deep, but recently I've really tried to look at things through John's eyes and tried to respond to things with the deep wisdom he so often brought to situations. It's somehow comforting that there is possibility for some of those seeds to come into full flower."

"I'd like that too," said Maria, "if some of Papa could bloom in me."

"There is some of your Papa in all of you," said Ellie softly, "but you, Maria, are especially much like him. You look like your Mama, but your personality is much like your Papa."

Maria reached for Ellie's hand and laid her head on her shoulder.

"Thank you, Mama!" she whispered.

"Do you think we should pack things up and get on over to the farm?" asked Jake. "Elda and Joseph will be looking for us."

As they turned the curve in the lane, Ellie's eyes were drawn to the sign and her memory hearkened back to the first days of their marriage.

Some dreams live on, even if they are in a different form than we expect, she thought. It was a strange feeling coming "home" when it really wasn't home any longer. The strange feeling only grew in spite of the hearty welcome they received when they entered the house. The rooms were the same, but the different furniture and wall hangings altered the look substantially. George wanted to explore the rooms right away.

"This is where my toy box used to be and this is where Mama's rocking chair was."

"George!" Ellie cautioned as he headed down the hall toward the bedrooms, "This is not our house anymore. You mustn't go where you aren't invited!"

"Oh, let him go," Elda said. "Harvey, you take George and show him the different rooms. Maybe the girls would like to go along."

As they gathered around the table and began to eat, the strangeness gradually ebbed and Ellie found herself enjoying the food and friendship.

After the meal, they all left for the walk to the woods—back along the riverbank and down over the little stream in the gully. As they started up the hill on the other side, Ellie paused to look at the tall pine John had pointed out to her. There it stood, tall and straight and true, just as John had stood in her life. Maria walked with the adults, but Marta ran ahead with George and Harvey and Edith.

"Here is the Dining Glade!" she heard George shouting. "This is where we always had our picnics. See that big old dead tree on the riverbank, Harvey? That is where the downy woodpecker likes to look for food."

When the adults caught up, Marta urged them, "Let's go on and see the Grand Matriarch now!"

"The what?" Elda and Joseph asked in unison.

"That's what Papa called the big old oak tree. Come, and you will see why," George advised.

When they reached the clearing, Joseph let out a whistle. "She sure is a big tree! I can see why your Papa called her the Grand Matriarch."

"It's not just because she's so big, Uncle Joseph, it's because she's got a lot of babies. See all the young oak trees around her?"

"Sure enough!"

"Did you know, Uncle Joseph and Aunt Elda," asked Marta, "that two of her babies are growing in your back yard? When they're big enough, you can hang a swing from one of their branches for your grandchildren or great-grandchildren to swing on."

Joseph and Elda laughed. "If it's for the great-grandchildren, we may be too old to tie the rope in the tree," Joseph commented.

"Maybe Harvey will have to do it for you," George said.

"Harvey, or even perhaps Harvey's son!" laughed Joseph.

"It's probably time we head back, or it will be dark before we get to Malden and home," Jake suggested. "Come along, children!"

By the time they neared home, Ellie was glad they had brought sweaters along, for the air had become cooler. The sun was setting by the time they came close to Malden, and as if to give them a final blessing, the sky lit up in an awesome display of color. The dark purple clouds were lined with brilliant streaks of orange and gold. Above the purple the sky was a vivid turquoise. Even the clouds on the eastern horizon were pink and mauve. "Oh-hh" breathed Ellie in awe, "I don't know if I've ever seen a more vivid sunset. Look at that turquoise!"

Jake looked as if he wasn't sure what impressed him more —the sunset or Ellie's appreciation of it. Quietly, he observed, "The Master Painter does a magnificent job, given a canvas, whether that is the sky or our lives."

Ellie glanced up at him. "You are getting positively poetic, Jake! That is the second time in one day!"

"Oh-oh! Have I ruined my reputation?"

"No!— Far from it, Jake. I just hadn't seen that side of you before. Guess it's just the Master Painter showing me a different part of the canvas!"

Chapter Seventeen

Ellie was busy writing out an order for cleaning supplies when Mr. Mayer came out of his office.

"Mrs. Kurtz, the hotel has just been booked by the Tories for a small organizational meeting the second week in November. It's for a Friday night and there will be about thirty people for the evening meal. Do you think you could help out that evening? I will hire some extra girls to serve, but I would like to have a responsible adult to supervise and keep an eye on the tables to make sure dishes are kept filled, the glasses full and the plates removed when needed. Since it is a political meeting and our member of parliament will be present, I would suggest that you dress up a little more than usual."

"That will be no problem, Mr. Mayer. I will arrange my schedule to be here that evening."

It was difficult to tell with her boss, but she perceived that this was an important opportunity for him. She was flattered that he trusted her to oversee the occasion. The longer she worked here, the more satisfaction she gained in keeping things running smoothly. She was being given more and more responsibility for the day-to-day running of the hotel.

As the date neared, Ellie found out just how important it was. Mr. Mayer even asked her to order some new tablecloths and make sure the windows were washed and extra cleaning done. The great care Mr. Mayer was taking to have everything right made Ellie a little nervous. Jake assured her that she should just be her own gracious self and things would go well.

She took special care in her dressing that afternoon. She put her hair up in a fashionable do and got out the combs John had given her. Her shoes had been well polished, and as she slipped her silk-stockinged feet into them, she was glad for the slim ankles she had inherited from her mother, even though people couldn't really see them for her long skirt. Just knowing made her feel more confident. She searched through her jewelry chest and chose a cameo broach, another gift from John, to pin at the throat of her high-necked blouse. She looked in the mirror, pinched her cheeks to bring a bit of color to them and sighed.

"That is the best that I can do. I just hope it will be enough."

The children had come home as she was dressing. When she came down the stairs, they were there to meet her.

"Oh Mama! You look beautiful," they chorused.

"Thank you! I needed to hear that! I am a little nervous about tonight. It seems to be very important to Mr. Mayer, and I don't want to do anything to spoil it for him."

"Mama, there aren't too many people more gracious than you. All the girls that usually work there like you, so they will try to do their best too." Maria told her.

The tables were set with impeccable taste. The chairs were placed with care. Ellie had brought some geraniums and small pieces of fern to put in little dishes on the tables, giving them added grace and charm. Mr. Mayer nodded in approval when he saw them.

Finally, people began to arrive. Apparently it was a men-only evening. When one party arrived, she saw that one of them was Gerhard, and her stomach tightened into a knot. She hadn't seen him in years. If she had thought she was nervous before, she was certainly more so now. Rowena was probably at home, presiding over their new mansion with servants to help with the work. She wished she could just disappear, but she had a job to do. He was so busy talking she didn't think he had seen her yet. She slipped out to the kitchen to give the serving girls some last-minute reminders.

At last, there was no way to avoid the dining room. All were seated and the moderator for the evening was making some opening remarks. They were about to choose a president for the riding association and were glad to have their member of provincial parliament as a special guest. A gentleman at the head table said the grace and urged those present to enjoy the meal provided by the Malden Hotel and staff.

Occasionally, Ellie would glance at Gerhard. He was still immersed in avid conversation with those seated next to him. At first, Ellie had wished she could disappear, but as the meal went on and Gerhard had still not noticed her, she began to feel irritated. She supposed the serving girls—and she was probably lumped in with them—were part of the machinery necessary only to bring his food, and as such, not worthy of his attention! Couldn't he even say thank you when his glass was refilled or his plate served?

By what she had overheard, she began to surmise that Gerhard might be the top prospect for the presidential nomination. So-oo! He was moving up in the world! Just over a year ago, she had heard that he and Rowena had, indeed, moved onto that large estate of which he had dreamed. He was also already a partner in a textile firm. Now he was apparently getting into politics. She felt her irritation growing. She almost collided with one of the girls headed toward the kitchen with a stack of dishes. She shook her head at her stupidity and started to lecture herself. *Ellie Kurtz! Don't you go and blow your opportunity by getting into a jealous snit!* Jealousy? Was that it? Was she really jealous? It was something she needed to think about and face up to, but now was not the time.

After the dessert and the coffee and tea were served, the moderator called for the kitchen staff and servers to come for a round of applause. It was then that Gerhard saw and recognized Ellie. His eyebrows lifted in surprise. There was to be a short break before the actual meeting began. Ellie began to supervise getting the tables fully cleared when she felt a tap on her shoulder.

"Ellie! What a surprise!" Gerhard said. "I was so sorry to hear about John's death. How are you doing?"

"Thank you, Gerhard. I am doing quite well. I am living here in Malden now. And how are you?"

"Very well, indeed. I don't know if you are aware, but we are living on that estate near Bolton now. We have two sons and Rowena is expecting another after Christmas."

"Congratulations! I overheard enough to surmise that you are also a prospect for the presidential spot tonight. That must be an honor!"

"Yes, that would be an honor, but that remains to be seen. My first priority is still Benham Textiles, but politics are of interest to me as well."

"It's been nice talking to you, Gerhard, but I have my duties to fulfill, so I should be going."

"Do you work here full time?"

"Usually just six hours a day. With the children all in school, it gives me something to do."

Gerhard raised his eyebrows. "Guess I'd better get back to my meeting too. Have a good evening."

Ellie wondered what those raised eyebrows meant. She remembered that he was not in favor of women working outside the home. In fact, he didn't want his wife to work much at all if he could provide servants for her.

It took some time to get everything cleaned up, but finally Mr. Mayer said she could go. On the way home she thought about her reaction to Gerhard. By the time she reached her house, she had come to the conclusion that her jealousy was based mostly on the fact that Gerhard and Rowena were still able to enjoy each other and she was left alone. Speaking to him had helped her realize she was rather happy she didn't need to climb the social ladder of Gerhard's pursuit.

All was quiet when she came into the house. The girls must have managed well, for the dishes were all cleaned up and the house was in order. *Maria is a responsible young woman, and although Marta is much more outgoing and takes less time to contemplate her moves, she is also responsible for her age, and usually pleasant and cooperative.* George, she thought with a smile, was more apt to be argumentative. Well, really maybe not so much argumentative as needing to know the reasons for everything before he could accept anyone's word.

She kicked off her shoes and picked them up to carry them upstairs. She sank down onto her chair and stared out at the starry sky awhile before she lit the lamp and undressed. Hanging her dress in the wardrobe, she took John's remaining shirt off the hanger and buried her face in it.

"I would trade any social prestige for ten more years with you anytime, John," she whispered. "It's probably silly of me to keep this one shirt, but it still gives me comfort to see it hanging there and to wrap it around myself occasionally."

Slowly, she hung it back in its place and went to the bed. She pulled the covers back. *How I wish you were here to cuddle up to, John!* She sank down and let the tiredness seep out of her body.

Monday morning, Mrs. Mayer made a point of coming over to compliment her on a job well done.

"Mr. Mayer was very pleased with your poise and the decorum which you displayed. He was especially happy with the added touch of flowers. Did you bring them from your own home?"

"Yes, I did. Our geraniums were blooming so well I thought it would add an extra touch to the tables. I also have a very large fern which needed a bit of a haircut."

"That was very generous of you, Mrs. Kurtz! If there are other occasions such as last night, we can probably get the flowers you need. Just add that to the supplies you order. You may not always have so many on hand," she smiled. "I must get back to the house now, but I am aware it is hard for Mr. Mayer to express these things and I thought you should know how pleased we are with your services."

"I thank you very much. It is nice to know I am doing the job the way you wish to have it done."

In the beginning, even with Mrs. Mayer's more friendly ways, Ellie had sometimes felt nervous in her job because of Mr. Mayer's curt comments. More and more, she was feeling comfortable and more understanding of Mr. Mayer. She was feeling more confident of herself and thoroughly enjoyed her work. It was nice, though, to be complimented for her efforts.

The days were getting shorter. Snow had come early and stayed. George came down with the mumps at the beginning of December, necessitating Ellie's missing a few days at work. She managed to go to the hotel for a few hours after the girls came home from school to do some of the ordering and a few of her other duties, but she had hoped to take a few days off closer to Christmas, and now she did not feel she could ask for it. They were just going to have to do with a little less of the baking and decorating she usually did.

She managed to get gifts for the children by doing some shopping over her lunch hours or after work. She wanted to get something for Jake to say thank you for all he had done for their family since John had died. She puzzled over what it should be. It shouldn't be anything too personal, yet she wanted something that he would use and appreciate. After looking for many days, she decided on a nice leather-cornered blotter for his desk with a matching ink well and pen stand.

On one of the more clear days, just a week before Christmas, her parents stopped in at the hotel in the morning.

"I hope you don't mind, Ellie," said her mother, "but I've come to take over your kitchen today. I figured, with you working, it would be hard to get all the baking and things done for Christmas."

"Oh Mama!" Ellie objected, "We were planning to make do. You don't have to do this."

"I know we don't, Ellie. Just think of it as our Christmas present to you. Are there any special things you would like me to make?"

"If you really want to do it, I would be glad if you would make some shortbreads and pfefferneus or springerle. Oh, thank you, Mama!"

Ellie went about her work with a lighter heart. She knew how much some of those traditional treats meant to the children, but she just hadn't known how to manage everything. Had she known they were coming, she would have asked her father if he would bring a small tree along so they would have a Christmas tree.

Before she opened the back door, Ellie could smell the pfefferneus.

"How nice to come home to my mama's baking!"

There was a large batch of shortbreads and some springerle. The last batch of pfefferneus was just coming out of the oven. Ellie gave her mother a big hug.

"You don't know how much lighter my shoulders felt today!"

Papa had his hands in the dishwater, washing up some of the baking dishes. Ellie came up behind him and put her arms around his waist.

"I think you deserve a hug too!" she laughed. "It's not often I've seen you washing dishes!"

"Oh, come now! I often helped dry dishes when you children were little, but I suppose by the time you remember, Regina was old enough to take over. Since mother and I are alone, I often help again."

"Well, I sure do appreciate your help. Would you stay for the night? "

"Perhaps some other time. We should get going soon, while it is still light. There have been so many stormy days we don't want to be storm-stayed so close to Christmas. We do have our family coming Sunday, you know."

"Yes, we'll be there if the weather cooperates and there are no more cases of mumps or any such things. Marta must be resistant to them, for she didn't get them when Maria did years ago, and she hasn't got them yet. The time is almost up. Martin and Tina said they would come and pick us up."

After her parents left, she finished cleaning up and putting the cookies away. Her heart was full of gratitude for their help. She thought of a wool throw she had seen in town when she was looking for gifts. She had noticed the last time she was at her parents' house that the one her dad always used for his after dinner nap was getting rather threadbare. Her mother often used it over her knees if she was cool. She would get the one in town for them for Christmas. The adults usually didn't exchange gifts, but she thought this was an exception. She wanted to do this for them. They, too, had been very supportive in the past year.

The smell of baking and spices still lingered when the children came home from school.

"You been baking Christmas cookies, Mama?" George asked, looking hungry.

"No, George, I haven't!" replied Ellie with a straight face.

"What smells so good, then?" he inquired.

"Oh, you smell something?"

"It smells like pfefferneus," added Marta.

"Well I didn't do any baking!" their mother maintained.

"Mama! You are teasing us! I can see by the sparkle in your eyes!" declared George.

"Maybe this is what you smell," said Ellie as she got a small dish of pfefferneus out of the cupboard.

"Mama! You said you didn't bake any!" George remonstrated. Marta looked puzzled. They heard Maria stamping her feet on the back porch.

As the door opened, Ellie laughed.

"I didn't! Grandma and Grandpa Kessler came today and did some Christmas baking while I was at work. So, although I didn't do any baking, we are blessed with some good cookies. I put most of them away, but I saved a few to sample."

"Did I hear something about sampling?" a deep voice said. "Could I be of help?"

Jake looked in the door. He disappeared only to appear once more with a spruce Christmas tree in front of him.

"Jake! You must be a mind reader. I was just wondering today how I was going to manage getting a tree. My parents were here for the day and I wished I had known they were coming so I could have asked my father to bring one along."

"I'm glad you didn't, for then you would have had two. Show me where you want to put it, and then we'd better get on with that sampling that you mentioned." He winked at George and put on his hungry dog act.

George laughed at him. "Maria and Marta, doesn't Jake look like a hungry dog when he does that?"

The girls joined in his laughter. "He most certainly does! Let's get that tree in place before he drools on the floor!"

Some chairs and furniture were moved so the tree could be placed in the parlor bay window.

"It looks perfect there!" Marta sighed.

"Can we decorate it, Mama?" asked George.

"Don't you want to join in the sampling?"

"Oh yes!"

"We'll have some tea and cookies, then you can get the boxes of decorations from the closet under the stairs while we get the supper on. After you have done your homework we will decorate the tree. You will stay for supper, Jake?"

"Only if I am invited!"

"You are! After all, there wouldn't be a tree to decorate if it weren't for you. Thanks for doing this for us."

"I thought I would keep up the tradition we started last year! Can't break one of such long standing, now, can we?"

Ellie laughed as she poured the tea, but inside she was giving thanks for one more dilemma she needn't face.

Chapter Eighteen

Christmas that year had a lot of new things associated with it—a different house, different places to hang the stockings, town living instead of open country—yet there were some things that remained. The Kessler family held their gathering, as usual, the Sunday before Christmas. On Christmas Eve, Claude and Moira Gilbert and their family came to the door with a large fruit basket and some extra Christmas goodies tucked inside.

"We just wanted to wish you a Merry Christmas. We have been so thankful to have you as neighbours."

Ellie invited them to come in for a while, but they said they had deliveries to make to some other folks.

It was only moments later that Roy and Dorothy Wilson came with a beribboned square of fruitcake and a basket of turnip and squash.

"Just a bit of something for your Christmas dinner," Dorothy told Ellie. "We wish you a Merry Christmas and a Happy New Year!"

As Ellie closed the door, she wondered if she had neglected to be neighbourly. She hadn't even thought of getting gifts for them. Maria saw the concerned look on Ellie's face.

"Now, Mama," she remonstrated, "You just be thankful for good neighbours. They know you are busy with work and everything. They probably just wanted to do this to show their support. Don't spoil their gift by feeling guilty!"

Ellie smiled and gave Maria a hug. "Aren't you perceptive! How did you know what I was thinking?"

"I saw the look on your face, and maybe I know you better than you think!" Maria hugged her tightly. "You do so much for us and for everybody else. This time it's your turn to receive, so do it gracefully," she laughed.

"You sound like your father!"

"Thank you for the compliment, Mama. I don't think anything could please me more."

Ellie put a hand on each side of Maria's face and kissed her cheek.

"I know we were joking, but it is true! You do often remind me of your father in what you say and the attitudes you take. I do love you so, and I am proud of the woman you are becoming. Your papa would be too."

"Thank you, Mama!" Maria whispered in her ear.

They had their own family time on Christmas Day, opening their stockings then having their traditional breakfast, after which they opened their gifts. Everyone agreed that they must then gather around the Remembrance Trunk for storytelling. Each one of them related memories that were precious to them. Ellie smiled when George repeated, from past times, a memory of "our first Mama." She did not correct him. She had wanted them to feel like one family, and so they were.

Ellie had bought a plump chicken to roast for their dinner, and since Jake would have spent the day alone otherwise, he came to join them for the meal. When he knocked at the door, George ran to open it.

"Merry Christmas!" Jake sang out. "Do you want this in here?" he asked, holding up a sled with a big red bow wrapped around it. "The snow is a little too soft to use it right now, but when the conditions are right, I promise to come and show you how it's done. There's a nice hill just outside of town that is perfect for sledding."

"Can we put it beside the tree, Mama?" asked George.

"Why don't you say thank you first?" his mama suggested.

"Oh, yes, thank you, Jake! I can hardly wait to try it."

"It's for all of you—even your mama, if she wants to try it."

There was a lot of merry chatter around the table as they ate. Afterward, she nodded to Marta, with whom she had made arrangements beforehand. Marta went and brought Jake's gift to him.

"What is this?" he asked.

"It's something from all of us to say thank you for all you do for us," Marta explained.

Jake opened the wrapping and withdrew the contents. "What a nice desk set! Won't that look impressive on my desk? Thank you all. I think your family has given me more than I have given you." His eyes rested on each of the children, and then he turned to Ellie. "Much, much more!" he added.

Jake has become such a comfortable part of our family life, Ellie thought. He had shared good times and bad. He empathized with them in their grief and difficulty, but he was so good at interjecting humor. Sometimes, in the midst of difficulty, a good laugh served to break the tension and stress. This she had learned through Jake. Especially since their move to town—with the regularity of his visits and the convenience of calling on him when she needed extra help or advice—she had begun to depend on him.

It had frightened her when he had made the comment about finding a bachelor to care for her. She hadn't been ready to entertain the thought. Now, comfortable in her job, and with life in more or less of a routine, she wondered what it would be like if he were a permanent part of the picture.

She mustn't let herself think that way! She scolded herself. He might just be one of those men who don't want to commit to family life. He certainly had given her no reason to believe that he wanted more. She didn't want to go and fall in love with someone who had no interest in marriage. Better to concentrate on life as it now was. She had much to be thankful for, and Jake did fill a need in the children's lives.

"Ellie? Where have you been?" Jake asked.

"Right here!"

"I don't think so," Jake teased, "I said your name the third time before you answered."

"Oh! I'm sorry, I guess I was lost in my thoughts," Ellie apologized. "What were you wanting?"

"I know John's family is having their gathering on New Year's Day. My folks have the same day for our gathering. I was planning to go and stay overnight. I just wondered if you would like to go along and stay at Uncle Abe's for the night. We could come back then the next day."

"Could we, Mama? I like being on the farm. Erik always takes me to the barn and shows me stuff. Last year he showed me a little room he had made up in the hay mow."

"Things, George, not stuff!"

"He shows me *things*. Mama, can we? Can we, please?"

Ellie smiled. "I guess we have one vote in favor. What do you girls think?"

"Sure, Mama! I like to visit with Heidi, and Marta and Lottie always like to be together. Maybe we could even spend the night with them."

"Even if I was not for the idea, I have been out-voted! However, I look forward to it as well. I don't get to see John's parents a lot now that we live in Malden."

"Then it's settled. I will come for you about nine on New Year's Day." Jake seemed buoyed by their acceptance.

For all the snow and stormy weather they'd had, the new year came in with the snow almost melting. The sun shone brightly as the five Kurtzes started their journey. There was a comfortable flow of conversation. A feeling of solidarity and ease settled around them. When Jake's arm brushed hers as he guided the horses, Ellie was conscious of their closeness. The thought came of its own volition, *Wouldn't it be nice if we really were a family?*

Jake was not quite as tall as John had been. His curly dark hair gave him more of a boyish look, but he certainly was handsome in his own way. He did have the same big, strong hands as John. It was silly, but somehow that mattered to her. It would be nice to have a man's arms around her again—a strong chest to lean on when the going got tough. *Ellie Kurtz, there you go again! Jake doesn't seem to be thinking about anything except making sure the children get to see the Kurtz side of their family. Don't go building castles in the clouds.*

Ellie and the children were deposited into the welcoming arms of Abe and Sarah Kurtz, and Jake took his leave to go to the adjoining farm. The day passed, as always at the Kurtz's, with noisy chatter, singing, games and fun. It was hard to keep track of everyone, for they were spread throughout the rooms of the big house. Finally, most of them departed for their own homes. The children had, indeed, been invited to spend the night with their cousins. At last, only Ellie was left with John's parents.

"Let's have a cup of peppermint tea. It's been a noisy, busy day. I always enjoy the bustle, but I guess I'm getting older, for I enjoy the peace and quiet when everyone has gone home too!"

"I think I'll go to the barn. I can maybe help with the chores since it was so late when they got started," Abe said as he put on his boots. "I'll have my tea later."

"You just sit down and let me make the tea, Mom," said Ellie. "You've been on your feet much of the day. "

"Bless you, Ellie! That does sound good."

When they were seated, drinking their tea, Sarah leaned forward. "Ellie, tell me how it's really going. We don't get to see you as often as we'd like. Don't just tell me what you think others may want to hear. I want to know how it really is—that is, if you care to tell me."

"Thank you, Mom. It's so nice to know someone wants to hear how it really is. I have often found when people ask they seem to expect me to say 'Oh, it's going well,' or some such innocuous thing. I'm not sure if they could handle it if I would tell them how lonely it really feels and how much I miss my husband's presence, even after more than a year. They would probably turn away in embarrassment if I told them that something as small as an unexpected smell or sight of something we enjoyed together can make the tears flow all over again—even if I think I have been totally drained of tears. But that does happen."

"I know, Ellie!" Sarah said as she reached out to pat Ellie's hand. "I came across a lock of John's baby hair in my drawer just last week, and the sight of it had me crying as though he had just died yesterday. Your babies shouldn't die before you do!"

"No, Mom, they shouldn't. We both grieve for John, but even I can't understand what it would be like to raise a child and then lose him in the prime of life."

They sat sipping their tea for a while, then Ellie continued. "I think our move to town has been good for all of us. Jake often comes to do things with George...well with all of us, but George, especially, needs that male influence—then again, maybe not more than the girls. They need it as well. My job has been good for me. It gives some definition to my days and keeps me busy enough and thinking of other things. It has also helped us out financially. I have been blessed in many ways."

"Ellie, if you ever need any help financially, please do tell us. We don't have a lot, but more than enough for the two of us, and we would be glad to share."

"Thanks, Mom. I really do appreciate that, however things are going well if nothing unforeseen happens."

"Ellie," began Sarah hesitantly, "Ellie, I don't know how to say this, and perhaps you may think it's none of my business—but have you ever thought of getting married again? You are young yet and could have some good years with someone else. Now, you don't have to answer that. I just wanted to let you know that we would support you if you did. You will always be a part of our family and we would welcome any new husband you would choose."

"Mother, that is very kind of you," said Ellie, with tears in her eyes. Through the tears, her eyes began to sparkle. "I have already declined one opportunity!"

"You have?"

"Do you know anything about Gordon McLean who lives the next road over from our farm?"

"Isn't he that dirty old bachelor who lives alone since his mother died?"

"He's the one! Last March he came calling and offered to help me out with 'the farm and such.' Thought 'mebbe we could get us married!' Poor man! I really think it took a lot of courage for him to do it. However, I declined. I told him I didn't think I was quite ready for that step. I wasn't sure if he felt defeated or delighted that I refused. I decided right then and there that there might be worse things than staying a widow."

Sarah chuckled as Abe came in from the barn.

"What's so funny?" he asked. Sarah repeated what Ellie had told her.

"I think you made the right decision on that one," Abe laughed. "By what I hear it could be a lifetime job to get that house cleaned out, not taking into account getting him cleaned up first. I think you could do better than that!"

As Ellie drifted off to sleep that night, she thought about the conversation with her in-laws. They had always been a very accepting, warm family, and she had no doubt that she would continue to be a part of the family no matter what, but it was nice to hear them not only voice it, but to actually desire a new life partner for her. Being with them always made her feel closer to John. It still hurt that John wasn't a part of those family gatherings, but the paradox was in how the comfort now outweighed the hurt.

Chapter Nineteen

The trip home went quickly, for the children had much to talk about. The day was warm enough that talking was possible. Even Maria was talkative as she told them how she and Heidi had compared their experiences in Continuation School. Heidi was in another school district and traveled by horse and sleigh or wagon three miles back and forth each day. In the winter, when it stormed, she would stay over in town with Isaac and Emma. Jake asked her, "Did you also compare the boys at your schools?"

"Jake!" Maria protested, even while her cheeks turned red.

"Don't worry," Jake laughed quietly, "I had enough sisters to know that, at fifteen, that topic must have been one that you discussed—but I won't ask you any specifics!"

What a nice day for January, Ellie thought. To have two such nice days in a row was out of the ordinary for this winter. They passed a farm pond where there was a whole group of children skating.

"That looks like a lot of fun! It's a long time since I was on skates. We had two pair in our family, so we had to take turns. We did most of our skating on the flats at the Turner farm across the road. Some winters there was good ice and some winters went by without any. Did you skate, Jake?"

"Yes. We, too, had to share, but we had the pond on the Wright farm down the road, so we skated quite frequently. After I moved into Malden I got a pair for myself because they have a rink there. Of course, that depends on the winter. The men of the town take turns to flood it. They use the Fire Brigade water tank to do it. Some evenings they have adult skating. Maybe we should get you a pair and we could go skating together."

"Oh, I don't know how good I would be at it any more. I would hate to break a leg or something."

"With my strong arm to lean on? Come on, now! I hope you trust me more than that!" Jake protested.

"Lottie thinks it would be great to go to a school just a few town blocks from where you live," Marta interjected, "and to have a room with only a few classes rather than eight different grades. I hope they can come and visit us sometime. I would like to show her our house and our school."

"Maybe we could invite them sometime in the summer when the days are longer," Ellie suggested. "Look up ahead on that hill there. See the sleds coming down?"

"Hey! Maybe we can try out our sled when we get home!" In his excitement, George almost jumped out of his seat.

"Whoa there, little man!" Jake cautioned, "We have to get home first! With this bit of melting, if we get a good freeze, it should make good sledding conditions and I will make good on my promise to take you."

"Goody, goody! I can hardly wait!"

Jake did as he said. Through the night the temperatures plummeted. The very next afternoon, Jake quit work early and was at the door clad for sledding. "How many takers have we got?" he asked.

"I'm going!" chimed George and Marta at once.

"What about you two?" Jake asked, looking at Ellie and Maria.

"If it wasn't quite so cold, I would come and watch, but I won't be taking any rides down the hill!" Ellie told him.

"Would it help if I dared you to go?"

"I really have no suitable attire for sledding, so no, it wouldn't help a bit!" she laughed.

"Maybe I'll go and watch," Maria decided.

"Make sure you dress warmly," her mother admonished.

It took time to get everyone bundled up, but finally they left in a merry frame of mind. Ellie settled down at the table to make use of the time to catch up on some letter writing.

Some hot cocoa and warm cinnamon biscuits would taste good after an outing in the cold weather, she decided. She laid her letter aside and went to the kitchen. The biscuits were just coming out of the oven when she heard merry laughter as the returnees were sweeping the snow from each other on the back verandah.

"Good timing!" she thought. She went to open the door. "Boots on this rug, please, and I'll lay the wet mitts on the oven door. You must have had some spills! Even your coats are covered with snow!"

"We even got Maria to take a few rides!" George gloated. "You should have heard her scream when she thought she was going over the creek bank!"

"George! You don't have to tell everything, you know!" his sister protested. "It was sort of fun, though," she admitted.

Jake, stripped of his snowy garments, elbowed George. "Do you smell something?" he asked. He began to lick his lips and roll his eyes.

"Mama! We have to feed this hungry dog!" George laughed.

"It just happens that I have some fresh cinnamon biscuits. Do you think that is what he smells?"

"I think so! Can we all have some?"

"That is why I made them. After fresh air like that, I thought hot cocoa and fresh biscuits might taste good."

The way those items disappeared proved Ellie quite right.

It was just two weeks later one Saturday night that Jake came, bearing a pair of ice skates to clip onto Ellie's boots.

"Be prepared, fair lady, we are going skating tonight! Maria, you will look after Marta and George for a few hours, won't you? If you do, I will take you next Saturday night."

"Oh Jake!" Ellie feebly protested, "What if I make a fool of myself?"

"Thou shalt in no wise make a fool of thyself so long as thou hast me to lean on!" Jake intoned as though he were quoting directly from scripture.

Everyone laughed.

"Go on, Mama! You'll have fun!" the children encouraged her.

At the rink, Jake knelt to fasten her skates to her boots. With that done he sat on the bench and put on his own.

"Now, lady, until you get your feet under you and gain some confidence, let's cross hands like this. It will make you feel more sure of yourself."

He started off slowly. His arm was so solid she felt perfectly safe. It wasn't long until she was gliding along with considerable grace.

"Now, let me put my arm under yours and hold your hand."

What a lovely feeling it was, gliding along with synchronized strokes. Jake was so sure and steady, it was not difficult to keep in rhythm. Oh, to go through life with that same feeling of togetherness! Arm in arm with Jake, she felt a strong desire stirring within her. The evening passed all too quickly. As they left the rink, Jake took her arm again.

"The sidewalk is slippery in some places. It would be too bad to have an evening of skating, then to fall and break your leg on the way home!"

"It was a lovely evening. I really enjoyed skating, even if it has been a long time. You make a very good skating partner."

"Why, thank you, madam!" Jake said, with exaggerated politeness, "You were a fine partner, yourself, and probably didn't need my instruction as much as I thought!"

"Oh yes, I did! I would have fallen flat on my face if you had not helped me get the feel of it!"

"I've promised to take Maria next week, but if the weather holds, perhaps we can do it again!"

"I would like that, Jake."

The weather did hold and Jake and Ellie repeated it not once, but three times by the second week of February. Each evening left Ellie with both deep satisfaction and an equally deep longing. Jake, it seemed to Ellie, enjoyed the time for the activity alone rather than the togetherness. He made no comment or suggestion otherwise, so life went on in the routine that had been established in the past months.

1898

It was the night before St. Valentine's Day the following year. Ellie was helping Marta and George finish the cards they were making for their school friends. Jake had been there for supper and now sat discussing some of Maria's lessons with her. Usually he went home before this time, but he seemed to be enjoying the history project on which Maria was working. He kept questioning her and drawing observations from her. Gently, he would probe some of her reasoning until she would either understand a different viewpoint or state hers with more clarity.

Looking at the clock, Ellie said, "It's past bedtime for all school children. Close up everything now, and off you go."

"Aren't you going to tuck me in and hear my prayers?" George asked.

Ellie looked at Jake, but he had picked up Maria's textbook and was reading it.

"All right, I will. I'll just put this paper away and I'll be right up."

Still Jake read on. Ellie followed the children upstairs and did the usual bedtime routine. When she came back downstairs, Jake looked up.

"All tucked in and ready to sleep for the night?"

"Yes. Bedtime doesn't take as long as it used to, but George still wants to be tucked in. Even the girls like to share a few words about their day and say good-night."

She looked at him with an inquiry in her eyes.

"You have some big question marks in your eyes. I suppose you are wondering why I am still here."

"I can't hide much from you, Jake, can I?" she smiled.

"Nope! I can usually read you like a book! But right now, I want to tell you a story. Sit down here, beside me." He patted the sofa. She sat down and looked expectantly at him. What was he up to?

"Ellie, do you remember John and Regina's wedding?"

"Of course I do."

"Do you remember me from that day?"

"Not that well. All John's family and your family were there. That makes quite a few people I had never seen before. I am sorry, but I'm afraid, even though you were best man, I guess I was all caught up in the romance of my big sister getting married to John."

"Well, Ellie, there weren't so many in your family, but even if there had been, I still would remember you from that day. Now understand, I was eighteen and you were only fourteen. I remember the color of your green dress and the way you had those chestnut curls fastened up on your head. I remember the way your eyes sparkled with delight when John and Regina kissed. Do you want to know what I thought?"

Before Ellie had a chance to reply, Jake continued, "I thought, 'Now there is a lovely rosebud getting ready to bloom. That one is worth watching and waiting for!' I thought I would like to be the one to put that sparkle in your eyes by kisses of my own."

He saw the surprise in Ellie's eyes, but he hurried on.

"Trouble was, I was a little too far away to keep a close eye on you, and before I got the opportunity, I found out that you were seeing Gerhard. I was upset with Gerhard for taking you away, but then when you broke your engagement and married John, what was I to do? He was my favorite big cousin and he had gone through so much. Remember, when I was helping with the wood that fall, how you teased me about being afraid to ask someone?" Ellie's eyes reflected immediate sympathy and alarm. "I understood you had no way of knowing, but oh, that hurt!"

"Oh Jake!" Ellie put her hand on his arm.

"I saw the love growing between you and John, and I was happy for you. I tried to find someone else, but somehow I kept comparing each woman to you and all my trying was in vain. I had decided that bachelorhood was the life to which I was destined. I, too, grieved when John died. He was a special cousin who felt, in many ways, more like a brother. However, I thought this time I was going to watch you very closely."

He reached out for her hand.

"I hope I haven't made a nuisance of myself. I know it still isn't two-and-a-half years since John died, but I couldn't wait any longer to let you know how I feel. Ellie, I have loved you for a very long time. Spending time with you and your family has only increased my love for you. Your children have always been special to me. Sharing meals and special times, your warmth and acceptance of me, inclusion in so many of your family activities—all of these things have made me feel so close to you. You don't need to answer right away if you want time to think about it, but I do want to marry you, if you will have me. Ellie—dear Ellie, do you think you can love me?"

Ellie couldn't believe the emotions she experienced as she listened to Jake's story. As he went on, she realized anew how comfortable their relationship had become. She knew she already loved him in many ways. When he asked his last question, she put a hand on each side of his face and looked up into his eyes.

"Jake, if you can read me like a book, look and see if you can read my answer."

"My darling Ellie! Is it yes? Oh, it is! But let me hear you say it!"

"Yes, Jake. Yes, yes! A few times I wondered if you had feelings for me— before I was really ready to hear it. But you hid it so well. I thought perhaps I had just imagined it. I had begun to think that it was just the companionship and the children you enjoyed. Since last Christmas, I often found myself wishing it could be more. Now that I know I can let myself go, I will be delighted to explore these feelings. I already do love you, Jake."

Jakes arms were around her and he held her as though he would never let her go. Finally, he released her enough to find her lips in a long, lingering kiss. She was surprised to see his eyes filled with tears.

"Oh Ellie, sometimes I thought this day would never come."

For a long while they just sat, reveling in their happiness.

"Do you think we need to wait for awhile yet?" Jake asked.

"Jake, remember to whom you are talking. I'm not exactly one who stands firm on conventional waiting periods! I married John after only six months. I can't see why we should wait any longer. Why don't we plan for May?"

"Do you mean that? Even three months will seem like a lo-ong time. I don't know if I can wait, but it's a lot better than September!"

Ellie's eyes sparkled, "Well, perhaps we could manage April!"

"Oh Ellie! You precious woman! You are anxious to get married too. Could I mention March, or is that pressing my luck?" he asked, with mischief in his eyes.

"First week in April! Take it or leave it," she laughed.

"No way I'm going to leave it! Sweetheart, you have made me a happy man."

Jake drew her closer again and gave her another lingering kiss.

"How often in the past two years have I wanted to do this? It was so hard, darling, to watch you suffer and go through those difficulties and not be able to take you in my arms to comfort you."

He looked deep into her eyes.

"Do I read a responding happiness in those eyes, my darling?"

"That you do, my dear Jake."

She drew his head down to give him another kiss.

"You must understand that there is part of me that will always love John and cherish the memories of him, but just as love expands to include each child that arrives, there is plenty of room in my heart to love you. I know John would approve of this."

"Oh Ellie, I would never want you to forget what you had with John. Just as I can in no way replace John. I expect our love to be a whole new relationship."

He held her as they sat in silence, enjoying the peace and joy their love brought. "Do you think the children will approve? When do you think we should tell them?"

"I have no doubt they will approve. George already looks to you as a father figure, and the girls have loved you since they were very small. I think they will be very happy to have you here all the time."

"So when do we tell them?"

"Why don't you come for supper Friday night? After supper we can tell them."

Jake was uncharacteristically quiet for a time.

"You know, Ellie, how much I have enjoyed those children since they were born. The prospect of parenting them almost overwhelms me with joy, even if I will only be a step-father."

"Jake, technically I'm only a step-mother to Maria and Marta, but it doesn't feel that way. All three are equally my children. Now they will be yours too. Parenting is much more than procreation. You've already been parenting them this past year and more. Our marriage will only make it official."

It was late when Jake finally tore himself away from Ellie to go to his own house.

"I'm glad I can see an end to this before long," he remarked with heartiness. "In less than two months, we can go upstairs together rather than me leaving for my lonely abode."

"And my bed will be lonely no more!" was her glad reply. "Goodnight, my love—my sweet valentine!"

"And a goodnight to you, sweetheart!"

Ellie watched as he walked down the moonlit path to the street and until she could see him no more. Slowly, she ascended the steps and went to her room. She set the lamp on the table and undressed. Pulling a robe around her, she sat on the chair beside the window. She blew out the lamp and sat in her room, glowing with moonlight, marveling at the change in her life.

"Dear Heavenly Father, you have blessed me again with the love of another good man. This time, I do not need to learn to love him, for I love him already. All that is left is to discover more ways to love him—more things to love about him. Father, I commit myself again to you, and ask your blessings on Jake and me and the children as we learn to be a family. In your dear Son's name I ask these blessings, Amen."

The room was cool, and she shivered in spite of the warmth in her heart. She dropped the robe on the chair and hurried into the warmth of her bed. For so long, she had yearned for John to be there with her. Now she could begin to anticipate having Jake to share that space. Her heart leapt at the thought. She fell asleep with a smile on her face.

Chapter Twenty

Supper on Friday night was a merry affair. Jake was in rare form as he joked with the children and teased them throughout the meal. Occasionally, amid the laughter, his eyes would meet Ellie's and the love in his eyes would beam into hers. His happiness in their new relationship was evident in their shining depths. As they finished their dessert, he told another joke, at which the children giggled. Jake looked at Ellie with a question in his eyes. She did not need to ask what it was; she just nodded in the affirmative.

"What do you children think I should do with a little bachelor house I no longer need? Should I sell it or rent it out?"

Three pairs of eyes were rapt in their attention. They looked as if they didn't know if this was the beginning of another joke or if he was serious. Finally, Maria asked, "What are you going to do—move into your office or build a bigger house?"

"Nothing like that! I thought, since I'm here so much, I may as well move in here. Your mother said it was all right. What do you think?"

More confusion was mirrored in their eyes. They looked at their mother, then back at Jake, and once more at their mother.

"You had better tell them the rest, Jake."

"Oh! Maybe I had!" Jake chuckled. "Actually, I asked your mother if she would marry me. She said she would. We have had some good times together in the last few years or so and I love you all dearly. I think we could make a charming, happy family. Don't you?"

Marta was the first one to answer.

"Oh Mama— Jake! I think that would be nice."

George stirred from his shock.

"All right!" he exclaimed, jumping out of his chair and onto Jake's lap. He thrust his arms around his neck. "It will be nice to have a papa again!"

Jake hugged George and tousled his hair, but his eyes went to Maria's face.

"I will try my best, George, but I want you always to remember your own papa as well."

Still his eyes questioned Maria.

Maria got off her chair and walked over to where Jake sat. She put her hand on his shoulder.

"Jake, if anyone is to take Papa's place, I am glad it is you. You have always been a special person to me ever since I can remember." She kissed the top of his head. "You are probably the best horse I have ever ridden," she added, with uncharacteristic humor.

Jake threw his head back with laughter.

"Now that is the kind of recommendation I like!" he chuckled. "So, I take it we have your blessing?"

He looked from one to the other of the children.

"Oh yes!" they chorused.

"Are you getting married tomorrow?" George asked.

"No, not quite," Ellie answered. "We thought the first week of April."

"Why not tomorrow?" asked George. "I'd like to have Jake here right away! Why do we have to wait until April?"

Jake looked at Ellie. She could see that Jake would have liked to agree with George. In fact, so would she in some ways.

"Well, George," Ellie began, "I'm sure glad that you like the idea. I can understand that you are in a hurry, but we will want to make some plans and that takes a little time. We'll have fun doing that together. Before we know it, April will be here."

Ellie rose to begin clearing the table.

"Perhaps you and the girls would like to think of ways we can celebrate such a special day. Do you think we could have the wedding here in our very own parlor? I'm sure your grandparents would like to be here too, as well as Uncle Henry and Aunt Sarah. See, there are a lot of things to think about."

"We'll all need new dresses too, won't we, Mama?" Marta asked.

Jake put one arm around Ellie and one around Marta. He winked at Maria.

"New dresses, indeed! My girls will be decked out in their finest for that day. I would have it no other way. And George, my little man, I think we fellows should have new suits as well, don't you? We're not going to let the women outshine us by too much, are we?"

All hands were on deck to help with the dishes, for everyone wanted to be in on the discussion of wedding plans. When bedtime came the children were reluctant to leave the excitement of the evening. However, they were eventually settled upstairs. Jake, with shining eyes, took Ellie in his arms.

"Phew! I think I agree with George! Why not get married tomorrow? I don't want to wait either!"

He nuzzled her neck then kissed her full on the lips.

"Ellie, I really can hardly wait! But oh, what a family I will have. Your children are so precious! There didn't seem to be any reservations for any of them."

He paused and looked deep into her eyes.

"Much as I love them, their mother is the greatest gem! My dear, dear rosebud!"

The tenderness and longing in Jake's voice made Ellie's heart swell with love.

"Jake, my darling, I am almost overwhelmed at the love I hear in your voice. To think that I had been persuaded that you enjoyed us just for the company and that you were probably not a man committed to family life."

"Oh Ellie, nothing could be further from the truth. I just had to keep it to myself until now."

"I'm glad I was wrong!" Ellie laid her head on his shoulder and held him close to her. "I can still hardly believe my good fortune." She raised her head. "Kiss me again, Jake!"

"With pleasure!"

Jake acted on her request, to her satisfaction.

"Maybe you'd better go now, before I move the wedding date closer. We wouldn't want to take away the excitement of the children's new clothes!" Ellie teased, while gently pushing him away.

Jake went into his hungry hound dog mode, eyes rolling, his tongue rapidly flicking in and out. He reached out for her with an exaggerated, lecherous look on his face.

"Out with you!" Ellie laughed. "Go home, boy!"

Jake didn't need a tail between his legs to add to his look of dejection as he went whimpering, with slow steps and shoulders sagging, to the front door.

"Oh Jake! You joker! I'll see you Sunday in church, if not before."

He turned, with a smile and a wink, to blow her a kiss before he closed the door.

The smile lingered on Ellie's face even as the warmth in her heart continued while she blew out the lamps and went up the stairs to her room. She set the lamp on the little table in the window and sat on the chair. She picked up the picture of her and John. *I think you would be as pleased as I am at this turn of events, my beloved. You gave so much to me and helped me grow and mature. Jake is so different in many ways, but he is giving me what I need at this time in my life. I know you liked him too—that is one reason I know you would approve.*

Slowly, she set the picture on the table once more and bowed her head. "Lord God, I thank you for your goodness and grace. Thank you for the gift of Jake and his love. Thank you for the happiness and contentment that fills my heart as I anticipate life with him. Help us always to keep our life and our love centered in you."

She rose to undress and slipped between the covers. The memory of the desire in Jake's eyes washed over her. Ellie's own desire rose in response. The coming six weeks, she realized, could not go fast enough for her, either. With a contented sigh, she turned to her side and drifted off to sleep.

Her heart was still light when she rose to face a busy day. There was the usual washing and cleaning to be done. As the family joined around the breakfast table, it was hard to know whose excitement was at the highest level. George was full of plans for what he and Jake could do when they were living in the same house all the time. The girls were mostly caught up in wedding plans. They began by making suggestions as to what kind of dress their mother should wear, then planned what color it should be. They thought they should choose colors for their own outfits that would blend well with their mother's.

As they went about their work, the conversation continued, with ideas being presented and thrown out as fast as new ones came. Ellie thought about how Jake had remembered the color of her dress for Regina and John's wedding.

"What do you think of a soft apple green for my dress?" Ellie asked. "April is the harbinger of spring and that would be a nice spring-like color. Maria, with her dark hair and fair complexion, would look nice in a soft rose, and perhaps you, Marta, would look nice in a darker shade of the same green as mine. Your chestnut hair would look good in that color. Of course, we will have to see what is available."

"Do you think we could make mine and Marta's with a placket down the front? Marta's could be edged in rose stitching and mine in green. That way it would really tie them together," Maria suggested. "Jake and George could have green ties."

"Mama, could we get new shoes too? I would like to have patent leather ones!" Marta interjected.

"We'll have to see," Ellie cautioned. "It will cost quite a sum for us all to get new dresses, and then we may want to decorate the parlor a bit. If we could bring in some forsythia and pussy willow branches, we could force the blooms. That could add a bit of color to go with our ferns and begonias."

"We should get some of those tissue paper bells that fold out, and hang them over the bay window with some crepe paper streamers!" Marta enthused. "You and Jake could stand under the bells when Pastor Schwartz marries you! Those should be pink, to go with Maria's dress and spring, and maybe we could get some pink flowers for you to carry. Mrs. Mayer lets you order flowers for the hotel. Maybe she would allow you to order some through their suppliers for the wedding."

"What a great idea, Marta!" commented Maria. "Mama, if you would get married in the morning, maybe we could all go to the hotel for lunch. I know it is usually you who does the supervising for banquets at the hotel, but the girls are quite used to what you do by now. They could handle it for once, especially if you have it all planned out before. There would be only twelve to fifteen people."

Ellie smiled. "You girls are going to have it all planned before the day is through. I could see what the Mayers think about having the luncheon at the hotel."

It was after lunch already when Maria asked, "Are you going to have a wedding cake, Mama? It should be made soon, shouldn't it? You always say a fruit cake should have at least six weeks to ripen."

"You are right! Maybe I should go and get the things this afternoon yet."

"Why don't you go right now?" Marta asked. "The washing is done and we can finish the cleaning while you are gone. We could all work together to cut the fruit and everything. We can do the ironing and other things while it bakes. We may have to stay up a little later to get it out of the oven, but then it would be done. It would be hard to get it baked before next Saturday otherwise, with you having to be at work."

"Are you sure, girls?"

"Yes!" they chimed. "Take George with you to help carry the parcels back," Marie added.

Ellie got out her recipe book to make a list, then picked up her grocery basket and called for George.

"We should be back in an hour."

"You don't need to hurry! We'll be finished with the cleaning before you get back."

The day was pleasant for February. The snow from last week's storm had settled and the sun was warm enough that the snow was melting in spots. George chattered away and Ellie listened in gratitude for his happy spirit and natural curiosity. It was interesting to observe the things that caught his attention. For a moment he was quiet, and Ellie's mind went to organizing the baking of the cake.

"Mama!" George's insistent voice penetrated her hearing.

"Yes, George?"

"Didn't you hear what I said?"

"I'm sorry, George. I guess I was off thinking other things. What did you say?"

"I asked if you remembered the time I came to Malden with Papa when he needed to get some parts for the plough."

"I can't say as I do. What do you remember about that?

"I thought it was a long way from home. When I saw some children playing in front of one of the houses, I wondered what it would be like to live in town. I felt sorry for them because they didn't have any fields around them or fencerows to explore and hunt for birds and rabbits and things. I never thought I would live in town."

"Do you still feel sorry for children who live in town?"

"No! It's fun to have other children nearby. It's a lot easier to get together with other boys to play ball and stuff. And Jake's been a lot closer. We get to see him a lot more. It would be different if Papa were still here. Then I would like to be with him and help him on the farm. But now, if Jake is going to be my dad, we can do his kind of stuff and I'll still like living in town. I do like to go back to the farm sometimes, though. I like walking back to the bush and along the river, and I'd like to go fishing and maybe swimming in the river. Jake will take us out there sometimes, though, won't he?"

"I'm sure he will. He's already taken us out there several times, and he likes doing things with you children. Of course, the girls will soon want to do more with their friends—more grown up things, but they will always like walking back to the bush on the farm."

What a difference in children! Ellie thought. She was sure that George loved his papa just as much as Maria had loved her mama. Although George wasn't much different in age than Maria had been with her first loss, he was much more expressive of his grief and much more accepting of the change. Even his fear of death seemed to have faded into the background. His inborn enthusiasm for life wouldn't be squelched, even with the death of his papa. He seemed to embrace the thought of having Jake as his new dad. The girls, older now, seemed well adjusted and happy for the change too.

When George and Ellie got back home with their purchases, not only was the cleaning finished, but the table was ready with the big baking board, mixing bowl and spoon. Three knives lay ready to chop the fruit. The clothes that needed ironing had been brought off the line and were rolled in the basket to keep them damp.

"My, you girls have been busy! I see everything is ready to go," Ellie complimented them as she shed her coat and hat.

She reached for her apron. "Let's get started. George, you get the Christmas cake pans from the bottom cupboard, and Marta, maybe you can help him line them with a few layers of brown paper and then grease them well."

Everyone was assigned to his or her respective tasks, and before long the cake was mixed and ready for the oven. Maria and Marta offered to make supper and do up the dishes if Ellie wanted to do the ironing. By the time they finished supper, the spicy aroma of the cake was beginning to fill the house. Ellie opened the oven door a crack to check how it was progressing.

"It's coming along nicely, but I think it needs another hour or so."

"It smells good!" George commented. "I wish we could eat some right away!"

"Fruit cake is not nearly as good right away as it is when it has had a chance to ripen," Ellie told him. "We'll wrap it in rum-soaked cloths and put it in the big cookie tins and store them in the cellar-way. The week before the wedding I will need to make almond paste to cover them, and then I'll put the icing on just before the wedding day."

The work was done and everyone bathed by the time the cake was ready. Even George didn't want to go to bed before it was done. The tops were nicely browned. The bits of fruits made little bumps on top and the smell was tempting indeed. They were duly admired before Ellie covered them with clean tea towels.

"They will have to cool overnight. On Monday morning I will wrap them and put them in the tins. Now it's bedtime. We have had a big day and we've done a lot of work. I am so proud of my children and how responsible they are. What a big help you all are to me!"

"It was fun for us today too!" Maria remarked. "It will be nice to have Jake here, so it's fun to work toward the wedding. I know, from what you have told me, when you and Papa got married it was a rather quiet celebration because of Mama having died just before. I hope your wedding to Jake can be a bigger celebration. I know that if I ever get married, I want to have a nice celebration!"

"Why, Maria! How kind of you to think of it! I never minded that our wedding had to be a quiet affair, for your Papa was such a kind and loving man. He made me feel special from the beginning. I guess every girl dreams of her wedding day. When your day comes, we will do everything we can to make it special. It's the loving and growing together after the wedding that makes it most special, though, and that's something from which your papa and I weren't deprived. Let's all go upstairs and we'll have a prayer in George's room before we go to bed.

After the prayer she kissed George and tucked him in. "I am so glad for my son," she told him. "I love you so much. Have a good night's sleep!"

The girls had reached the hall when she caught up to them. "I know you are too old to be tucked in, but I want to give you each a hug before you go to bed. No woman could ask for better daughters. Thank you so much for all your hard work and your love too!" As she embraced them she whispered, "I love you Marta!" then, "I love you, Maria!"

"Good-night, Mama. We love you too!"

Chapter Twenty-One

The next weeks were busy ones. One afternoon, after school, the girls and Ellie went to the dry goods store to choose fabric for their dresses. Ellie found the perfect shade of green in a medium weight silk. She chose some very fine lightweight lace material in a light ecru. She thought the silk could act as a lining for the upper part of the dress. If she placed the scalloped edge of the lace toward the center, the silk could be exposed down the middle, with a placket and small fabric-covered or pearl buttons. She would make long full sleeves with wide cuffs, closed with the same small buttons. The high, standup collar could be edged in lace. The skirt would be silk alone, with only the bottom edged in ecru lace. A wide belt with a covered buckle at the back would finish it off with an interesting touch.

The girls were able to find the fabric they wanted as well. They found silk thread for the topstitching and small iridescent buttons that picked up the colors of both their dresses. She also got fabric for Tina, who would be her witness. It was in a deeper shade of green.

When Jake stopped in that evening, he asked how the day went. The girls were all excited about their purchases.

"Are you going to show them to me?" he asked.

"We'll show you our fabric, but you can't see Mama's until the wedding day!" they told him.

"And why is that?" he asked.

"Don't you know it's bad luck for the groom to see the wedding dress before the big day?" Maria asked.

"And even if it wasn't, it should be a surprise!" added Marta. "You'll like it, though. Mama is going to look absolutely beautiful in it!"

"Of that, I have no doubt." Jake granted.

When Tina heard about the wedding plans, she offered to help with the sewing. Ellie knew Tina was an excellent seamstress, so she gladly accepted her offer. In fact, many others offered their help. Everyone seemed happy for Jake and Ellie.

When she approached Mr. and Mrs. Mayer about having the wedding dinner at the hotel, they insisted on giving that to Ellie and Jake as a wedding gift. When Jake came for lunch that day he was congratulated by both Mr. and Mrs. Mayer. The offer was repeated, and Ellie and Jake consented with thanks.

Before Ellie left that afternoon, Mr. Mayer called her into the office. In his usual straightforward manner, he asked, "Your marriage plans probably mean you will be leaving our employ?"

Startled, Ellie replied, "Mr. Mayer, I hadn't given it any thought. I thoroughly enjoy my job and would like to continue. I will discuss it with Jake. If it is all right with him, I will stay on."

Mr. Mayer looked relieved. "That would please Mrs. Mayer and me. You have certainly been a great help to us and have done your work well. We would find it difficult to find a good replacement."

That is quite a speech, coming from you, Mr. Mayer! Ellie thought. With a gracious smile, she only replied, "Why thanks, Mr. Mayer."

When Ellie saw Jake next, she told him about Mr. Mayer's assumption.

"Well, of course you can quit," Jake assured her.

"But Jake, I don't want to quit. I really enjoy my job and have found a lot of satisfaction in it. Do you mind if I keep on working? We have adapted to the schedule and I can't see that having you in the house is going to make that much more work—unless you are extremely messy!"

Jake reached to take her in his arms. "Are you sure that is what you want, Ellie?"

"Oh yes! My work hours aren't that long, and I still have lots of time for my flower beds and garden in the summer and sewing and other things in the winter. I enjoy keeping things running smoothly at the hotel and the challenge of arranging meals for groups. I think I would miss it greatly if I quit."

"Far be it from me to deny my lady love something that brings her joy. I want to add joy to your life, not take it away." Jake paused, "I just don't want anyone thinking that you have to work, or that I'm not willing to provide for you."

"Oh Jake! We can't control what other people think. I know most of the married women around here don't work outside their homes unless they really have to. Some will maybe say things like that, but we know that is not so. That's what really matters! Maybe some of those people are just jealous!"

"Then, my dear one, you can tell Mr. Mayer you will continue. If I continue to get my noon meals there, at least they will be graced with your presence!"

"I'll be glad to have my meals with you there if Mr. Mayer agrees to that. I can't see why he wouldn't, for I eat there anyway, and it may as well be with you. I ate in the kitchen before, but I am sure he will allow me to eat in the dining room with you."

"Make it a condition of employment!" Jake suggested, with a grin. "And tell him if he doesn't allow it you will have to quit and feed me at home. That way he would not only lose a valued employee but a faithful customer as well!"

"I'm sure that would do it!" Ellie retorted with a smile. "Who else eats there as often as you have in the past?" She looked into his eyes. "Seriously though, thanks, Jake, for understanding how important this is to me. It's just that I have found the job so fulfilling, and I don't think it will interfere at all with our marriage." She reached up to give him a kiss.

"I want what makes you happy, my love!" Jake kissed her in return. "But be forewarned! I will claim some of your time! I have years for which to make up, and I intend on doing just that. In fact, Mr. Mayer may have to give you a day off now and then—if I see my way clear, and the spirit so moves—to run off with my beautiful wife for a picnic or a frolic or an overnight at a hotel in some romantic spot!"

"Ooh! That sounds absolutely terrific! I hope the spirit moves easily and frequently!"

"Oh Ellie!" Jake held her close. "We haven't talked about after the wedding. Can we take the train to Niagara Falls and stay for a few days? Maria should be able to manage the other two, shouldn't she?"

"I'm sure that Mama and Papa would stay with them if they would rather. It would be nice to have a few days to ourselves."

"Then I will make some reservations. You talk it over with Maria and Marta and your folks, if that's what the children want. We're getting married on Wednesday. We could stay in Strafford the first night and go on to Niagara Falls the next day. We could make the return trip on Tuesday. That way your parents could go home Tuesday morning and we would be back before the children were home from school. I'll make reservations at a hotel. I will also make an appointment with a photographer to have pictures taken Thursday morning before we leave Strafford."

He paused. "March can't go too fast for me, Ellie! I know I told you that we could wait until fall if we needed to, but after all those years that I thought my dream was gone, now that it is coming to pass, I don't want to wait. Knowing you want it, too, fills me with delight!"

"Our time of waiting is almost half gone, Jake. Tina was in last night for dress fittings. Even though they aren't finished, it made me anxious to be walking down the staircase to meet you in the parlor. The day can't come too soon for me either, sweetheart."

She leaned her head on his shoulder. "By the way, I received postcards from both your parents and John's, saying they would come to the wedding. I think John's parents are as happy as anyone else about our wedding. They told me over a year ago that they would be glad if I found someone else to share my life. It probably doesn't hurt that you are so close to the family."

"Uncle Abe's family and ours, in some ways, were almost more like one family than two, because we lived so close and worked with each other so much. I know they rejoice for both of us."

March went out like a lion that year. The afternoon of the thirtieth the wind moved around to the northwest, and before nightfall, snow came whipping in on strong gusts of wind, making it difficult to see even across the street. By morning there were great snowdrifts across the front sidewalk and the streets. Ellie's heart sank. Only six days until the wedding. She had counted on it being at least a little spring-like. How were Jake's and John's parents going to be able to make it into Malden?

"Father, you are in control of our plans and of the universe. Help me to keep my trust in you. Most important are the vows Jake and I want to make before you. Help me to keep things in perspective."

Later that morning Jake came around to see if they needed any shoveling done. He knocked at the door and opened it without waiting for anyone.

"Any frozen wedding plans need thawing out?" he asked.

"Oh Jake! Who would have thought of getting such a snow storm this late in March?" Ellie commented as she came to kiss Jakes cold cheeks. "You maybe need some thawing yourself! I was really upset this morning at first, but then I thought as long as Pastor Schwartz and you can get here, we will have the most important ingredients for the wedding!"

"Now that's the spirit!" Jake agreed.

"We'll be here as witnesses!" Maria added. "But maybe we'll get a real thaw and all will be well before next Wednesday."

As it turned out, Maria was right. Saturday morning the sun was shining, and as the mercury climbed throughout the day, the snowdrifts trickled away and shrank in size. The days kept up their warmth, and by Monday, one could hardly believe the snowstorm had ever existed. The forsythia blooms and pussy willows in the living room were bursting on their branches as if in reassurance to Ellie.

On Tuesday, as she put the final icing on the two-tiered cake, Ellie paused occasionally to look at the beauty they had created in the parlor. It did look very spring-like. Marta and Maria had done a splendid job of putting up bells and streamers in a very tasteful manner. The ferns and flower branches in the bay window and immediately to the right and left made a nice "altar" at which they could stand. Marta had covered one of the parlor tables with a lace tablecloth, on which the marriage license could be signed. Mayers' had ordered flowers enough for her to carry some pink rosebuds and fern and have one for the bud vase on the table. These extras were not necessary to make a good marriage, but she found enjoyment in the planning, especially since the girls were getting such satisfaction and pleasure out of it as well. Ellie gave one last glance before going to add the finishing touches to the cake. Jake was going to take it over to the hotel yet tonight so that it would be there for tomorrow's dinner.

While she worked she thought of the dresses hanging in the closet upstairs. She was pleased with the outcome of hers, and the girls had been ecstatic at the sight of Tina's efforts on their own. Tina had added some extra little touches that made them look very professionally done. Jake had taken them all to the shoe store last week to get new shoes. He and George had made a trip on their own to get suits, but they all went to the shoe store together. Jake had teased the girls, asking if it was all right for the groom to see the bride's shoes before the wedding. The girls thought that shoes wouldn't hurt their good fortune.

Chapter Twenty-Two

Wednesday morning, April 7, dawned bright and sunny. Ellie woke quite early and treated herself to a long bath before anyone else was up. What a luxury to have a bathtub! Her parents were coming quite early to help with any last minute things that might come up. The girls had planned that by ten-thirty they would have Ellie and Tina in her bedroom to get dressed. At ten-forty-five, Jake and his brother Levi would join George in his room to put on their suits; then they would go downstairs to join the minister and the other guests until the service was to start at eleven fifteen. John's dad, who said he'd provide some violin music to which the bride and her attendants could come down the stairs into the parlor, would begin playing at twelve minutes past eleven. She smiled as she thought how the girls had laboriously written out the schedule so everyone would know exactly when to do what.

When they gave Jake his copy, he laughed.

"Really, I am not sure that I need this. As long as I am dressed and in the parlor a bit before the lovely bride and her attendants descend the staircase, I think I will be doing fine! But I will take it up and put it on George's dresser, just in case." Then he added, with a twinkle in his eye, "You just make sure your mother is coming down those stairs at the right time, or I will have to come and carry her down. I don't want to wait one minute over time!"

"Oh Jake! You wouldn't really!" Marta remonstrated. "That would spoil the whole affair!"

"Don't tempt me, then! Get your mother coming down there right on the dot!" he had laughed.

Jake was so much fun, but Ellie realized that the joshing about his hurry was only partly in jest. He seemed to feel he had waited long enough and was anxious to be married to her. It was such a marvel to her to feel so deeply longed for, so utterly cherished. She had felt cherished by John too, as time passed, but in such a quiet, deep, abiding way and it had grown slowly. Perhaps with Jake it would become deep and abiding as well, but right now, his cherishing was much more flamboyant and urgent.

Ellie heaved a deep, contented sigh, got out of the bathtub, and toweled herself dry. She had washed her hair yesterday and Maria and Tina would help her put it up later. For now she twisted it into a bun and held it in place with hairpins. The girls were moving about in their bedroom. Apparently no urging was needed to get them on the move this morning! Ellie's heart filled with thankfulness as she contemplated the pleasure the children were experiencing in this change in their lives.

The morning sped by and it seemed like no time at all until Ellie was back in her room. She had put her dress on and was shrouded in a cotton sheet while Tina and Maria fussed with her hairdo. The two of them had long ago decided that the chestnut hair would be upswept, letting it pouf out to frame her face with elegance. The ends of the long strands would be fashioned into a pile of curls towards the back and top of her head. They had tried it out the week before, with much laughter and several attempts until it was perfected. The task went much better and more quickly this time.

"I brought a bit of baby's breath and some fine green ribbon to tuck into the curls," Tina informed Ellie. "Is it all right with you if I do that?"

"That will really be nice, Mama," Maria encouraged her.

"Sure, I trust your judgment," Ellie assured her.

A few more minutes, and Tina held a mirror behind her so she could see what the back of her head looked like in the big mirror of the dresser. "What do you think?" she asked.

"Oh, that does look pretty! You should have been a hairdresser."

"Stand up, Mama, so we can see the full effect with your dress and everything." Marta suggested.

Tina removed the sheet, and Ellie stood.

"Oo-ooh!" they all chimed.

"What a beautiful bride!" Marta said. "Wait until Jake sees you!"

Just then there was a tap at the door and Jake said, in a low voice, "We're going down. Make sure you are in time, girls, or I will carry out my threats!"

"Oh, go away, Jake! We'll be there!" Tina scolded.

"The three of you had better get dressed or you will be late," Ellie told them. "You are supposed to go down the stairs before me, and you only have fifteen minutes to go!"

Ellie watched and helped do up buttons. Tina and Marta's dresses were two different shades of the same green as Ellie's dress. The soft rose of Maria's dress added color to the spring greens. The tones were flattering to each of them.

"My attendants are lovely too. What a lucky bride I am to be surrounded with such beauty and love."

They heard the first strains of the violin from downstairs.

"I guess it's time to go."

"Don't forget your flowers, Mama!" Maria said, handing the little bouquet to her.

"All right, Marta, you go first. When you are down five steps, I will come, when I am down five steps, you start, Tina. Mama, you wait until Tina is off the bottom step, then you come."

Ellie nodded and stood at the doorway as Marta began. She looked upward and silently she said, "John, please give me your blessing. I think you would be happy for me."

Tina was beginning her descent.

"Heavenly Father, walk with us and grant us your blessing too."

Warmth seeped through her being. As she moved to the top of the steps, she knew her prayer had been heard. Her face reflected the joy she felt as she, too, began her way down the curving stairs. She first could see only Jake's trousers, with Levi and George standing beside him, but soon she caught Jake's eyes when he became visible through the door. His face beamed with pleasure; his eyes were full of love as she neared him.

Pastor Schwartz greeted those present and then announced the happy occasion for which they were gathered on this day. The scriptures he had chosen were encouraging, as were his comments on marriage in general and theirs in particular.

His inclusion of the children in his comments touched Ellie's heart, acknowledging that this was a ceremony for all of them, a time of committing to each other to become a family. He encouraged them to continue giving God a central place in their marriage and in their home.

Their "I do's" were expressed with joyful commitment; their kiss sealed the vows. They signed the register, with Levi and Tina as witnesses. When that was finished, Pastor Schwartz asked Maria, Marta and George to come and join hands so that the family stood in a circle as he offered a prayer of blessing on the new family.

"I now present to you the Kurtz family—George, Marta, Maria and their parents, Jacob and Ellie Kurtz."

Immediately, they were surrounded with the love and well wishes of their parents and family. After several minutes, Levi reminded the group that the hotel was expecting everyone to be there soon after twelve. Everyone moved to retrieve their wraps, and they began the walk to the hotel.

It was difficult to believe that a week ago there had been a blizzard raging. The sun shone, and although there were still bits of snow on the lawn, the grass looked to be greening and the birds were chirping. Other than having to dodge a few wet spots, the walk was a pleasant one and everyone was in high spirits.

"You're really going to like the dinner at the hotel, Mama!" George said, excitedly.

Maria took his hand. "Yes, they will. Mama has planned everything, George, and the Mayers will have it all ready for us."

When they arrived at Main Street, they turned the corner to the hotel. The Mayers were at the door to greet them. Mrs. Mayer, smiling broadly, offered her congratulations. Even Mr. Mayer seemed jollier than was his wont.

"Come in, come in!" he urged.

They stepped in from the front foyer. There they saw tables set up, not only in the dining area, but also in the sitting area. White tablecloths were immaculately set with the good silver and china. On each table were little vases of the same pink roses that Ellie had carried. Half of the tables were already filled with Jake's and Ellie's and John's siblings and their spouses. They shouted as one, "Surprise!"

"What?" both Ellie and Jake asked, shock, surprise and delight washing across their faces.

"Are you surprised, Mama?" asked the girls, merriment sparkling in their eyes.

George was jumping up and down. "Jake, Mama, do you like the surprise?"

"Who was it that planned this?" Jake bent down to ask George.

"Maria and Marta and Tina thought it up. They didn't tell me at first because they were afraid I would tell you, but I didn't, did I?"

"That is why you thought we were going to like our dinner, was it?" Ellie asked.

"I thought he was going to spoil the surprise at the last minute," Maria said, "That is why I quickly took his hand."

"But I didn't tell, Maria!" protested George.

"No, you didn't, George. We are both very surprised. Thank you all for coming!" Jake told the crowd before he took Ellie by the arm. "Now let me get my lovely bride seated since we are both weak-kneed and trembling at the unexpected turn of events."

There was good-natured ribbing as they made their way to the head table.

"Are you sure the trembling is from the surprise? It's probably from losing your bachelor status!" one of his brothers called out.

"Maybe he's trembling at the thought of the chivaree that we'll have for him to pay back for all the ones he's planned for others!" someone else suggested.

The happy celebration became all the merrier with the presence of the extended family. The Mayers and their staff served them a lovely meal. The cake was brought out for the bridal couple to cut, and with the extra guests, more of the two-tier cake was eaten than Ellie had anticipated.

As they drank their tea, Levi stood.

"It has been my privilege to stand beside this brother of mine today as he and Ellie took their vows. I know their train leaves in an hour or so, but I think it would be fitting, before they leave, to speak a few words. Over the years, we all wondered what Jake was waiting for. There has been many a lovely lady who tried to win him with her charms. Wherever he went, it seemed, the children found a playmate in him. They swarmed around him at family gatherings and church. But our Jake, although he enjoyed the company and attention, seemed impervious to all those charms and steered clear of any commitment. We don't know what you did, Ellie, to make him want to change his status, but seeing you in your beautiful dress and with those glowing eyes today, we may begin to understand. Whatever it was or however you did it, we'd all like to wish the two of you much happiness and God's blessings on a long life together."

Everyone clapped and whistled. "Speech, Jake! Give us a speech!" they began to call.

Jake looked at Ellie. "Will you stand with me?" he whispered in her ear.

She nodded. Jake got to his feet and helped Ellie stand. He put his arm around her.

"You all know how shy I am!" he began.

This was met with an uproar of laughter.

"One would think I am not believed," he said, in an incredulous tone. "Well, believe this. I want to start by thanking you all for coming. We thought we were planning a small wedding, but it sure has been nice having you all here to rejoice and celebrate with us. You wonder what kept me waiting, but do you really need to wonder when you see the beautiful woman I have on my arm? She has been well worth the wait!"

He turned to kiss her before he continued.

"I thank you all for your support, but I want, especially, to thank our parents—and I would be remiss if I did not mention Uncle Abe and Aunt Sarah. We really appreciate your kindness, understanding and encouragement. Perhaps most of all, we want to thank Maria, Marta and George for their enthusiastic help in planning this day. I guess we also need to make special mention of Maria, Marta and Tina for planning the surprise. We had no clue that anything like this was going on. Mr. and Mrs. Mayer have also made our day special in providing this lovely meal.

"Now, although I have waited and made you wonder for many years, I do not wish to delay any longer. Our train will be coming through before long, and we still need to pick up our bags, so we shall take our leave."

With that, they began to make their way toward the door as everyone clapped and shouted good wishes. Levi had gone out before them, for he was taking them to the station in his buggy. The children went to the door to say goodbye and Ellie hugged them all.

"I'm so proud of you!" she told them. "Have fun with Grandma and Grandpa. We should be back before you get home from school on Tuesday."

"We will!" they assured her. "You have a good time too."

Chapter Twenty-Three

Finally, Jake and Ellie were settled in their seat on the train. There were only a few other passengers in their car, and they had chosen a seat at the back for added privacy. As they pulled out of the station, they both sighed deeply in relief. They laughed at themselves.

"It wasn't that great a trial, was it?" Jake asked.

"I think the sigh, for me anyway, was more that the festivities are over and we're finally alone."

"If we could only dispense with the train trip in the twinkling of an eye!" Jake sighed again. He squeezed her hand. "I'd like to be in our room at this very moment."

In spite of their impatience, it wasn't long until the train began to slow down as the conductor called, "Strafford!"

Jake reached for their bags. "I asked the hotel to have a carriage ready to pick us up."

The rig was waiting beside the platform. The driver came to take the bags to stow them away and Jake helped Ellie to her seat. Jake sat beside her with his arm around her shoulder.

"When we get checked in, we will go to the photographers. We can have a light supper afterward and then..."

Jake stopped speaking but his eyes eloquently told her the rest. Ellie's eyes answered with an enthusiasm to match his.

When they entered the photographer's studio, fleeting thoughts about Toronto and the time she and John were photographed came to Ellie's mind. This time the photographer asked her to sit on a tall stool. He gave her a single rose to hold in her hands. Jake stood slightly to her right, his left hand on her shoulder. He took several shots in this pose, with their heads in slightly different positions.

"May I try something a bit different?" the photographer asked. "I'd like for you to stand facing each other. Mr. Kurtz, you hold your wife's hands up about four inches under her chin. Now look into each other's eyes. Mrs. Kurtz, could you lift your chin a little higher? Step a little closer. Yes, that's it. Now, think of one of the happy moments you have shared."

Jake's eyes did an exaggerated roll and then twinkled in his unique combination of shared humor and eager love. Ellie's eyes reflected the intimacy of their affection. They were barely aware of the flash that caught the moment.

"Perfect!" the photographer exclaimed. "Did you want to pick up the portraits when they are finished in about ten days, or do you want me to mail them to you? Once you have seen the poses, you can order the ones you like the best."

"Why don't you mail them?" Jake suggested. "When we decide what we want, we may make the trip to Strafford to place the order and make the payment. It might be a nice excuse for another get-away."

With a broad smile, the photographer agreed and took down the necessary information.

"Congratulations, and have a nice wedding trip," he said, reaching out to shake their hands.

They went back to the hotel dining room, but their supper didn't last long. They were both still full from the Mayers' wonderful meal. Their appetites were more for love than for the sandwiches and tea they had ordered.

Finally, they were in their room. Jake drew Ellie into his arms.

"Let's get this finery on some hangers."

He unbuttoned his jacket and loosened his tie. Ellie began to remove the baby's breath and hairpins from her hair. "Would you undo the buckle and the buttons at the back of my dress?" she asked Jake as he finished hanging his suit.

"With the greatest of pleasure!" he exclaimed, making short work of removing the belt. "It's going to take ten minutes to undo all these tiny things all the way down your back," he complained.

Ellie chuckled. "Oh, the foibles of fashionable wear! You did like the dress, though, didn't you?"

"You looked lovely, Ellie. You chose the same color that you wore to Regina's wedding, but you looked even lovelier today. A rose bud is beautiful, but the unfolding reveals more of its splendor. In spite of, or perhaps because of, all you have lived through, your beauty has been deepened and enhanced. I am so blessed to drink in the beauty of my rose!"

As he opened the last button, Jake gently lowered the dress and his hands caressed her bare shoulders. Ellie shivered in delight.

"Oo-oh, Jake!"

She lowered the dress to the floor and stepped out of it. Stooping down, she lifted it up and quickly hung it on the hanger. Jake went to turn back the covers of the bed.

The weeks of their waiting were over. Their love, fully and beautifully expressed in exquisite ecstasy, left them touched to the core of their beings. As they lay in each other's arms, Ellie felt tears well up in her eyes.

"Jake, sweetheart, it feels like my heart has come home," she whispered.

Jake's arms tightened around her.

"I couldn't have said it better myself. How long I have waited for this moment! You are finally my wife, Ellie—my loved and cherished wife! My darling."

He lifted her chin to kiss her once more. "I will treasure you for the rest of my days, my lovely one."

"I think I can handle that," Ellie murmured.

Even though they woke before seven, it was eight-thirty before they entered the breakfast room. They didn't need to be at the station until eleven to catch their train to go on to Niagara Falls, so they had a leisurely meal before packing their bags and leaving the hotel. Jake then asked their driver to take them on a little tour of the town before they went to meet the train.

When they reached Niagara Falls, there were many carriages waiting to take passengers to their respective hotels. Jake hired one to take them to their reserved room. As they neared the hotel, they could hear the thundering water across the street. The room was lovely and had a nice view of the Falls. They stood at their window for several moments, awed at the sight. After awhile, they unpacked their valises for the stay.

"Do you want to take a stroll before we go for supper?" Jake asked.

"Let's have a cup of tea first, then maybe we can go for a short walk and come back for supper," Ellie suggested.

She came to put her arms around his waist.

"We have several days to enjoy the sights. Right now I am most anxious to enjoy my husband."

Jake's eyes lit up. "No argument there, honey!" He went into his hungry dog mode. "See! I'm all for it!"

"Oh Jake, you clown! One could think you see me as a dish of dog food!"

"Not dog food, my dear, but you sure are a dish! And that you can't argue about, because that is my unalterable opinion."

"That appraisal I will accept," Ellie laughed.

They had their tea and their first look at the mighty Falls. After a nice meal they browsed through the hotel gift shop, inspecting the souvenirs. They decided that, before they left for home, they would get a little something for each of the children. There were countless items—everything with a picture of the Falls on it. Perhaps they would get a china plate for each of the girls, and small tin box for George. However, they decided to wait until they looked at some of the other shops.

Ellie was examining a glass paperweight when Jake whispered in her ear, "Psst! Let's do some browsing upstairs!"

"Very well, sir." Ellie replied, in a formal tone and a faint smile. "I believe that would be a fine choice!"

He put his hand under her elbow and guided her out of the shop.

The activities of the next few days were divided into long exploratory walks, watching the never-ending rush of water over the Falls, and time in their room. The garden close to their hotel was a fascinating place, with lovely benches where they could sit. Saturday afternoon the sun was so warm it felt more like the end of May. There was a nice breeze that made their stroll, all the way to the side of the Canadian Falls, a pleasant one. They were on their way back when the wind shifted, sending the heavy mist from the thundering cascade right into their path. Hand in hand, they ran to escape the drenching downpour, laughing all the way. In spite of the warmth of the April day, it was still not enough to counteract the temperature of the moisture. By the time they got out of the mist, they were not only wet, but also decidedly cool.

"We'd better get these wet clothes off," Ellie panted. "Look at our hair! How are we going to get dried out? I guess one should carry an umbrella in these parts!"

They hurried to their room.

"I didn't think I really needed a cold shower," Jake commented.

Ellie's hair was plastered to her head, but Jake noted the flush in her cheeks and the laughter in her eyes. His own eyes softened.

"If that bit of rain thought it could wake me up from the bliss of being married to you, I've got news for it! Rain or shine, I will always live in the delight of having you as my wife."

Jake reached for her and gave her a kiss to prove the truth of his statement.

"Come, let's towel dry as much as possible, then we'll get into bed to get warmed up again. I don't want you to be going home with the pneumonia or anything!" He reached to unbutton her wet dress and hung it on a hanger for her.

They had inquired about churches on Saturday morning and decided they would attend the service at a Lutheran church nearby on Sunday morning. They felt a little awkward as they went in the door, but the church must have been accustomed to greeting visitors, for several people, including the minister's wife, came to welcome them.

Mrs. Nielsen asked if they were just visiting the Falls, or if they had friends in the area. She must have talked to her husband before the service, for in his welcome, he greeted visitors and mentioned the newly-weds among them. His prayer also included a blessing for them.

Afterward, both Mr. and Mrs. Nielsen asked if they would join them for lunch at the manse. At first they demurred, but when they were assured that the Nielsons were prepared for company, they accepted.

As it turned out, Mr. Nielsen's first parish had been in a small town near Strafford, and he was pleased to connect with the area through Jake and Ellie. They knew some of the same people. They had a delightful lunch and a pleasant visit. There was not a great deal of difference in their ages and they shared some of the same interests. Jake and Ellie assured them that, if they ever wanted to come to visit their area, they would be welcome to stay in their home. When Jake and Ellie took their leave, they knew that Miles and Catherine Nielsen would be lasting friends.

The weather was still very warm and sunny, so they took a long walk through the streets to the edge of town. They walked past the grand buildings of a monastery and down a stairway and path over the cliff, down to the walk along the river and Falls.

Their conversation, for the most part, was quite jocular. Jake, with his teasing ways and wordplays, kept Ellie laughing. She was getting more and more adept with retorts that surprised Jake and made him laugh too.

By the time they reached their hotel they were tired and hungry. The inn served them a tasty dinner that they ate in leisurely comfort. Ellie couldn't help but think about the difference in the first days of her two marriages. Those days she shared with John were precious, and really not to be compared with her present situation, she realized, for both she and John had still been close to their grief. There had been so much learning and responsibility for her following her marriage to John. There was, she acknowledged, a depth that came with such circumstances. Being with Jake was so much fun it made her feel younger and more light-hearted than she had felt in a long while.

Monday dawned decidedly cooler, with the threat of rain. It was not conducive to outside pursuits. They visited displays and a few shops to make some purchases for the children. Jake then suggested they get a Niagara Falls cushion top for her parents, to thank them for staying with their family, and a glass paperweight as a souvenir for themselves. Since they needed to arise early to catch their train, they wanted to go to bed early. When they were ready for bed, Ellie put her hand on Jake's arm.

"Can we sit here on this couch for a bit?"

There was a question in Jake's eyes as he sensed her serious mood, but he sat down and encircled her with his arm.

"Is something wrong?"

"No, no," Ellie assured him. "I was just wondering if we could pray together."

She took a deep breath.

"These first days of our marriage have made me feel so light-hearted and almost young again. I couldn't help but remember the somber feeling that permeated the first days of my marriage to John. We did a lot of praying together. Sometimes I wonder how we would have made it without that. Of course, we were both still grieving. I am so thankful for what you and I have, and that our first days don't need to be so clouded—that we don't need to learn to love each other, for you and I were in love before we were married. But I do want us to be able to pray together too."

She looked into Jake's eyes to see if he understood. What she saw was unshed tears.

"My dear, dear Ellie! Of course we can pray together. Let's!"

He drew her close and began, "Dear Heavenly Father, thank you for the beautiful gift you have given me in Ellie. The years I have waited for her have only made her all the more beautiful and precious. Thank you for being with her through all the hard times she has experienced, for all the growth and maturity that she gained in the midst of the trials, the growth of love out of difficult circumstances. We thank you for the love and the time that she and John shared. We acknowledge your faithfulness and your wisdom."

Jake paused, "Now you have brought us together in joyful union—a union, Father, on which we feel your blessing in every moment we share—a union that satisfies us and brings us such pleasure. In our elation, we give thanks and acknowledge your goodness. We seek your guidance that our union may also bless our children and those around us so that it may bring honor and glory to you, our Lord and Saviour. Amen."

Jake opened his eyes, but Ellie kept hers shut.

"Precious Lord, I, too, want to thank you for the way you work in the sunlight and shadows of our lives. I thank you especially for the sunlight that Jake has brought into my life; for the faithfulness of your love that you sent Jake to let his love banish the shadows and let me, once again, feel cherished by a good man. Thank you for the influence and stability he has already brought to these children that are now ours. My heart is so full, Lord. Please accept my praise and thanksgiving, for Jesus' sake. Amen"

Jake lifted her chin and kissed her. "Thank you, Ellie, for suggesting we pray. I think we should make a habit of it. What a blessing you are!"

She laid her head on his shoulder.

"Do you know the scripture that says 'A cord of three strands is not easily broken?' I think that can apply to our marriage relationship. If we let God be the third strand in our marriage, we will have a strong one."

“Right again, my love!” he whispered. “Now we’d better get to bed, for it’s back to real life tomorrow!”

Chapter Twenty-Four

1900

Ellie stood at the bay window looking down the street. She smiled as she saw Mrs. Schwartz across the street moving her curtain to look out. It didn't really matter if curiosity or care was the motivating factor, but her family was sure being carefully watched these days. Ellie's hand rested on her burgeoning stomach and she felt the movement of the baby.

"Are you impatient, little one?" she asked. "Mama can hardly wait either, and your Papa is just as eager as the both of us. Your big sister would like if you would make your appearance before she goes off to Teacher's College. Do you think you could come a few days early?"

The baby was due the second of September, and Maria had to leave on the sixth. Today was already the twenty-eight of August. It was going to be nip and tuck if Maria was to be there when the baby arrived. Marta would be starting her last year in Continuation School, and George would be heading into the sixth grade. Her family was growing up, and now she and Jake would be starting over with this new little one.

Ellie smiled as she thought about the ecstatic look on Jake's face when she had told him she was pregnant. He had been perfectly happy with their family as it was, but she sensed how pleased he was to have fathered a child of his own. He did think of the others as his own, but she was pleased, too, that this baby was on the way.

After her previously miscarried pregnancies, she had been quite surprised that it could happen so easily. For the first three months they had kept the news to themselves, for they could hardly believe it would really continue. But here she was—things had progressed smoothly and she was close to giving birth.

Everything was ready. She'd had several months to do all the sewing and preparation, since she had quit her job in her sixth month. The Mayers, thankful for the extra two and a half years Ellie had given since her marriage, hired a replacement and let Ellie do the training. There was implicit understanding that she would be welcome to come back any time she felt ready. Ellie didn't think that would happen until their child was ready for school. Would she feel too old to go back to work then? She had so enjoyed her job. Ellie moved to the rocking chair and settled down with the awkward movements of any woman this late in pregnancy.

Dr. Mitchell isn't far away this time, nor is Mrs. Dunkirk," Ellie thought. *I'm so glad that Mrs. Dunkirk is willing to come yet this time, even though she is retiring. I know I will feel more comfortable with her than I would with a new person.* She picked up their wedding picture from the parlor table. The photographer certainly had captured the essence of their love for each other in that last shot. Now, that love had borne fruit in this little one she was carrying within her body. One more child was coming to add its own unique gifts to the interesting mix that was their family; yet they were intertwined into one unit and all loved equally.

Much as they had been in love, there had been some adjustments to living together. There still would be difficulties, as in any relationship, but most of the time, Jake and Ellie were still amazed at the gift of their love. She set the picture back on the table and rocked slowly, immersed in her contentment and joy.

George was over playing at the Gilberts' and the girls had walked downtown for some last minute school supplies. The supper was in the oven and she could smell the ham and scalloped potatoes already.

She had been thoroughly spoiled in the past month. Jake was so careful for her welfare, and Maria and Marta had followed his example, doing most of the housework and urging her to take care. Even though it felt good right now because she was so big and awkward, she was anxious to get back to a more ordinary routine.

Ellie smiled. *Ordinary is maybe a relative term. Feedings every four hours, night and day, certainly is not the ordinary I've experienced for quite a few years now.*

The back door opened. Her heart leapt as Jake called out, "Ellie?"

"Yes?" she answered as she struggled to get out of the rocker. "Is something wrong that you are home early?"

Jake came through the door to the living room.

"Just stay seated, my lovely rose," he hastened to assure her. "Nothing at all is wrong. Things were slow at the office and I have this beautiful wife, large with child, awaiting me at home. I decided to close early and come spend an extra hour with her." Jake leaned over to kiss her, then went on his knees before her and gently kissed her stomach.

"Hello there, little one. Papa came home early to see you and Mama. There is nothing wrong with that, is there, little one?"

Ellie ran her fingers through Jake's curly hair.

"Oh, sweetheart, there sure is nothing wrong with that! But do help me up out of this chair so we can sit together on the sofa. You'd better save those knees for horse rides in a few years," she laughed.

Jake chuckled as he rose and assisted her.

"You may just be right about that. My knees aren't as young as they were when I used to give the girls rides on my back."

"I'm not as young as I was when I had George either, yet I feel so much more serene and at ease this time. I think age helps in that way. I just hope age keeps me feeling just as serene when I need to get up for night feedings!" Ellie laughed.

Jake smiled as he helped her lower herself to the sofa, and then sat beside her, an arm around her shoulders.

"This child will be so loved he or she will not mind one bit having old fogies for parents!" He kissed her. "I have been so happy being a father to Maria, Marta and George—you know I have. But Ellie, I am so excited about this new little one. Up until now, when babies were born, I was on the outside looking in. This time I will be in on it from the very beginning. I will be Papa from day one!"

Before Ellie could reply, George came bursting through the door, letting it slam behind him.

"Is supper ready soon, Mama? Colin Gilbert wants me to go with him and his dad to pick up some things at the train station after supper. Can I, Mama and Papa, can I?"

"*May* I?" Ellie reminded him.

"Oh Mama! May I go with Colin and his dad?" George conceded.

"Here come the girls. Since Papa is home already, we can get the supper on quickly, then, as far as I am concerned, you may go with the Gilberts.'"

"No signs of the littlest Kurtz being early, Mama?" Maria asked.

"No, Maria, I am afraid not."

"If things don't happen soon, I am just going to have to save enough money to come home the first weekend after his or her arrival."

"Don't worry, I will do baby duty until you get here, Maria," Marta offered.

"Sure, worm your way into the baby's affections before I get a chance!" Maria teased.

"Now, now, girls!" Jake remonstrated, "I am sure you will both have a special place in your sibling's heart. And you, too, big brother!" he said as he tousled George's hair.

In spite of everyone's readiness, the days passed without any eventful moments. Maria left, with her packed bags, ready for her new adventure in Normal School. Ellie was so glad that Maria's best friend, Rose Arnold, was also going to become a teacher. They were going to room together.

Marta and George had just left for their third day at school when Ellie felt the first twinges of labor. By the time Jake came home for lunch, Ellie suggested that perhaps, after he had eaten, he should go for Dr. Mitchell. They were already seated at the table, but Jake jumped from his chair.

"Are you in labor?"

"Yes, Jake. I have had contractions on and off all morning, but now they are coming a little more regularly."

"Then I will go for Dr. Mitchell right away!" said Jake, reaching for his hat.

"Jake, sit down and have a bite. Things are not that imminent!"

"Are you sure? What if Dr. Mitchell is called out before I get there?"

It took a bit of persuasion on Ellie's part, but Jake finally sat down and quickly gulped some food. Serenity enveloped Ellie and she smiled at Jake's obvious case of nerves. She only sipped a bit of tea.

"I shall go upstairs and get everything ready while you bring the doctor," she said as Jake started for the door. He turned and drew her into his arms.

"Oh Ellie! The time is here, and I am nervous. How can you be so calm?" He gave her a kiss. "I love you!" He went out the door and Ellie started up the steps.

She had just finished getting the bed ready, having had to stop several times, as her abdomen contracted in earnest.

"Oh-hh!" she gasped. "I hope Jake and Doctor Mitchell hurry! Maybe I should have let Jake go when he first wanted to."

She situated herself on the bed as another wave enveloped her and she felt the urge to push. The arrival of the baby was almost upon her when she heard the door downstairs.

"Hurry!" she managed to scream.

Three sets of footsteps rushed up the stairs. As Dr. Mitchell came through the bedroom door, he saw the urgency of the situation. Mrs. Dunkirk quickly moved to the side of the bed to assist. Less than two minutes later, Katherina Joy let out a lusty howl to announce her arrival. Jake stood in awe as Ellie wept in joy.

"A daughter! Oh Ellie! Thank you, thank you!"

Ellie looked at him with shining eyes.

"Our little Rina! Kiss me, Jake, then say hello to our daughter."

Mrs. Dunkirk handed the baby to Jake. He held her close, looking at her with wonder and delight. Gently, he placed her on Ellie's chest, and then mother and daughter both were enfolded in his arms. The happiness emanating from Jake's face and the radiance in Ellie's eyes seemed to fill the room with warmth and light.

"Another strand for the cord of our family, Jake," commented Ellie, kissing little Rina on her forehead.

Epilogue

1998

Rina sighed in contentment as she closed her eyes. The love of her parents had always been a steady influence in her life. Even now, long after they were gone and she herself way beyond the age to which they had lived, the security of her Mama and Papa's love was a comfort to her. Rina knew she had often tried their patience. She had been continually anxious to enthusiastically tear into any new adventure that presented itself. Perhaps her birth had set the tone—dashing impatiently headfirst into life. Her father was forever telling her to slow down, that not everything had to be experienced in one day. He often admonished her to enjoy something for awhile instead of immediately setting off on a new quest—"escapades" her mother would call them.

Rina grinned "I suppose some of them were, but all in all, I did have a good life and a lot of fun—almost a hundred years of living."

That was another, different chronicle!